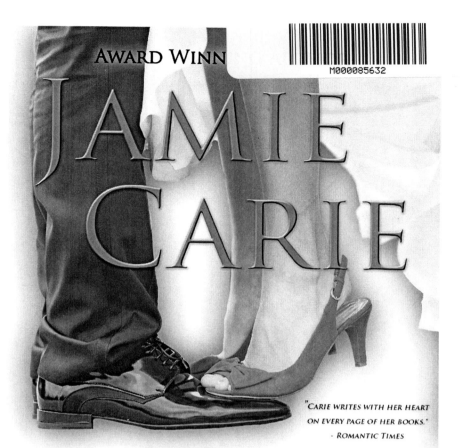

Award Winn

JAMIE CARIE

Rush To The Altar

Rush to the Altar

by

Jamie Carie

Dedication

This story is dedicated to my husband, Tony. We are embarking on a new adventure with this book and I couldn't have done it without you. You always believe in me and I believe in you and us. I am blessed among women to have you as my husband.

CHAPTER ONE

The phone rang with a soft trill, breaking the quiet of the evening.

Maddie lifted her head from the story she was reading to Max as her mother answered it. She paused to overhear who had called, ruffling Max's hair.

"How are you doing, Sasha? How's your mom? Umm-hmm...that's good." A short pause ensued while Gloria walked into the living room. "Oh, she's just reading to Max. I'll get her. Hold on."

Maddie rose, taking the phone. "Mommy will just be a minute, sweetie."

Max, at twenty-six months—okay, okay, two years old; it was just hard to let go of the month-counting stage—shook his head and held up the book. "Read it, mommy."

"I'll be right back, Max." Maddie gave her mom a pleading look and walked toward the back door, the clear night air and a moment—alone—with a phone call of her own.

"Hello?"

"You'll never guess what happened."

"Hi, Sasha." Sasha never started a call with "Hey, it's Sasha, what are you doing?" or anything normal like that.

"Of course it's me. Who else? Anyway, guess what happened!"

Who else, indeed? Maddie hadn't connected with many of her old friends since moving back home and was thankful Sasha, her best friend from high school, had picked right back up from where they had left off. "You know I hate guessing games. Just tell me."

"Oh no, this is too good. Three guesses at least."

Maddie groaned. "You won the lottery." Deadpan voice.

"You always guess that first. Come on. Be creative."

Maddie smiled. "You had a blind date last night. Turns out he's a doctor and wild about you. He proposed."

Sasha laughed. "Now that's more like it. But no, try again."

Maddie laughed. "You won tickets to the Ice Capades!" Mock excitement laced her words, but she couldn't help her smile.

"Oh my gosh. You're so close!"

"Really? Tell me."

"Okay, are you sitting down?"

"Yeah. Of course. Any news this important would have me sitting down." Maddie plopped down on a wobbly lawn chair, leaned her elbows onto her knees and grinned into the phone. "No more stalling. Out with it."

"Okay, okay. You know that morning radio show I listen to like a groupie? Well, all of my hard efforts have finally paid off. I won tickets to a Racers game!"

"Basketball?" Maddie couldn't help the deflated tone after such a buildup.

"What'u mean basketball? It's the religion of the Midwest!"

"Shhhh. My mother might hear you." The smile was back in Maddie's voice.

"You have to go with me! Front row seats and everything."

6

"Really? Front row?"

"Well, maybe not *front* front row. Maybe we won't be able to feel the flecks of sweat off their brows or anything like that, but close seats, great seats."

"Oh, Sasha, I don't know…"

"Now come on, Maddie. You haven't been out in weeks. You need to have some fun."

Maddie sighed into the phone. "Yeah, maybe, but a basketball game? I can think of 'funner' ways to play my babysitting card."

"Do you know how many guys I could ask out with these tickets? And I called *you*. You are my priority."

Great, just what she needed. Another person's responsibility. Like moving back in with her parents wasn't bad enough. "Listen, Sasha, I appreciate it, really, but why don't you ask Rob? He's a sports fanatic. He would love it."

"Out of town again," Sasha explained in a disgusted tone.

"What is it this time?"

"Something stupid. His mother had a sneezing attack or some such crisis. He doesn't do anything without her approval. I'm really ready to call it quits, Maddie. I don't think I can hang on much longer unless there are some real changes."

"Sounds worse than I thought. I'm sorry, Sasha. Maybe you should start dating again. What about that guy at work? Chad, wasn't it? Ask him to go. It might be the beginning of something."

Sasha snorted into the phone. "Didn't I tell you? He went out with Lana, the five foot nine, 120-pound receptionist with long blond tresses. I don't have a chance."

"Well, you never know. Racers tickets might just do the trick."

7

"Yeah, well, if he didn't notice without the tickets then I don't want him noticing with them. So, you'll be my date, right?"

A brief pause. "Okay, if my mom can babysit. When is it?"

"Next Saturday. And Maddie, don't paint your face blue or anything, okay? I want to get on TV and all, but not that badly."

Maddie threw her head back and laughed. "It's the price you pay for dragging me out. You know what a crazy fan I am."

As their laughter died down the silence grew long and serious.

"How are you doing, Mad, really?"

"You mean, am I thinking about him?"

"Yeah."

"Not as much. Not hourly anymore."

"Oh, girl."

"It's just that…Max looks so much like him."

Another pause.

"Sometimes he'll look up at me from his breakfast cereal, grinning at something funny on the box, that goofy grin that I know so well…and I…I just stop inside. Everything stops. Oh Sasha, I wish he didn't look so much like Brandon sometimes, and yet I feel so awful for wishing that. I should be thankful. You know, to have something so real to remember him by, and yet," her voice lowered to a near whisper, "I wish Max looked like me. Am I so terrible to wish that?" She swallowed back the tears from her throat.

"Of course not," came her voice of reason. The voice that had saved her countless times from tipping over the edge of grief these past few months. "But someday you'll be glad. Someday it will all make sense."

8

"Really? I don't see how."

"I know. I know."

Another pause.

"Love you, Maddie."

"Thanks, Sasha. Love you too."

They hung up.

It was how they ended every call these days.

~~~~~~~

Sasha and Maddie made their way across the crowded isles to their seats in the huge arena at Bankers Life Fieldhouse, stepping over purses and feet, squeezing between knees and people's backs as best they could. Laughing, they finally arrived at the only two empty seats around and plopped down.

"Can you believe these seats? I told you they would be great," Sasha gushed.

"Everything's so huge. I can't believe I've never been here before."

"Just wait until the players come out. They will be giants from here."

"I just wish I *liked* basketball." Maddie made a comical face. "I think I would enjoy this more."

"Shhhh." Sasha looked around at the people near them. "That's like saying 'I wish I liked God' in church. You gotta pretend, girl."

Maddie compressed her mouth tight and said through barely opened lips, "Okay, okay, I forgot."

A loud buzzer rang and the announcer began the evening's presentations in a booming voice. Maddie saw that all the major networks' television crews were there, along with the local stations. A DJ sat behind a long table loaded with equipment, queuing up the music. The excitement rose as the Racemates entered the stadium looking even more tanned and beautiful in person, if that was possible. And then everyone came to a fevered pitch as the players arrived, their names in lights with giant photos of them on the flashing screen overhead in the middle of the arena.

A popcorn vendor stepped close and Sasha motioned for two, paid for them and sank back into her chair with a contended sigh. "This is gonna be great." Her dark brown eyes were glued to the players as the opposing centers made their way to the middle of the court for the first tip-off.

"I knew they would be tall but what was God thinking?" Maddie asked in awe. "He was thinking they would play great ball," Sasha answered without taking her eyes off number 14. "Can you believe how tall he is?" She said it quietly, so only Maddie could hear over the roar of cheering as the Racers won the tip-off. Maddie poked her in the arm and answered back with a laugh. "Now I get it. You are crushing on one of the players. Who is he?" Maddie looked at number 14 and nodded her head. He was tall, dark and incredibly handsome.

"Jake Hart. And I'm not crushing. I'm just impressed by his…by his…rebounding stats. That's all."

Maddie laughed. "Sounds like you've been studying."

"Just a little internet research. I wanted to be educated for the game and got a little…sidetracked." Sasha grinned and shrugged, a woman who rarely felt the bite of guilt, which was one of the many reasons Maddie loved her so much.

Sasha sighed. "He's even better looking in person."

"Well, why don't you ask him out?" Mock innocent tone.

"Yeah, I'll just get his phone number after the game."
Sasha had the sarcasm down pat. "He'll just hand it over the heads
of all the interviewers when he notices how beautiful I am."

"You are beautiful."

Sasha, Asian-American, with her coffee-creamy skin and
the sloe-eyed slant of a courtesan, sighed louder in mock long-
suffering. "Only to those who know me."

"Well, that's the best kind. Lots of people are only
beautiful *until* you know them."

"Aww, shut up. You're going to make me cry right here
under all these bright lights."

Maddie grinned and stayed silent for a while, taking in the
game, the squeaking sneakers, the blaring horn that marked their
plays, the power of the players' movements, as if they had figured
out some secret weapon against gravity. It didn't take long to
become totally immersed, her heart pounding when they
approached the basket, praying it would go into the little round
hoop, clapping and cheering with the fans all around her, becoming
one of them.

It was surprising. How caught up she became, how
immersed and loving the feel of being a part of something so big,
so wonderful…so united, as if she had stepped into a perfectly
harmonious moment of time.

A loud horn blared, signaling the end of the first quarter.
Maddie turned to ask Sasha if she wanted to go and get something
to drink when there was a tapping on her shoulder and a squeal
with her name attached to it. Turning, she found herself looking
into the slightly older face of a high school friend she hadn't seen
in years.

"Barb?"

"Maddie! Oh my gosh, I can't believe it's you." She edged
around an irritated fan and squeezed into a nearby seat behind

11

them. Grasping Maddie's hand, she squeezed it tight. "How are you? Are you in town for long? I heard you live in Muncie now."

She obviously hadn't heard about Brandon's accident. "Um, I'm great. In town for a while. It's so good to see you. What are you up to now?" Please God, let her talk about herself.

Barb raised her eyebrows and nodded her head with her typical exuberance. "I started my own dance academy a couple of years ago, which is doing really well. Kids mostly, but we've pulled together an adult team, up on the northeast side of town. It's been lots of fun." She laughed, a little self-consciously. "Lots of headaches too, but you know what I mean."

"That's so great. You always wanted something like that. I'm really happy for you."

"Hey." She paused, looking at Maddie with a considering gleam in her eyes. "This is going to sound strange, I know, but you were always such a great dancer in show choir and a quick study, too. My team, the adult team, is doing a little halftime show. We were supposed to be here," she motioned around them, "in the main court, but somehow they overbooked and bumped us to the practice court. We'll be performing for some kids from Coburn Place; it's an awesome facility for abused women and children. Anyway, it'll be very low key and since one of my girls couldn't make it…well, we could really use another dancer to fill the spot."

Maddie shook her head, eyes wide. "No way. I haven't danced like that in years. I don't even know the routine."

"We'll have twenty minutes to warm up. I could teach you."

"Barb, you're crazy."

Barb leaned in. "It's some older moves. Not so different from some of the stuff we used to do in high school. Come on, it'll be fun. And think of the kids. Their moms are trying so hard to make life normal and great for them."

Barb didn't know it. She couldn't know it. Of course, she didn't know she had just played the ace card. Maddie knew all about trying to make things feel as normal as possible. Knew about that moment when Max was about to ask about his father again, and how she would jump in with something, anything to distract and distance them both from the truth. There wasn't any other reason under heaven that could have made her say yes, except that one.

And Barb had said aloud what she hadn't even voiced.

Maddie hesitated and then nodded. "Yeah, okay, if you really need me."

Sasha gasped, grabbing her arm. "Are you joking?"

Maddie turned to Sasha. "It's in a practice court, for the kids. What harm can it do?"

Sasha nodded, understanding lighting her eyes. "I get it. Okay, go break a leg, or not, or whatever it is they say." Then, grumbling under her breath, "Leaving me here all alone with my popcorn and glimpses of Jake Hart so you can go be on TV. I'm so abused. See if I ask you to a game again."

Maddie grinned and gave her a peck on the cheek. "Thanks. And I am not going to be on TV, silly. I would die first." Turning to Barb she said, "Halftime is coming up soon, isn't it? Can we get into the court now? I will need all the time I can get."

Barb nodded. "They've assigned us a practice room that we should be able to get into. Come on."

The two wriggled through the crowd to the aisle, dashed up the stairs to the main level and hurried down the long corridor to the designated room. There were already a couple of the dancers inside.

Maddie could only blink in horror at what they were wearing. Like Olivia Newton-John throwbacks from the eighties, each woman sported matching pastel headbands and leggings with coordinating leotards and white tights. Worse, some of them should have known that their leotard-wearing days were long behind them. What had Barb been thinking?

"I'm not wearing that!" It came out of her mouth before she had time to stop and think how it would sound. Quickly, to smooth it over, Maddie added, "Barb, we didn't think about the costume. I can't dance. I don't have anything to wear."

Barb grasped her arm and pulled her further into the room, making Maddie feel like a fish on a hook. "Oh, we have several extra outfits," she assured cheerily. "Just go over to that box and dig around in there. You'll find something."

This wasn't happening.

Maddie slowly walked over to the box, crouched down and plowed through spandex and polyester blends. Sure enough, there were extra leotards in her size—medium. She might have been able to fit into a small before Max was born, but after a year of breastfeeding, her chest had never gone back down. Was there a sports bra in here? Oh no. She suddenly remembered she was wearing her black lacy bra, the one she hadn't worn since Brandon's death, and didn't know exactly why she'd put on tonight, except that she had wanted to pretend to need it. It was going to show through the pale pink leotard for sure. God help her, with her D cups bouncing around in black lace showing through pastel pink…she was going to look like an eighties streetwalker in this getup.

It's only for the kids, she reminded herself. They won't notice. I'll be in the back. I'll make sure to be in the back.

There was a small screen set up for changing and Maddie rushed behind it before too many of the other girls showed up to change. Everything fit, kind of—too much cleavage for comfort. On the bright side, she'd been doing her exercises and her thighs shouldn't jiggle too badly in the tights, but a headband? Did she really have to wear the silly headband?

14

She shook her long, wavy hair out of her ponytail and put the headband on the best she could without a mirror and stepped out from behind the screen.

Barb came over and whistled. "Boy, good thing we are in front of young children or we would have to change the rating on this show! You look phenomenal."

"I very much doubt phenomenal is the word to describe this outfit. What's with the Olivia Newton-John look?"

"We're called the 'Eighties Ladies.' Gives us a marketing edge, you know. Something to set us apart."

"I can see that." Maddie tried not to sound as appalled as she felt.

"Come on, you look great. Now let's work on the routine before the others get here."

Barb plugged her phone into the speaker's dock and turned up the volume. To Maddie's further despair, I Will Survive started to blare from the tiny speakers. She wanted to ask if that was really an appropriate song considering the audience, but Barb had begun to shake her hips and move to the music and Maddie could only attempt to follow along and learn the steps as quickly as possible.

Slapping her palms to her hips and twisting around for the first time in ten years, she glanced at the ceiling briefly. "You owe me for this one."

She talked to God a lot these days, and not much of what she said was very nice.

CHAPTER TWO

A sweet-faced woman was leading a line of children into the practice court where the dancers had gathered, ready to begin, when a tall, lanky man with a gray beard and mustache, eyes bugged and panicked, arms waving, stopped them.

"The show has been moved. Please, take the children back to the stadium. The children need to find their seats immediately."

Barb stepped up to the man, questions rushing from her hot-pink lips.

Maddie just stood frozen, deer in the headlights, knowing that something really bad was about to happen. Some sixth sense told her, or maybe it was the ecstatic smile on Barb's face, either way, Maddie could feel the weight coming toward her, about to run her down, squashed into the pavement by life again, and there wasn't going to be a thing she could do to get out of it. No brilliant rolling to the side of the road for her. No dodging the truck coming right for her torso. No. She was about to get good and flattened.

The other dancers, faces registering different degrees of shock and awe, surged toward the man.

Barb turned to explain, breathless, eyes alight, like a cheerleader on speed, with something Maddie had long ago hoped she would never see in Barb's eyes again—heaven help them, "Barbarian Barb" was back. "Mr. McKlesky just explained that one of the halftime acts had a bus accident on the way here and won't be able to perform. No one was injured," she assured them in a rush, "but they won't make it here in time for the show." She paused for effect, eyes wide, lifted her arms and turned her hips to one side, then announced with a dazzling smile, "Ladies, we've been bumped to the halftime show at Bankers Life Fieldhouse." Seeing some of her students' faces, she quickly added, "Now, don't be nervous. Our routine is all of four minutes and we know it beautifully." Her voice lowered to a growl. "We can do this."

They had little time to debate it as Mr. McKlesky motioned them to follow the children out the door. "Ladies, ladies, please, we must get into position. Everything is very precise timing around here. Now, let's move."

As if an army drill sergeant had spoken, the women lined up and followed Barb out, suppressing nervous laughter as it echoed across the high-ceilinged hallways.

Maddie was careful to wait for the back of the line before moving, hoping for some miracle to save her. Maybe she would trip on the stairs and break something, she thought hysterically. Or maybe she could just slink away. Yes, that was it. She would disappear from this nightmare, run to the car and call Sasha's cell phone, then avoid Barb for the rest of her life.

The idea had no sooner lodged into her thought processes when she was slowing down, letting the line of dancers get further and further ahead of her. Just a few more feet and she could dash down an upcoming hallway.

One of the girls coughed, causing Barb to look back and frown at them, seeing Maddie so far behind she motioned with her arm and hissed, "Come on, girls. Get a move on. This is our big break!"

Her eyes were truly feverish now.

The corner of the hall loomed and Maddie made to sidestep into it when she felt a hand clamp down on her shoulder.

"Where do you think you're going, missy?" It was Mr. McKlesky. "No nerves now. No time for that."

He turned her back toward the line and gave her backside a smack. She squeaked with outrage. Had he really just done that? She couldn't believe it! She stopped and spun around to give him a piece of her mind, only to find him gone. Somehow disappeared. Turning back, fuming, she took another few steps and found herself on the floor of Bankers Life Fieldhouse, the bright lights now taking on a whole new meaning.

Her skin prickled and flushed to her hairline as thousands of eyes stared at her and then she groaned as their gazes seemed to slide down from her face to the black bra. She walked in front of the rows of players' chairs and poised at the end of the line, waiting, feeling like her backside was coming out of the leotard and wanting desperately to tug it down, but knowing she couldn't possibly. Her mind went completely blank as she followed the dancers to the middle of the glossy yellow floor. She could almost see her reflection in it; the thought buzzed like a numb distraction, then she laughed, a brief expelled breath of hysteria.

This was a nightmare. She would wake up at any moment in a cold sweat.

She pinched her leg, felt the slight pain and nearly passed out.

Maybe God would have pity on her now and send an earthquake to open up this overly waxed wood floor and swallow her whole. Massive deaths and the carnage of falling spectators raced across her imagination. Okay, too violent just to save her pride. A small tornado, taking only her? A lightning bolt. Just a little zap to get her out of here. That would really be perfect.

No such luck. Before she knew it, Maddie was standing in the middle of the court, at the far right side and in the front—no one in front of her and no one behind her—black lace bra exposed to a bazillion fans. How could she have forgotten the dancer at the end of the line stood in front for the beginning of the dance?

Well, it had happened. The worst thing that could possibly happen to her at a public sporting event had actually come to pass, so she might as well have fun, right? After all, there were the precious children, sitting right there on the second row. They looked so eager, so sweet and excited…Maddie paused, squinting her eyes. Were those two boys talking behind their hands and pointing at her?

18

A giant television camera seemed to come out of nowhere and zoomed in on her as the crackling of the music started on the million-dollar sound system.

They were not broadcasting this on television, were they? Thousands of eyes just turned into millions.

She heard Barb give the count as she pasted a bright smile on her face and started moving. Slap to the right hip, slap to the left, turn, pivot, freeze, turn, pivot, freeze. Rock step to the right. Flash hands overhead. Rock back to the left. Turn and look over one shoulder.

Barb hadn't exaggerated that the steps were ancient. It had all come back to her and really, it *was* kind of fun. After all, what a great story to tell Max when he got a little older.

Lemonade. Lemonade. Lemonade.

~~~~~~~

Sasha sat in the stands, eyes wide, mouth hanging open with an "oh no" coming audibly from her lips.

"Hey." A big man leaned over into her space, causing Sasha to lean sideways and stare warningly at him. "Isn't that your friend? That pretty gal who was sitting beside you?" His stale breath wafted over her face.

"No. It isn't." Sasha turned back toward Maddie, ignoring the snorting sound coming from the man, and shook her head. "She's gonna *wish* I didn't know her when this is over," Sasha whispered.

~~~~~~~

It was over almost as soon as it had begun. Maddie had no idea how they'd done, could hardly remember even dancing as they marched off the floor and back up the stairs to the rehearsal

19

room. It was over. She would change now and go listen to Sasha retell the whole thing until Maddie threatened to kill her. Life would go on. She would never, ever wear a black bra again, but life would go on.

Minutes later, amid the dance troupe's excited chatter and different states of undress, Mr. McKlesky stormed into the room, face red, eyes bulging.

The girls shrieked and tried to cover themselves.

"Who's in charge here? Who owns this monstrosity?"

When no one answered and it appeared that Barb was going to remain hidden behind the changing screen, he leapt at the one closest—Maddie.

"You…the cowering one…I should have known you would be disastrous." Grasping her by the arm, he shook her hard, causing her neck to snap back and her shoulder to wrench. "Do you have any idea what you've done? Do you? My career is at stake here! I'll be fired over this! Do you know how ridiculous and horrible your team was? You've made me a laughing stock."

Maddie cried out in pain and tried to pull free.

"I'll have your heads for this. You'll never perform again!" His murderous gaze swept the room and then lit back on Maddie. Unable to contain his rage, he shook her again.

The door opened behind them and Maddie saw a man in an expensive suit enter the room. He strode over to Mr. McKlesky, gripped the arm that was still holding onto Maddie and must have squeezed hard enough so that Mr. McKlesky abruptly let go.

"What are you doing, Frank? What are you thinking?"

Mr. McKlesky, or Frank it seemed, slowly came back to reality, looked back and forth from the nice-looking man to Maddie and then back again. "I quit," he shouted, turning to run. "I quit!"

"This isn't going to go away that easily, Frank. Wait for me outside the door."

Maddie and the rest of the room watched as Frank McKlesky realized what he had done, his face dawning in degrees of horror and fear. He stumbled from the room.

The man turned to Maddie. "Are you all right? Do you need a doctor?"

Maddie's open mouth snapped closed. She rolled her shoulder around and found it surprisingly fine. She grimaced but shook her head. "I don't think so. I think I'm all right."

The man led her toward a quiet corner. "I'm Jordan Tyler. I work for the Racers, and rest assured that we will take care of this. Would like me to call the police? Would you like to press charges?"

The combined events of the last hour finally took its toll on Maddie, and to her complete mortification she began to shake.

Mr. Tyler looked alarmed. "Are you sure you're okay?"

Words she hadn't spoken to anyone since the funeral poured out to this kind and well-meaning stranger. "Okay? Do I look okay? I just danced in front of thousands of people under excruciating bright lights in this," she looked down at her leotard, motioning with her hands toward her hips, "horrendous get-up with my underwear showing through. I thought the worst was over. Then I come back here and get accosted by a deranged man who claims that I ruined his career. I was out of practice, sure, but I'm not *that* bad a dancer." To her great dismay, she started to tear up and shake in anger and frustration. "I didn't deserve to be shaken like that."

"Of course not." The man took off his suit jacket and placed it around her shoulders. "He will be fired immediately. Stay here." He reached into his pants pocket and pulled out a phone. "We need to call the police."

He dialed the number and the next half-hour was spent reliving the event over and over. Barb stayed, genuinely concerned, but she couldn't really be of much help as she'd been hiding behind the changing screen most of the time. Several of the other women, though, had seen the whole thing and were quick to give their accounts to the police. Mr. McKlesky was found trying to leave the parking garage and taken to the police station.

When they were all gone, Mr. Tyler came back over to her and touched her gently on the shoulder. "I'm sorry you had to go through this, Mrs. Goode."

"I'm, um, a widow. You can call me Maddie."

He reached out to grasp her hand. "I'm so sorry. Was it recent?"

"A little over six months ago."

"You're so young."

"Yes, that's what everyone says. He was very young too."

The man looked into her eyes for a moment, silent and searching. "I am truly sorry."

He sounded so sincere, like he would say something better if he knew what to say. Maddie gave him a wobbly smile. "Thank you, Mr. Tyler."

"Please, call me Jordan. I'm not quite old enough to be your father." He smiled kindly at her. "You've been through a lot lately, haven't you?" He paused, looking into Maddie's eyes again, and then asked with sudden intent, "Do you live here in town?"

Maddie nodded. "My son, Max, and I just moved back in with my parents. I'll get a place of my own after I find a job."

He stared at her thoughtfully. "You need a job?"

Maddie sniffed, still cold and shaky. "Yes. I've been looking but there isn't much out there that pays well." She didn't mention the hours spent poring over the job ads and the "How to get a Better Career" articles online.

The man nodded at her in understanding. "It can be tough to get back into the workforce. What kind of experience do you have?"

Maddie shook her head, wishing for a tissue, telling herself not to swipe her running nose against the back of her hand. "Office work. I was a regional assistant to a sales manager at one of those weight-loss places and then an office manager at a mobile-phone company. I worked so that my husband could get his MBA. And then, when I was going to go back to school, I got pregnant."

"Any college? What's your educational background?"

"I have a degree in communications from Ball State, before Brandon and I got married. Why are you asking me all of this?"

"Well..." He paused and stared thoughtfully at Maddie. "I can't make any promises, but I just happen to know of a recent job opening here, with the Racers. How would you like to interview for Frank McKlesky's job?"

Maddie sniffed again. "But I've only ever been in administrative assistant roles and a mom."

"We can train you on everything you need to know. Trust me, if Frank could do the job, I think you can. I think you will be better at it, because you've been there. You've experienced tragedy, just like many of the people we help."

"What was Frank's job?"

"One of three foundation coordinators for the Racers. A liaison between the team and the many charities we fund."

"That sounds...good." It sounded amazing.

"Here's my card." He reached toward his jacket pocket, which was currently covering her chest.

Maddie swatted his hand away.

Jordan swallowed. "Sorry, I, uh, my business cards are in that pocket." He pointed to Maddie's chest.

"Oh, sorry. I forgot I was wearing your jacket. I guess I'm a little jumpy after everything." Maddie took off the jacket and handed it back, cool air rushing over her.

Jordan reached into the pocket, scribbled his private cell phone number on it and held out the card. "Call me in the morning and we will get you scheduled for an interview. And call me sooner if you have any pain and need to get that shoulder checked out." He gave her hand a warm squeeze. "Again, my sincerest apologies on behalf of the Racers."

Maddie nodded, barely comprehending it all. Had she really just gotten a job interview with the Indiana Racers?

She changed back into her clothes, throwing the leotard back into the box, imagining burning it, the curling pink fabric going up in pretty flames.

Now, to find Sasha. And hope she wasn't laughing too hard.

CHAPTER THREE

"My mother will kill me if she catches me using this credit card. She's so worried I won't get the job," Maddie complained to Sasha as they walked into the department store.

"Oh, come on. You need work clothes and a killer outfit for the interview. What do you think they pay for a position like that? I'll bet you are going to make loads of money."

Maddie smiled, "I doubt loads. But wouldn't it be perfect? I might even be able to buy Max and me a house."

"Of course you will," Sasha encouraged. "How's your mom taking the news?"

The two veered toward career separates. "She's glad for me. Worried about a million things going wrong, like Mr. Tyler didn't mean it, like he was just trying to satisfy me and will really give me some lame excuse once I get there. And then, if I really get the job, she's worried that I won't be able to do it, of course, but she had tears in her eyes when I told her. She wants something good to happen for us."

"You'll be fine. How hard can fundraising and charity work be? It sounds so perfect for you." Sasha rushed over to a rack. "Oh, look at this."

Maddie had to admit, when it came to clothes, Sasha had a great eye. It was a dark gray jacket and matching pencil skirt that the store had paired with a light pink silk blouse. "I love it. Do they have a six?"

"Have you lost weight?"

"A little. Since Brandon...I just can't seem to eat much."

Sasha nodded, understanding in her brown eyes. "You're going to look great in this. Come on, I see some dark pinstripe pants and a sapphire blouse over there that will look great with your dark hair."

"Sapphire, is it? You've been reading fashion magazines again. You know what I told you about the dangers of fashion magazines."

"Ha! I've been reading Vogue since I was three. Well, looking at the pictures anyway."

Maddie grinned, then turned serious. "I'm so glad you came. I would have shown up at the interview in an old navy-blue suit or something outdated."

"Exactly," Sasha agreed, pulling out the pants and holding them up to Maddie's waist. "Just wait until we get to the jewelry. You're going to look so great they won't even care if you can type."

Maddie laughed. "Oh, I can type. I just don't know if I'll be able to do the rest."

"Just be confident, really…really…confident. And be yourself. Everyone who meets you loves you."

"I hope you're right."

"Anyway, you have a champion, right? What position does Jordan Tyler have in the company? He sounds important enough to push it through."

"His business card says he's the Vice President of Racers, Sports & Entertainment. He was probably afraid I would sue them."

Sasha stopped mid-rummage in a rack. "Hey, you could sue them, you know?"

"Probably, but I wasn't really hurt, so there's no point. I would much rather have the job."

After a couple of hours of trying on clothes and a hefty charge bill, the women left the store for lunch.

Maddie eased her older Nissan into the turning lane for I-69 and a new restaurant on the busy 96th Street. She thought of Max and wondered what he would be eating for lunch. Another bologna sandwich? Her mother seemed to have forgotten how to cook since Maddie and Michelle, her younger sister, had moved out. Every week since she'd been back at home lunch and dinner had revolved around a diet of bologna sandwiches, tacos from the store-bought kits, spaghetti and meatballs and chili. She'd offered to cook, but her mother never seemed to remember to get any of the ingredients she wanted. So mostly she and Max just ate whatever was there.

All she could think of now was a big, fat cheeseburger. Maybe she'd bring one home for Max. The pang in her heart reminded her of just how much she was going to miss him when she went back to work. She couldn't even be gone on a three-hour shopping trip without the image of his chubby-cheeked face popping into her mind. He was two, plenty old enough to be in daycare. But it didn't seem fair. She'd wanted to stay home with him until kindergarten, maybe even have another child before then. They had just started talking about another baby when Brandon had the accident. Now she might never have another one.

The sad, depressed feeling started to come upon her, so she quickly turned to Sasha and said, "I'm tired of thinking about my problems. Let's talk about yours." She grinned. "How are things with Rob?"

Sasha gave her that look that said "don't get me started" while digging into her purse for the pale lip-gloss she couldn't go an hour without. "Driving me crazy, as usual. Just when I think his parents are lightening up about us, and he'll finally get himself down on one knee and give me a big, fat diamond, some family emergency occurs and he has to fly back to Philadelphia. He says he loves me, but sometimes I wonder if he knows how to think on his own. He agrees with me when we're together and then turns around and agrees with them when he goes home. I just wish he would decide what he wants and then stick with it."

"I don't get it," Maddie put in. "Is it you they don't like, or the whole idea of any girl with him?"

"Both. I can't imagine that there will ever be a woman Rob's mother will think is good enough for her son, particularly not an Asian one."

"It's so unfair. She doesn't even know you." Maddie sighed, merging into the far left lane of traffic, then, seeing a Hummer boring down on her from behind, she stepped on the gas. She hadn't gone more than a mile, flying down the road, trying to stay well in front of the Hummer until she could get back over into the center lane when they saw it—police lights.

"Oh, no," they both muttered at the same time.

"Why is he pulling me over? That Hummer was going just as fast and obviously tailgating!"

The Hummer sped by unimpeded as Maddie signaled and pulled off onto the shoulder, the police car right behind her.

"It's called small car discrimination," Sasha remarked. "Someone important might be in that Hummer." Sasha adjusted the vanity mirror, trying to see. "Is he cute, at least?"

"No! Oh, this is just what I need, after spending nearly five hundred dollars on clothes today. A speeding ticket costs about two hundred dollars, doesn't it?"

"Depends. How fast were you going?"

Maddie didn't have time to answer as the tall, lean policeman stepped to the side of the car, leaned down and rapped on the window. "License and registration, ma'am." He looked to be in his late forties, all business with that military crew cut and motorcycle sunglasses. Never a good sign.

"Hi there, occifer, I mean officer." Maddie smiled and tried to be friendly.

"Have you been drinking, ma'am?"

Maddie's eyes widened. "Oh no! No, sir. I just said that because that's the way my son, Max, says 'officer' and I've gotten so used to repeating it because it's so cute." She grimaced and handed him her license. "Sorry."

The cop looked at her sideways as if he had some special method of judging whether or not she was telling the truth, some magic power behind the mirrored shades.

Almost unconsciously, Maddie corrected her posture, letting the D cups do what good they could.

Sure enough, his head shifted, then quickly snapped back to her face, wary of traps.

"Do you know how fast you were going?"

"Uh, not really. The Hummer was bearing down on me pretty hard and I couldn't get immediately back into the center lane, so I just sped up a little. Was it very fast?"

"Fifteen miles over the speed limit. I'm going to have to write you a ticket."

Maddie groaned internally. She really didn't have money for this right now, and who knew when her first real paycheck would come.

She was just about to switch tactics to begging when a movement in her rear view mirror caught her eye.

The police car was moving. It was moving right for them.

"Uh, sir? Is that your car moving?" Maddie turned around just as the cop spun on his shiny police boots toward his vehicle. The car was picking up speed and amazingly, it turned and headed out into open traffic, just missing Maddie's rear right fender.

Sasha started to sputter, squashing laughter.

The cop's eyes bulged and then he took off, running after his car. Vehicles came to a screeching halt as the highway traffic stopped for the runaway vehicle. Maddie joined Sasha, leaning over her steering wheel with choked hysterics as they watched the brown-uniformed sheriff chase after his car. He caught up with it, running straight up the highway, his carriage erect, arms pumping close at his sides. Then, leaning to grasp the door handle, he pulled the door open and dove in. He pumped the brakes, hit the police lights and started the vehicle. Before they knew it, he had sped up and disappeared over a rise in the highway.

"Should we wait? Will he come back?" Maddie asked the shocked face of her friend.

"Are you kidding? Let's get out of here. He would be too embarrassed to chase us down."

"Right. Right. But he has my tags. He knows who I am."

"Just go. We'll say we waited a little while if he tracks us down. Go, girl."

Maddie inched the car into the slow-moving traffic, got into the far right lane and made for the next exit. As soon as they turned off onto 96th Street they started laughing and laughing, Sasha whooping, her arm upraised outside the window.

A cheeseburger from just about anywhere would do fine after that adventure.

CHAPTER FOUR

The steps to the Bankers Life Fieldhouse were wide marble, the walled entrance long panels of tinted glass. Maddie took a deep breath, tottering a little in the new peep-toed, leopard pumps that Sasha had insisted were "just the thing" with the black suit. Her hair was done up in an elegant chignon. Her nails were a classic French manicure, her toenails a dark merlot and, to top it all off, she was wearing perfume. She hadn't looked this good or put such time into her appearance since her wedding day. Her only fear was that she'd overdone it. What if they were all in business casual? Would she look like she was trying too hard? A wannabe New Yorker? It was Indianapolis, after all.

And she would be working with charities. The real reason she was there slammed into her as she reached for the glass door. How was she going to look meeting with charities in this? Like a throw back from Knots Landing, that's what. Dear Lord, why did you let me listen to Sasha? She works at a Bloomingdales, for goodness' sake. She doesn't know what normal is.

Her heels clicked over the smooth, glossy floor as she forced herself to the elevators. There was no time to turn back now. Jordan Tyler was expecting her at 9am sharp. Just concentrate on what's important. The job. Helping the needy.

Sounding halfway intelligent.

She was supposed to go to the Founders Level. Her heart thumped in her chest when the elevator dinged and the doors slid open. Thankfully it was empty. She stepped inside and pushed the number four. It was four, wasn't it? Hadn't Jordan said the fourth floor? Stop it. Of course it was. She clasped her sweaty palms together in front of her and took a long, deep breath.

The doors opened and she walked up to an imposing reception desk, but no one was there. Glancing at her watch, she saw that it was five minutes until nine. She didn't have any time for things to go wrong. Clearing her throat, she leaned over to glance around the desk, hoping to see the receptionist's name, some clue that a real person was coming back, but there was nothing.

Turning, she walked around the reception area, looking at the photos on the wall—all of them of basketball players in various attempts at making a basket or keeping someone else from making a basket, faces grimacing in concentration. She glanced back at her watch—9:00. Where was that receptionist?

When nothing happened after five more minutes, Maddie decided to walk a little way down the hall to see if she could find Mr. Tyler's office herself. It just wouldn't do to be late.

The hall was filled with doors, most of them closed, but there was an open office with a woman inside—a beautiful, more-dressed-up-than-she-was woman. She was standing in front of the desk, bent over and writing with long, slanting handwriting on a piece of stationery. She wore a tight skirt that showed off long legs, a clingy knit blouse with a keyhole neckline and several long, beaded necklaces. She stood and turned as Maddie paused in the open doorway, her long blond hair swinging over one shoulder, her eye makeup giving her a feline stare. "Yes? Can I help you?" Her gaze sized Maddie up from head to toe in a nanosecond.

Maddie cleared her throat. "I'm looking for Jordan Tyler. Do you know where I might find his office?"

The woman's eyes narrowed. "Do you have an appointment with him?"

Maddie nodded. "An interview, at nine."

Her full lips smiled. Her eyes did not. "You're late."

"Yes, well, there hasn't been anyone at the receptionist's desk. I've been trying to find his office for some time now."

The woman tilted her head and smirked. "Wait, I know who you are. You're the woman Frank McKlesky accosted, aren't you? Jordan described you like a damsel in distress and now I can see why." Her top lip curled. "Follow me."

Maddie breathed a sigh of relief. Finally, she would have this interview.

The woman led her back to the lobby, looking even better under the bright, harsh lights in the entry and pushed the down button.

"But Mr. Tyler said to meet him here. On the Founders Level."

"Jordan is a little tied up right now. You'll be meeting with someone else."

That didn't sound good. It didn't sound right, and Maddie was feeling more and more like this woman just wanted to get rid of her.

"Who are you?" She plucked up the courage to ask.

The woman gave Maddie a nudge into the elevator. "Someone to be wary of, believe me. If you want to advance from the laundry department, you should make friends with me."

Was she crazy? "Laundry department? Oh, no, there's been some mistake. I'm interviewing for a coordinator's position for the Racers Foundation."

"Ah, poor dear. Didn't Jordan tell you? No one starts there. Everyone works at least a few weeks at the bottom of the food chain. Then you can move up." Her lips curved into a smile, but her blue eyes shot scorn. The elevator stopped and dinged. The woman stepped out and clasped Maddie's wrist, pulling her along, down another hall toward the locker rooms.

She stopped at a room with a sign on the door saying "Laundry," opened it and gave Maddie a little nudge. "There should be a uniform in there somewhere, dear. You really shouldn't dress up so much for a job like this, you know."

Maddie opened her mouth to protest. This couldn't be right, but the woman interrupted her.

"Remember now, we're friends." She pointed to herself. "Lillian Tyler, Jordan's wife." She smiled again, turned with a click of her heels, and was gone.

His wife? She didn't even work here, did she? Maddie stood blinking at the huge bins of white laundry, trying to put it together. This couldn't be right. Mr. Tyler had been so kind, so promising. He couldn't have planned for her to work in the laundry. But what if he had? What if her mother had been right and it was all too good to be true?

How was she going to tell her mother? Maddie looked toward the white squares of the ceiling for the answer.

Shaking her head, she decided to wait in the room for a few minutes for his wife to hopefully leave and then go back upstairs and track down Jordan Tyler. Even if she did belong in the laundry, someone had to train her, someone had to have her employment information, her social security number and…well…information. She wouldn't leave today without talking to him.

Gosh, it was hot and humid in here. Maddie could feel the sweat start to trickle down her back and around her hairline. Great, when she finally did locate Jordan, she was going to look like she'd been sitting in a sauna. Just wonderful.

Maddie walked over to one of the huge laundry bins, a big canvas bag on wheels, and unbuttoned her suit jacket. The camisole underneath wasn't something she would normally wear alone in public but she had to buy a little time in here and wasn't about to let her suit jacket have armpit rings when she finally got her interview. She laid the jacket across some clean towels.

34

Wow, what a lot of laundry. Standing beside one of the bins, she reached in, her brow wrinkled in curiosity, unable to identify the item. Grasping the side of white cotton, she pulled out an enormous pair of men's briefs. She stifled a giggle. Goodness, they were huge.

Maddie couldn't help but laugh as she held them out in front of her, seeing the familiar words on the waistband. Brandon had worn a 32, but these…she was just peeking inside the waistband to see the size when a loud commotion came from down the hall, coming right toward her. Before she had time to move a muscle, three giant men walked by, saw her, stopped and backed up.

Maddie stepped behind the bin, the underwear clutched to her chest.

"Whatta we have here?" one of the men asked, grinning with big, white teeth and friendly eyes.

Three men in Racers warm-up suits filled the doorway.

"Looks like one pretty lady to me," said the other black man. He looked her up and down, but somehow it didn't feel bad…it felt like he had just paid her a compliment. "And holding somebody's shorts." He cocked his head and looked at the third man. "Those yours, Jake?"

Any response Jake might have had was ignored in the ensuing laughter.

"You're not a stalker, are you?" the first guy asked with that dazzling smile, his chin jutting out as he spoke. "Yeah, we know your game."

"She can be my stalker," said the second man, who Maddie was starting to remember was Tyson Jackson, number 42. She had memorized most of the players just in case she needed to appear a fan for the interview.

35

The three walked further into the room, making it feel tiny. One of the players gently tugged the underwear out of her hands and stared at them. "I think these *are* yours, Jake." He teased the third man, who had black hair, smoky green-hazel eyes, and a very attractive five o'clock shadow.

Jake turned a little red as he stared at Maddie. He seemed to be waiting for her to explain, but she couldn't seem to push enough air out of her lungs for speech. After a couple of tries, she finally managed, "I, ah. You wouldn't believe me if I told you," she decided, grabbing her suit jacket and rushing her arms through the sleeves.

One of the men politely helped her into it, making her feel like a little doll he was dressing. They were so huge!

"Sure we would. Don't go rushing off. What's your name?"

"Maddie. Madeline Goode," she stated with as much authority as she could muster, straightening her jacket, the cami and her skirt with little tugs and twitches. "And I need to get back to the Founders Level. I have an appointment."

The man she recognized as Tyson laughed. "Maddie Goode. She sure do look good." He grinned at his teammates, then turned his attention back to Maddie. "What are you doing down here, baby? And clutchin' Jake's underwear. You a fan?"

Maddie shook her head. "I don't even like sports. Basketball especially. Now please, gentlemen, let me by."

The men moved out of the way, but Jake stopped her by touching her shoulder as she passed him. "Do you need some help? Did something happen up there?"

She started to say no, but then the image of her walking back into those offices with actual players beside her changed her mind. She needed this job, and not the laundry job. She might have a fight on her hands and it couldn't hurt to have a wall of Racers at her back. "Well, actually, I might need a little help."

She explained what had happened, leaving out some of the details, telling about the arm wrenching by Mr. McKlesky, but leaving out the embarrassing dance number. She also took the high road and did not mention how rude and strange the woman, Jordan's wife, had been, saying that it must have been a misunderstanding.

Tyson said, "We'll get you in front of Jordan. He's a good man. He wouldn't mess with you. If he said you could have the job, then he'll give it to you."

The other black man said, "Now Tyson, you know coach won't like it if we don't get to practice on time. Especially after last week. Let Jake go. His record is so clean it squeaks."

"But she's a damsel in distress, man. Coach'll understand."

"Yeah, like you haven't used that excuse three times already this month. Let's go. Jake, you got her?"

Jake nodded. "Go on. I won't be long."

The elevator, so large before, seemed crowded now with Jake in it. Number 14—Jake Hart. If only Sasha could see her now. Maddie thought she should get his autograph for her or something, but that seemed lame, especially since he was so serious and quiet.

"So, you don't like basketball, huh?" He leaned against the back railing of the elevator with an elegant ease that made Maddie's heart speed up.

Maddie blushed. "Sorry. I haven't been a big fan in the past, but honestly, I've only been to one game and that was last weekend when this whole mess started." She paused and then said with soft wonder, "I have to confess, during the first quarter something strange happened to me. I was really getting into it. They are in quarters, right?"

Jake let out a laugh and nodded, then pressed his lips together into a smile. "Yeah."

Maddie couldn't stop staring at his face. She probably appeared star-struck, a look he must be used to from women. She looked down at the buttons on the elevator, feeling like a traitor. Her husband was barely cold and here she was staring at her best friend's crush. She deserved the laundry job.

Trying to keep talking so that she wouldn't stare, she continued. "Well, I was really starting to enjoy the game, feeling the whole atmosphere and excitement of it. So," she shrugged, "who knows. I might turn into a fan after all."

They both realized the elevator doors had stood open for some time and were now closing again. Jake leaned across from behind her to hit the open button, brushing against her back with his long arm. She barely suppressed the squeak of startled excitement leaping from her throat.

"Let's see if we can find Jordan for you."

CHAPTER FIVE

It was as if she held a magic charm in her hand.

The receptionists, two of them, so pretty and smiling, welcomed them into the foyer, offered coffee and gazed, dazzle-eyed, at Jake. They listened attentively to Maddie's short version of the story and then buzzed Mr. Tyler. Like a well-oiled machine, Jordan Tyler came out, apologized for being absent earlier, the gross misunderstanding, and gushed thanks to Jake for lending his talented helping hand.

As she started off toward Jordan's office, Jake leaned down to whisper something into her ear. Her whole spine tingled in anticipation as he brushed back her hair with a hand and leaned in, his breath warm, her neck tense in anticipation. "Your shirt's unbuttoned. You might want to fix that." He stood back up, winked at her and was gone, a long-legged stride headed for the elevator and his home—the basketball court.

Maddie felt her face turn degrees of red. Glancing down, she noticed that the cami had come unbuttoned and was askew, showing more cleavage than was acceptable for an interview. Looking back up, she saw that Jordan had stopped, turned, and was staring at her, a patient smile on his face. She couldn't fix it now and draw attention to it. It was bad enough that it might look like she and Jake had just fooled around in the elevator. She pulled her jacket closer together, put her chin up, and followed Mr. Tyler to his office. Better to just brazen it out for now and look for an opportunity to fix it later.

Nodding and smiling, she caught up with him, sighing in relief to see that his office was empty. She sat down, pulled her resume out of her bag, the bag she'd bought Brandon when he'd gotten the job at First Old Bank of Indiana in Muncie, and squelched the turmoil of emotions that were rollicking within her.

"I thought you might like to see it," she stated nervously as she slid the short document across his desk toward him.

"Thank you, Maddie. And again, so sorry about the mix-up this morning." His voice quieted. "My wife and I are going through a divorce and it has been rather unsettling at times."

Maddie nodded, squashing the words "I can see why that would be the case" between her teeth. Instead she said, "I'm so sorry. This must be a difficult time for you."

It was what so many had said to her after the funeral and just popped out before she had time to judge whether or not it was appropriate.

Jordan just smiled and nodded. "We are both in a difficult personal time, are we not? But, that doesn't mean our work has to suffer. Have you seen the building? There is even a daycare across the street if you need one. You could have lunch with your son every day."

Maddie nodded her thanks, wondering suddenly how Max was doing at her mother's. Her mother meant well and tried to be a good grandmother, but she was so worried Max would hurt himself. She chain-smoked with the litany "Max, be careful. Max, don't do that." Or "Good lord, Max, you'll kill yourself climbing up that high." It was the last one that sent a spike of anger through Maddie's spine. She didn't want her child growing up like she had—half convinced she wouldn't see her next birthday. Maddie had written out her final will and testimony on her dad's fancy stationery at age nine, signing away all her stuffed animals, Barbies and the forty-three hard-earned dollars in her ceramic piggy bank. Every time she caught herself saying something like that to Max, she changed tactics and applauded him instead. It had been tough breaking that pattern, but she was determined.

She shook her head, feeling some of the hair in the coil at her nape start to slide. A big section came completely undone and piled on her shoulder. Oh, great! Her new boss was someone she desperately wanted to impress. She had to get this job! Maddie quickly reached up to fix her hair, not realizing the effect on the unbuttoned cami until Jordan's eyes glanced there. Looking down, she did a mental groan. Would something please go right today?

Forgetting the hair, she just let the rest of it fall, gave it a quick shake to settle it, hoping it looked halfway decent, and concentrated on the interview. "Tell me about the position. I am so…eager." God, help! "That is, excited to hear about it."

Jordan turned in his chair, found some papers on one corner of his desk and pulled them out.

"As coordinator for the Racers Foundation, you will be one of three team members in charge of managing the relationship between the foundation and the various charities we sponsor."

"I've been reading about the charities. The foundation is so generous."

Jordan nodded. "We have several reading programs for the kids, sponsor the Make-A-Wish Foundation, our own school, the Racers Academy for kids at risk, the Halloween party fundraiser, golf outings, several meet-and-greets throughout the year and so on."

"It sounds wonderful," Maddie said, and she meant it.

"Good. I have a feeling you will be perfect for this job. Now, the first thing is some paperwork to fill out." He slid a thick envelope over to her. "You will find our official offer with your full compensation package—salary, benefits, that sort of thing— inside here. Look it over and if you have any questions just come back to my office. I should be here all day today. I'll be glad to help." He stood. "Let's go have a look at your office."

The job was hers? It was that easy? She had her own office? Maddie rose, nodding, trying to keep her knees from knocking together.

They went a few doors down the hall and then Jordan paused, waiting for her to catch up. He turned the knob and smiled.

41

"Frank McKlesky hasn't picked up his things yet, but we boxed them up and left them downstairs at the main desk so you should be all set. He was more than relieved that you decided not to press charges."

Maddie just nodded. The man had lost his job over it, a job she was taking, and she just didn't feel she needed to punish him further.

The office was small and spare but had tons of potential, with tall ceilings and long, graceful windows. The only furniture was the desk, a lovely piece that looked like an antique in the Cabriole style. Maddie walked over to it and ran her hand along the leather top, admiring the ball and claw cabriole legs, imagining a velvet-cushioned bench as her office chair.

"You like the desk?" Jordan asked with a smile.

Maddie glanced up at him, pressing her lips together in a smile, trying to suppress her glee. "Oh, sorry. I have a thing for antiques. This is a really lovely piece."

"Don't apologize. After all that you have been through, I am happy to have something for you that you obviously appreciate." He looked around the room as if just noticing how bare it was. "Feel free to order furniture and decorate it any way you like."

"Thank you." She couldn't wait to get started.

Jordan took her to the window and showed her the view of downtown Indianapolis, looking over Pennsylvania Street, then he motioned her to follow him back out. "Let's introduce you to your co-workers."

He led her to two other offices down the hall. Randy Bentley was a middle-aged, slightly overweight and balding man with glasses and a big, friendly smile and handshake. "Frank was working on the Halloween party fundraiser," he informed Maddie. "Do you like to plan parties? That's about all there is to it."

Maddie nodded, memories of her last party flickering in her mind. They'd run out of ice, didn't have enough food and several of Brandon's friends had turned up intoxicated and obnoxious, staying the night because they lacked a designated driver. She wouldn't exactly call it a raving success.

Pushing those memories aside, she nodded and stated, "It sounds very exciting."

"I'll get you all the information and Frank's contacts. He was working with the caterers last week, as I recall." Shaking her hand again, he boomed, "Great to have you on board, Maddie."

In the next office sat a petite, pretty woman with short, blunt-cut dark hair and dark-rimmed glasses. She had on bright red lipstick that was pretty on women like her with creamy translucent skin. She wore a black dress that looked designer and fit her curves perfectly, high-heeled, black boots, the shiny kind that a woman had to wrestle up her leg, and gold jewelry, which completed the impact of success, confidence and wealth. Maddie was suddenly very glad of Sasha's help with her wardrobe.

The woman waved them in, talking on the phone and rising from her chair, motioning for them to sit down. Maddie listened as she articulated what she wanted from someone, flipping through papers and rattling off numbers. She sounded like someone who knew what she was doing and did it well.

Hanging up, she smiled and reached for Maddie's hand. "Katherine Hutchins. So good to meet you, Madeline. I heard what happened with Frank and can still hardly believe it." She shook her head, dark-brown bob waving back and forth. "He was a little strange, but we had no idea he would snap like that. You weren't hurt, were you?"

Maddie shook her hand, took the offered seat and smiled. "No, thankfully, my shoulder seems fine."

"Good. Now, I plan to show you the ropes and ease you into this. I understand you've been out of the workplace for some time and I want to reassure you that I'm here to help in any way I can."

Maddie felt a rush of appreciation. "Thank you. I'm sure I will need some guidance. But I am very eager to get started."

"Excellent." She turned to Jordan and smiled. It was such a different smile than the one she had given Maddie that Maddie found herself staring.

"Jordan, why doesn't she just shadow me today? I'm covered up, but I'm sure I can squeeze in some training as we go."

Had her voice taken on a silkier tone?

Maddie watched as Jordan Tyler fumbled for a response, seemingly mesmerized and unable to speak. Finally he managed, "That sounds wonderful. Thank you, Kat."

"Anything for you."

She said it like a caress. Was this the reason for his divorce? Maddie forced the shocked look from her face. Kat just grinned and waved him from the room.

"Now," she stated, staring at Maddie thoughtfully, "you're much too pretty to be left in uncertainty, so I will tell you. Jordan is taken." She smiled again, perfect white teeth showing as only a predator knows how to smile. "By two women presently, but that is soon to change. He is too old for you anyway."

Maddie could feel her eyes widen. "I, um, that is, I haven't any designs on Mr. Tyler."

"Good. Perfect. Now. Let's see what we can come up with for you to do while I make a few calls." She sat down and turned her laptop around so that Maddie could use it. "Look over my calendar and the files on the Halloween party. Frank was having trouble with the caterer, if I recall, and we'll need to make other arrangements for that. Also, there is a press release about a meet-

and-greet that we need to write up and send off as soon as possible. Can you write?"

Maddie thought back to her college English classes and nodded, but a bubble of panic was rising. "If you have a template, some examples, I'm sure I can manage it."

"Fine. And Madeline..." Maddie looked up and into Kat's startling blue eyes.

"What I've told you is confidential and a test. If you pass, you will find I can be a very good friend."

Maddie swallowed. Everyone seemed to want to be her friend for one reason or another. The only problem was they all seemed to have ulterior motives. "Yes, ma'am," she murmured.

Katherine shook her head. "Please, no ma'ams. Just call me Kat. All my friends call me Kat and I think you and I are going to be very, very good friends." She smiled again and Maddie didn't like it.

She didn't like it one bit.

CHAPTER SIX

Jake rode down in the elevator in something of a daze. He stepped out, making his way to the practice court, blinking and wondering what was making him feel like he'd just been punched in the stomach.

It wasn't like he hadn't been out with a pretty woman lately. He dated pretty women fairly often; he had taken out the lovely model, Maria Saberio, Saturday night after the game. He shook his head as if to clear it.

Practice was already in session when he entered the court. He brushed off the disgruntled look on his coach's face as he shed his warm-up suit and jogged out onto the floor. The ball came at him like a bullet with the phrase, "Where you been, Jake?"

Jake ignored Toshner, dribbled inside and sunk a basket. He was feeling on.

"Watch out," another player laughed, "Jake's gotten himself all hot and bothered."

His friend, Ricky Ballard, took a shot, missed, and Jake jumped for the rebound. "Who is she?" Ballard asked, laughing.

"Up in corporate. Pretty thing, all long legs and killer—"

"Tyson." Jake shot him a warning glance.

"Interesting." Ballard stole the ball and shot. "Where was I? How come you always get so lucky?" This time he made it, over the half-court line. There was some brief hand slapping as a couple of his teammates ran past, then the pace quickened and they all got serious.

A couple of hours later the team showered and regrouped in the media room to study the video from the last game. Jake sat next

46

to Ballard, near the assistant coaches and toward the front.

Ricky Ballard leaned close. "So, come on. Who is she?"

Jake shrugged. "I just met her, man. Maddie something. She needed some help getting in front of Jordan Tyler."

Ballard's bushy eyebrows lifted. "Really? That's it?"

Jake jerked his head toward the back. "You know how they are."

"She was pretty, though? A new employee?"

Jake breathed deep, once. "Yeah, she was real pretty."

"Hey, if you've got a thing for her, tell me now. You never know. I might run into her, and my charms are legendary."

Jake laughed. "Yeah, I know."

"Well?"

"Well, give me some time to think it over."

The replay started on the big screen so both men quieted down to watch. There were lots of notes to take, replay after replay to watch. Professional ball was as mental as it was physical. The smart guys knew best how to play the game.

As the second quarter wound down, the video ran into halftime and the team dispersed to stretch and take a lunch break. Coach Brown let the film run, everybody pretty much ignoring it as they reached for something to drink and eat from the spread of catering in the back of the media room.

Suddenly Tyson's voice broke through the chatter. "Hey, Jake, isn't that your new girl?"

All eyes turned to the big screen and a hush settled over the team as a group of horribly costumed, mostly overweight dancers

47

made their way to the middle of the court. There, on the far side of the line, stood Maddie Goode. Jake was sure of it.

Shock rippled through him as she strutted and shook her hips, the leotard looking too tight, a black bra showing through, a determined smile pasted on her face.

The men started laughing and Jake felt his face turning a shade of red.

Someone whistled. "Your girl sure got some curves, Jake."

"She isn't my girl. I just helped her find her interview," Jake growled.

"Awww, come on, she's smokin' hot. She got the full package, man."

Jake turned away, his stomach churning. There she was, big as life on the screen in front of them, the camera zooming in on her face. A spotlight-grubbing floozy disguised in a nice suit had momentarily blinded him. Jake couldn't believe he'd considered asking her out. He should have known better. He knew what women were all about—the money. He'd made that mistake a long time ago and it still stung when he thought of his longest relationship. Thankfully, he had seen what Maddie was really made of before it had come to making another big mistake.

Turning to Ballard, he said, "You can have her."

~~~~~~~

Maddie was exhausted as she pulled into her parents' driveway—rush-hour traffic, first day of a new job kind of tired. Her head was spinning with all the new information that Kat had rattled off to her from her pouty red lips. Her body felt as wiped out as she did during the first trimester of pregnancy. How had she managed to work full-time in an office during all of Max's pregnancy? She could barely move. Worse, at 6:00 in the evening, Max would be going through his cranky phase and her mom would be obsessing whether or not Maddie had survived the semi-truck jockeying on I-70 in her beat-up Nissan.

She put the car into park and just sat, for one quiet moment, in the driveway, closing her eyes and taking some deep relaxing breaths, turning up Sarah McLachlan on the car stereo. She felt the strains of the piano echo inside her body, felt the hum from her throat as she began to sing along, connecting with what Sarah called *a beautiful release*. She sang along, thinking that her voice still sounded okay. She used to sing in high school and then in a choir at her church, but after Max was born life had gotten so busy. She hadn't really sang in long time but listening to music had become something of a life-giving force since Brandon had died, giving her a cushioned landing place when the grief felt about to crush her.

As the song faded away, she turned off the car, pasted a big smile on her face and walked up the sidewalk to the front door. She opened it to see her mother coming around the corner from the kitchen, Max in her arms. "Maddie? Oh, thank goodness, I was getting worried. How did it go?"

Maddie dropped her satchel on the couch, feeling like it had been a lifetime since she had walked so excitedly out with it this morning. "It went really well." She gave her mom a perfunctory smile and reached for her son. "Max, come here to Mommy."

Max rushed into her arms, all fresh smelling from his bath, PJs on and grinning from ear to ear. He put his chubby arms around her neck, squeezing tight, making Maddie laugh.

Maddie buried her nose into his curly, golden-brown hair. "Oh, Max. I missed you today. Did you have a good day with Grammy?"

"He didn't eat his dinner," Gloria said, lighting up.

"Mom, can't you smoke that outside? It's not good for Max." Maddie hated to ever say anything negative to her mother, but this was one area that had to be addressed, especially since she wasn't home all day to monitor it.

Gloria nodded. "Oh, yeah, I forgot." She went to the door and hung her arm out, letting the cool, autumn air into the living room.

Maddie pulled Max onto the sofa with her, still cuddling him close. "So, what did you do today? Did you have fun?"

"Saw a doggie," Max announced with a big smile.

Gloria shook her head from her stance at the door. "I thought he was going to get bitten for sure. He chased after every dog in the park today, but he really went after this one cute puppy."

"Really? A puppy, Max?" Maddie ignored the near-fatal wounding. "What color was he?"

"Brown with a big white spot," said Max. "I think I loved him."

Maddie felt her heart expand and sudden tears rush to her eyes. "Oh, Max. Did you find out his name?"

"Doggie."

Gloria laughed from the door. "Her name was Doodles. The owner was a nice grandmother who thought Max was adorable."

"Which he is," they both said at the same time.

Gloria and Maddie laughed.

"I want a doggie," Max stated, crossing pudgy arms over his chest. "A big white doggie."

Maddie shook her head, still smiling. "Maybe someday. Maybe when we get our own house, then we will get a dog."

"Dogs are a lot of work, Maddie. You're going to have your hands full enough being a single parent to Max and working full-time."

Maddie nodded slowly and shrugged. "You're probably right, but you never know. We might be able to get one someday."

"How did your first day go? Did they really give you the job?"

"Yes. It was good. I think once I get over the learning curve, I'm really going to like it." She left out all the morning drama with Jordan's almost ex-wife. "I'm starving though, any dinner left?"

"Tacos in the fridge. I saved you two."

Tacos. Great. Maddie pulled Max closer into her arms and started for the kitchen. "Let's go warm up Mommy's dinner and you can tell me all about your day, okay sweetie?"

Gloria, thankfully, left them alone in the kitchen while Maddie heard Max's account of the day—the park, the cartoons he had watched, too many cartoons, and how grandpa had played horsey ride with him when he got home from work. Maddie nodded, smiling encouragement, popping bits of her untouched taco into his mouth while she asked him questions, trying all the while to steel herself against overwhelming feelings of loss.

It would crash in on her at odd times, like now, when she wasn't looking for it and hadn't the energy to steel herself against it. She wanted to fall in a heap on the cold kitchen floor. She wanted to bury her head into her hands and never look up again. But she couldn't do that. She had to be strong for Max. But she wasn't strong enough to block out the leaden litany of her heart drowning out the soft tones of her son's chatter. *Why did you leave us, Brandon? Why did everything have to change? I miss you so much. God help me, I miss you.*

The anger was lessening, though. Now she felt mostly a raw sadness that gnawed at her insides—moments that stole her breath away and left her aching for just one more time to be in his arms.

"Come on, Max," she coaxed, staring into the deep brown eyes of what she still had. "Let's read a story before bedtime."

Max nodded. "Daddy read it?"

Oh no. She really couldn't do this tonight. Not tonight. "Daddy's gone, Max, remember?" Her throat choked on the words, making her silently berate herself. "Mommy will read you a great story." Her voice sounded angrier than she wanted it to. He was only two. He didn't understand.

"Daddy's in heaven," Max said, pointing to the ceiling.

A tear escaped, darn it. Darn it! She would not cry tonight.

Gloria came into the room and scooped Max into her arms. "Yes, sweetie. Daddy's in heaven having a great big time up there with God. And someday we'll all be up there with them. But for now let's go read that story."

Maddie smiled at her mother through her tears. "Thanks, Mom."

Gloria nodded, smoothed down Maddie's hair like she used to when she was a little girl. "I'll read the first one and then you can come in and read him his favorite."

Maddie nodded, wiping her cheeks and sniffing.

Gloria looked deep into her daughter's eyes. "It's going to be okay, Maddie. It will get easier."

"Will it?"

Gloria nodded. "I promise."

Maddie watched her mother pad down the hall with Max's arms wrapped around her neck and tried to pull herself together. Taking a couple of deep breaths and blowing her nose, she pasted another smile, a mother's mask, on her face and followed them into the makeshift bedroom that had belonged to her little sister before Michelle had gone away to college.

They were lucky—blessed—to have this place to go to and parents who loved and cared for them. And she had a promising new job. She needed to focus on the good things in her life.

Maddie entered the bedroom and couldn't help the laugh that escaped seeing Max cuddled up under her sister's faded but soft comforter. There was another thing to be thankful for—thank God Max didn't seem to mind the bright floral wallpaper or her sister's big pink bed.

CHAPTER SEVEN

"I can't believe we're going to this fundraiser," Sasha gushed, climbing into the limo where Maddie sat, hands clasped tightly in her lap.

"I know! Oh, Sasha, you look amazing."

"So do you. Who knew fairies could be so sexy?"

Maddie laughed, looking down at her white satin gown. "It's not too much? I even have glitter eyelashes and a wand, see?" She waved it in front of Sasha's nose.

"You look ethereal. Really. Now, what about me?"

Sasha was dressed in black from the tip of her pointy hat to the low, jagged-cut black mini-dress, black fishnets and pointy-toed red sling-backs. "You make a very cute witch," Maddie assured her.

"Cute? Cute is *not* what I was going for." Sasha pouted.

"Okay, okay! Hot…sexy! You will steal the show!" Maddie giggled.

"That's more like it." Sasha burst out laughing.

The limo pulled with silken ease from the street outside Sasha's house, heading toward the Hilton Hotel where the Halloween party and fundraiser for the Racers was to be held.

When they were close, Sasha grasped Maddie's arm. "I'm so excited! Will Jake Hart be there?"

Maddie laughed. "I think so. But you promised to be good, Sasha, remember? This is a business event for me."

Sasha opened her mouth and jutted out her chin in mock offense. "What do you think I'm going to do, attack him on the dance floor or something?"

"Well …" Maddie giggled as Sasha's wand appeared, waving menacingly in front of Maddie's eyes. "Just don't change him into a frog and slip him into your pocket or anything, okay?"

"What a great idea! I knew there was a reason I brought you." Sasha grinned, eyes overly bright.

Maddie collapsed back into the leather seat with a howl of laughter.

When the laughter died down, Sasha asked, "So, you nervous about how this is going to go? You've been working so hard on it."

It was true. The last few weeks had been a whirlwind of hard effort and training. She had been given this fundraiser, one of the Racers' biggest fundraisers of the year, as the ultimate test. If she pulled this off then she could do just about anything else her job might require.

"I'll be glad when it's over, that's for sure. But really, I think it just might go off without a hitch."

"Your wedding was fabulous and you practically planned that all by yourself," Sasha reminded her as they turned into the hotel's parking garage.

"Yes, it was," Maddie agreed with a small smile and dreamy voice. "As long as there is plenty of good food and drinks…and the band, as long as they like the band, everything else should take care of itself."

The girls climbed out of the limo, admiring each other's costumes again, and then made their way up the grand staircase to the ballroom. It was early, but Maddie wanted to be on hand in case she was needed. It was a good thing, because the minute she walked into the door, Randy Bentley approached her, panic in his eyes. "We have a problem."

"What is it?"

"Two of the players, one of whom is supposed to speak soon, are in the bar, and they've already had too much to drink. We have to get those boys sobered up."

Boys? These were grown men. Multimillionaire, hard-disciplined, grown men. How was Maddie supposed to have any sway over them? "Are they here alone? Any wives or girlfriends?" Maddie had learned not to associate with the players much, especially the ones with wives and girlfriends. She'd learned to go through the women, make friends with them first, and then other avenues might be opened for her to be friendly with the players.

"No. They came stag."

"Who is it?"

"Hart and Cornell."

Hart? Her stomach flip-flopped. "Have you talked to them?"

"I tried, believe me." Randy pulled out a handkerchief and dabbed at his receding hairline. "They got me in a headlock and tried to pour a drink down my throat." He blushed against the white collar of his tuxedo shirt and admitted, "They said if I go back in there and bother them they'll do body shots on my…well, you girls probably know more about what those are than I do, but I'm not risking it. You'll have to give it a try."

Sasha laughed. Maddie rolled her eyes. "Great. Okay, I'll go see what I can do. Anything else going wrong? People will start to arrive in about fifteen minutes."

He shook his head. "You've done a great job, Maddie. Everything from the decorations to the food looks great, better than last year. I'll keep an eye on things out here. Maybe you and your

56

friend can use a little feminine charm to bring those guys around. Let me know if they give you any real trouble though, okay?"

Maddie nodded and took Sasha's arm. "We'll be all right."

Randy nodded, his relief obvious. "You look great, by the way. Both of you."

"Thanks."

Maddie led Sasha into the darker, adjoining room, where a dance floor, a stage, and a long, low-lit bar had been set up. "Come on, let's see if we can talk some sense into these guys."

"I can't talk to them yet," Sasha whispered, wide-eyed and suddenly nervous. "I pictured myself nicely inebriated before talking to any of the players. And 'Hart' means Jake Hart, right? I'm about to meet Jake?"

Maddie rolled her eyes and laughed, pulling her friend along. "Their size is worse than their demeanor. Now show some backbone. Come on."

Sure enough, as they came closer to where the two men sat, Jake's voice rang out, slightly slurred, "Would you look at that, Marcus. A witch and an angel, comin' to visit us."

Marcus whistled. "I'll take the witch over an angel any day." Then louder, directed to them. "Well hello ladies, come on over and have a drink."

Maddie and Sasha came up to them, Sasha standing right in front of Jake. "I'll have a drink," she said, ignoring Maddie's shocked stare. "Cosmopolitan, please."

Jake grinned at her, turned to the bartender to order her the drink and then swung back suddenly to Maddie with the question "What'll you have, angel?"

"I'm not an angel. I'm a fairy. And I won't be drinking anything."

"Wait a minute." His eyes squinted in the dim light as he stared at Maddie's face. His head nodded up. "You're that girl. Working for the foundation."

Maddie gave him a single nod. "Yes, I am. Now Mr. Hart, I've put a lot of time and effort into this event and you are supposed to say a few opening remarks, remember?"

"Of course I remember."

Maddie backed down at his tone. "Well, you seem a little…um, inebriated, to be precise, and I'd like to help you sober up before your speech."

Jake's gaze took on a sudden disenchanted sheen. "Oh yeah? How are you planning to do that?"

Maddie fiddled with her skirt, not meaning to draw attention to the clingy sheath of white satin. "Coffee, maybe? Have you eaten anything? Could I get you some appetizers?"

Jake laughed, low and dark. "Sure, let's go up to my room and have an appetizer together. Why not? I've seen you in your costume and I know how good you can move." His sarcasm was like a slap in the face.

Maddie took a shocked breath. "What are you talking about?"

"Halftime, at the game. You know, you had yourself sashaying all over that floor. Best girl there," he laughed, "not that any of them were much to watch."

Maddie felt sudden, angry tears gather in her eyes. Why was he attacking her like this? "Fine. Give your speech and make a fool out of yourself. It will only reflect badly on you, not me." She turned, choking over her shoulder to Sasha, who looked equally color-drained, "Come on, Sasha. You can't possibly have a crush on this jerk now."

Maddie stopped and turned back toward Sasha, wondering why she wasn't right behind her. She watched in suspended horror as Sasha grabbed her drink from the bar and said to Jake with a low, hissing voice, "You have no idea what you're talking about or who you're talking about. Maddie is the best person I know and was begged to dance that night, replacing someone who was sick at the last minute. She didn't want to do it. She didn't even know the routine. She did it for the kids at Colburn Place."

Maddie cringed when Sasha squinted her eyes until they were slits of anger. "You're not worthy to kiss the soles of her shoes, you, you, cad." With the look of a sudden decision, Sasha threw the red drink in Jake's face.

She turned, leaving two shocked, slack-jawed men in her wake, catching up to Maddie and rushing with her to the ladies room to freshen up.

"Oh, Maddie, how horrible was he?"

Maddie clung to Sasha's shoulder. "Why? Why would he say those terrible things about me? What have I ever done to him?"

Sasha handed her some tissue. "Who knows? What a conceited monster! I can't believe I wasted hours of my life daydreaming about him. Are they all that awful?"

Maddie shook her head, blowing her nose. "I hope not. I've only met a few. But it's so strange. He was so nice in the elevator my first day."

"Elevator? You didn't tell me about any elevator encounter with Jake Hart. What happened?"

"I didn't tell you because I knew you would be mad that I didn't get his autograph for you. He was helping me get past the ex-wife to my interview. Remember? I said one of the players escorted me back to Jordan's office?"

"Oh, yeah, you just didn't mention who. I wouldn't have been mad. Gosh, especially not now. If I had his autograph, I'd

59

staple it to his forehead and throw darts at it."

Maddie giggled, imagining it. "Thanks for sticking up for me. I—I didn't know what to do."

Sasha dug into her tiny black-sequined bag and held out a pale pink lip-gloss. "Here, get some makeup back on and we'll get right back out there and ignore him and his friend for the rest of the night."

Maddie nodded. "You're right. I have to get back out there and pretend it didn't really upset me." She grimaced when she looked at her blotchy face and smeared mascara. "Men," she muttered as she reapplied the eyeliner, cleaning up the smudges under her eyes. "My makeup was perfect."

"Hurry. We don't want to be missed."

After fixing Maddie's face, they turned and rushed out the door. Maddie was shocked into stillness to feel a hand on her shoulder and a tall presence looming at her back.

"Maddie?"

She turned slowly to see Jake Hart, devastatingly handsome in black tie, even with the cranberry-colored wet spots on his white shirtfront from Sasha's drink. He looked from Maddie's surprised face to Sasha's and then back again, a frown between his brows.

"I came to apologize. I, um…" He seemed completely sober now. "Seems I jumped to some conclusions about you. And I'm sorry." He looked to Sasha again. "You were right. I really don't know her at all. Thanks for setting me straight."

Sasha visibly gulped.

Maddie could only stare.

"Will you forgive me?" His voice was so deep and quiet and sincere. Maddie felt herself go warm all over and found that her head was nodding and shaking at the same time. "Of course," she managed out of a tight throat.

60

"Will you save me a dance? I'd like to get to know the real Maddie Goode."

Maddie thought she might faint, but took a deep breath instead. "Okay, I guess."

He smiled, a real, warm, inviting smile that made her head swim like the time she had a terrible cold and a touch of vertigo.

"Good." He lifted her hand to his lips and brushed a kiss across the back of her fingers. "I still think you're an angel...no fairy looks this pure." Then he was walking away with his long-legged stride down the hall. He turned at the entrance to the men's room and grinned at Sasha, teasing, "You think I can get this stain out of my shirt before my big speech?"

Sasha grimaced. "Sorry," then she shrugged, a half-pained, half-happy expression on her face. "But you did deserve it and I've always wanted a good excuse to do that."

Jake laughed and disappeared into the men's room.

They turned toward each other, both wide-eyed and staring.

"I can't believe it. A monster one minute and a prince the next. Do you think that was real?" Maddie questioned.

"Wow. If it wasn't, he's a very good actor. Maddie, he asked you to dance!"

Maddie brushed back her hair nervously. "I know. Do I know how to dance?"

"Of course you do, you're a great dancer. Now let's go mingle and get some food. Best thing to do is act like it was no big deal. Let's ignore him for a while."

Maddie nodded with a tight smile. "Okay. I'm so glad you're here, Sasha. I truly think I would ruin my life without you."

CHAPTER EIGHT

After cocktails, there was a four-course dinner. A bowl of either French onion or cream of artichoke soup made up the first course, followed by a finely chopped salad with creamy parmesan dressing. Maddie had agonized over the main course, finally settling on a choice of roast beef or salmon, steamed veggies, asparagus with mustard cream sauce, twice-baked potatoes loaded with anything they could want on a potato and huge yeast rolls. Dessert consisted of vanilla flan with amber-colored caramel sauce or creamy chocolate mousse, all of which Maddie had gotten to sample before choosing a caterer. That had been a great two weeks, sampling food and being acquiesced to as the Racers representative.

Now she hung back, overseeing the guests, a few she recognized, many she did not, but knew them mostly to be distinguished community leaders. The mayor and his lovely wife sat at one of the round tables in the center toward the front of the room with another politician, a university president, a doctor who was a close friend of the mayor's family and a local celebrity, the current Miss USA. She was gorgeous in a sequined gown, Miss USA sash and tiara, which Maddie presumed was the costume of a beauty queen.

"Must be nice to look like that all the time," Sasha had whispered to Maddie when they'd first seen her.

Their table looked happy—plenty of food and a handsome waiter at their beck and call. Her gaze roving, she spotted a gentleman growing loud and animated. Gliding near the table she casually studied him, waved over the waiter for their table and whispered, "Water down Dr. Sinclair's next vodka tonic a bit, yes?"

The waiter nodded, understanding and a slight smile of respect lighting his eyes.

Maddie turned to circle the room one last time before sitting down to her own dinner and nearly walked into a wall of muscle.

"Oh," she exclaimed, stepping on his foot with her silver sandal. "Excuse me."

Low male laughter. "That wasn't how I envisioned getting you back into my arms, but I suppose it will do."

Maddie's head jerked up to look into the eyes of someone familiar, though at first she couldn't quite place him. The lighting was low, candles everywhere, reflecting the colors Maddie had chosen of gold, yellows and reds, making it difficult to see the man's face, standing in the shadows as he was.

Suddenly it clicked. "Greg? Greg Foreman?" She took a step back.

"Maddie. It's been so long since I've seen you. What are you doing here?"

"I...I work for the Racers." Incredibly, he looked better than he had in college.

"Really? Wow. What do you do?"

"I am a coordinator for the Racers Foundation. How are you? I saw all the names on the guest list but don't remember seeing your name."

"Really? Well, I *was* invited." He was sounding a little heated.

"Of course, you were. It's a wonderful party, is it not?" Her gaze swept the elegant room.

"Maddie...you've changed so much, I hardly recognized you. You look really... spectacular."

Maddie wasn't sure if that was a compliment or not. She smiled, knowingly, remembering his smooth talk. She *had* changed a lot since their brief stint of dating in college and wasn't quite so naïve. "Thank you. What are you up to these days?"

"I'm an orthodontist. I have a practice in Carmel. It's very…" He pretended humility with a shrug. "…Successful."

Maddie laughed, unable to help it. "Well, your teeth look wonderful. How about personally? Are you married?"

Greg ground his teeth. "I should be."

"What do you mean?"

"Divorced." He sighed heavily. "I found her…in bed with another man."

Maddie didn't know whether to believe him, he was acting so strange. "I'm sorry. How terrible for you."

"Yeah, I didn't think I would get through it, but I did. Meeting sweet women like you puts the game back in me. You taken?"

Maddie didn't want to go into that. "I'm in a relationship."

"Anyone I know? Wait, it's not one of the players, is it?" He asked it like it was an impossibility and though Maddie knew she shouldn't, she couldn't quite help herself.

She shrugged delicately.

"No kidding. Who?"

Maddie allowed her gaze to wonder over to Jake. It wasn't as if she was out-and-out lying, not really. Just leading a cad to think something that might buy her some peace tonight."

"No way. Jake Hart? I should have snatched you up when I had the chance."

Maddie wanted to roll her eyes but feigned neutrality. "We both know that wouldn't have worked out. I'm sure you will find someone, Greg."

"Sure I will. I've found lots of someone's, but I'm looking for someone really special. Someone like you."

Could the malarkey, as her Irish grandfather always called it, get any thicker? Maddie pasted a smile on her face, tilted her head to one side and remarked. "You didn't think I was so special when you dumped me via email during our sophomore year. What makes me so different now?"

"Look at you!" Greg gushed. "I hardly recognized you, you look so good."

Again the backhanded compliment. Maddie was getting bored. "Greg, it was so good to see you again, but I have to go." She smiled a tight smile at him. "I'm working, remember?"

An angry yet panicked look flashed across his face. "Can I call you?"

Maddie shook her head. "I'm sorry, Greg. I think we can both agree that it wouldn't work out. Take care."

She glided away toward her table, where she could hear Sasha laughing at something the handsome, successful owner of a retail chain was saying.

At least someone was having fun.

~~~~~~~

Jake's gaze slid over to Maddie again. Who was that she was talking to? And why did he care so much? He looked purposefully away but it wasn't long before his eyes sought her out again. He just couldn't seem to help it. He couldn't get her out of his mind. Every time he tried to turn his attention to someone else, someone bright and glittering at his table, he would sense

Maddie's presence, know just where she was standing in the room, who she was talking to, trying to place the decent-looking guy she was talking to right now. Was that a flirtatious laugh? Did she know him? He watched her touch his sleeve with familiarity and had to stop his feet from marching over there and taking the guy by the collar. He turned away, taking a long gulp of his drink. This was ridiculous! He had never wanted a woman to notice him this badly and he was determined to disregard it. It wasn't sane.

He just had to ignore her. It wasn't as if she was the only captivating woman in the room. He looked up and across the table at Lisa Montgomery, a model, aspiring actress and a blond knockout. Usually he would be interested, wonder how long it would take to reel her in, but he couldn't seem to drum up the chase instinct, and that scared him.

He'd heard some of the other happily married players talk about how their wives had captured them and he'd always thought of it as enticement, though they'd never called it that. He saw how happy and connected they were with their wives, always on guard around the attractive female fans, and he had privately thought the women in their lives had finally won the game, put the ol' ball and chain around their million-dollar necks and won the prize. But now, for the first time, he had this glimpse of what they felt. He couldn't get over it. He couldn't believe in it. He wanted to fight it and yet...he wanted to take her into his arms and kiss her; it was all he could think about tonight.

The image of her, in her light fairy costume and glittering eyelashes over those shocked and hurt eyes, eyes the color of the blue waters in the Caribbean, staring at him in hurt disbelief as he'd berated her for her dance routine and accused her of wanting to seduce him, haunted him. He found he wanted to banish the hurt, put salve on the wounds he's caused and draw her into his arms. And she'd been gracious enough to accept his apology. That alone was impressive. She could have played that card in a lot of different ways—revengeful or calculating, taunting or tantalizing. Instead, she'd melted—sincere, sweet, openhearted acceptance—and promised him a dance.

The dance. Dinner was over, the speeches were over and the party had migrated to the other room, where the band was testing their mics and the sound system. The dancing would soon begin.

Jake took another sip of his drink and found Maddie at the back of the room, talking and laughing, a barely touched martini in her elegant hand. He debated his options. The third song, if it was a good one. He couldn't ask her before the third song if he wanted to look better than desperate. He'd already forgotten his promise to ignore her.

Jake's spine straightened when he saw out of the corner of his eye the man she had been talking to earlier come up to her and ask her to dance the first song. It was a fast one, and only two women, one dressed as Wonder Woman and the other as a tennis player, were making their way to the dance floor. He saw Maddie shake her head, then clenched his teeth as the man grabbed her hand and pulled her to the floor anyway. Jake stared openly at them now, anger beating in the pulse at the base of his throat. What was it about Maddie that everyone thought they could manhandle her like that? He would have to get her into self-defense classes. Teach her some street moves to protect herself.

He stared while Maddie acquiesced, though he could tell her heart wasn't in it, she didn't give the man eye contact and her body was barely moving to the music. The guy, however, was obviously intoxicated and getting handsy with her. He was just about to go out there and do something about it when he heard "Hey, Jake" from just behind him.

He turned to see Marcus Cornell, a fellow player and the friend he'd come here with. "Marcus." He nodded to him then looked back at Maddie. She looked miserable.

"You really got a thing for her, don't ya?"

"Why do you say that?" He wanted to know how he was being so obvious.

"Come on, man. You've only got eyes for her. You haven't even noticed Jill Parkinson is here, or that other woman you dated, Tiffany something or the other? Didn't you go out with her?"

Tiffany Daniels. His only serious relationship outside of a college girlfriend. "Tiffany's here?" He'd really been in love with her until she had left him when he said he would never marry without a pre-nup. It hadn't taken her long to find another rich boyfriend. "I wonder if she married that guy," he said.

"She's a beautiful woman, that's for sure," Marcus agreed. "Hey." Marcus motioned toward Maddie on the dance floor. "Is it just me or is that guy getting a little too friendly on the dance floor with your girl? I don't think she likes it, either."

Jake grasped Marcus on the shoulder. "Thanks, man. That was all I needed to hear." He made his way through the crowd toward them as the song wound down. The man's hands kept wandering over Maddie's arms and side in a way that made Jake want to plow a fist into his face.

Maddie was shaking her head and trying to back out of the man's touch when Jake arrived within earshot. "No, thank you, Greg. Now, please. I'm finished dancing. I need to see that the auction is set up and ready to go."

Greg didn't seem to want to pay any attention to her feelings, but as he looked up and beyond Maddie's shoulder and locked eyes with Jake, he suddenly let go and backed away.

Greg held out his hand toward Jake. "Jake Hart," he gushed. "I'm a big fan. Dr. Greg Foreman." When Jake ignored his hand and turned toward the stunned face of Maddie, he asked her, "Maddie, are you okay? This guy bothering you?"

Maddie shook her head, sidestepping toward him so that her slim shoulders were right at his chest level, almost touching him.

"Now don't be upset," Greg scolded him. "Maddie and I are old friends from college and it was just an innocent dance." He looked at Maddie and said in a stage whisper, "Looks like we got your boyfriend jealous."

Jake really wanted to slug him now; the vision of it played in his head until he had to look away from his overly groomed face and back at Maddie. Instead, he contented himself with playing into Greg's misinformation. "Yeah, I'm the real jealous type so you better keep your hands off my girl if you know what's good for you."

Greg's hands went into the air, false innocence on his face. "It was just a dance, man." He looked at Maddie and mumbled, "You take care, Maddie," and spun on his heel to leave.

Jake stopped him by grasping his shoulder and squeezing, saying into his ear, "I mean it, *man*. Don't call her, don't touch her, don't ask her to dance…don't even think about her. She's mine." He gave the doctor a firm pat on the shoulder, hard enough to make him stumble, and then turned his back on him, taking Maddie's hand into his.

~~~~~~~

Maddie tried to gulp back her shock. She hardly knew what to say as the band began playing one of her favorite songs and she felt Jake's big hands reach for her.

"Sorry about that," he whispered, leaning down a little to speak into her ear, pulling her close and beginning to sway to the music.

"About rescuing me?" Maddie looked up into his eyes. "I…I thought I could handle him, but I think I underestimated his, uh, determination. Thank you. I didn't want to make a scene and possibly lose my new job by stabbing him in the foot with the heel of my shoe, but that was my next plan of action if he didn't get his hands off…" She faltered, embarrassed.

69

"Yeah. I saw," Jake stated with intense eyes. "I think I convinced him not to even look at you anymore."

Maddie laughed, a little lightheaded. "Yes, I think you did." Jake smelled so good. She wanted to get closer, turn her head and lean against his chest, smelling the cologne on his neck and letting the music take them away, but she didn't.

Jake Hart was an NBA star. She was little more than a recent widow, a new employee and a broken-hearted woman who had little trust in enduring love. As happy as she felt now, she knew the pain that could come from this.

She took a step back from Jake's tall form and gave herself an internal shake. Life could break your heart. This man could certainly break hers and there wasn't much left intact to conquer.

She was a mother, with responsibilities.

She had better remember that.

CHAPTER NINE

"Having a good time?" Sasha asked, after Jake escorted her back to her chair and left to get them fresh drinks.

Maddie looked at Sasha's face and felt a pang of guilt. He was, after all, the one player Sasha had been interested in—never mind that she "sort of" had a boyfriend, or that they never thought in a million years that they would actually meet him. "Yeah. He's a really good dancer for someone so tall. I'm sure he will dance with you too. I can ask him when he gets back." Maddie slid into the chair next to Sasha and lifted her brows.

Sasha shook her head. "No way! I think we know who he is interested in and it's not me. You two looked pretty involved out there."

"Oh, no. We did? This is my job. I have to be careful."

"Are there rules about dating the players? Could you get fired?"

"I'm not dating him, but no, I don't think there are rules against it."

Sasha grinned at her. "Well, don't worry about it. Only I know how much you were enjoying yourself out there because I know you so well." She looked around at the gregarious crowd. "No one else would realize it." She reached out and grasped Maddie's hand, squeezing it. "I haven't seen you dance like that since…well, you know."

Maddie groaned, pulled her hand away and dropped her head into one palm, her elbow braced on the table. "I'm a terrible person. How could I?"

"What, be attracted to someone? Come on, Maddie. First off, he is Jake Hart. Secondly, he's drop-dead gorgeous and third, as if we needed a third, you were used to having a man's…" she

71

lowered her voice to a whisper, "...you know, attention, on a regular basis. Six months is a long time when you've been married."

Maddie gasped. "That's not it."

Sasha's eyebrows rose. "Isn't it? Just a part?"

Maddie felt her cheeks heat up and was thankful it was so dark in the room. Sasha had a way of speaking the truth right out loud, leaving people spinning to catch up and admit to it. "Well...it did feel good to be in a man's arms again and—"

She was saved from having to expand the thought as Jake returned with three drinks in hand. He handed the first one to Sasha. "Cosmo for our sophisticated witch. I heard it's your favorite concoction."

He winked at her, speaking in that teasing, deep-voiced way that had even the pragmatic Sasha dreamy-eyed and ready to melt. "Thank you."

Jake turned to Maddie. "And for you, I brought you something new to try." He held out a martini glass with a milky-white liquid inside. "Eggnog," he said with a proud grin.

Maddie blinked several times. "I...um, thank you."

"But Maddie..." Sasha interjected, shock in her deep-brown eyes. "You hate eggnog," she stated in a hissing whisper from between her teeth.

"What's that?" Jake asked. "You don't like eggnog?"

Sasha shook her head emphatically. "Oh, no. Threw it right back up the first time she tried it."

"That was a long time ago. I'll try it," Maddie assured him.

"No way," Jake said, taking the drink. "I want another dance later, and I'll not have you leaving early because you're sick." Then he took a sip himself. "Not bad. You can have my drink. A shot of espresso."

Maddie looked at the dark-colored liquid in the small cup and smiled up at him. "It looks a little scary. I take mine with like a gallon of cream."

"Don't sip it. Just a couple of big gulps," Sasha advised, smirking.

Jake's shoulders were shaking with compressed mirth while Maddie took Sasha's advice and downed the steaming brew.

Hot. Burning throat. Maddie started to gasp and cough, putting the cup down on the table. "Oh my! That is strong!" She turned mock-accusing eyes toward Jake.

Jake let out his compressed laugh. "That bad?"

Maddie nodded. "I prefer it weak."

Marcus walked up to them and clasped Jake on the shoulder. "Hey, man. Let's get this party started." He grinned big, looked over his shoulder at the dance floor and pointed back to it with his thumb. "It's pretty slow out there." His gaze shot to Sasha and brightened. "Do witches dance or just cast spells?"

Sasha took a gulp of her drink, stood and put her hand on his arm. "Witches can do anything they want, haven't you heard?"

They both laughed as Marcus led her to the dance floor.

~~~~~~

Jake sat down next to Maddie, noticing that she had relaxed against the back of her chair and had a dreamy smile hovering around her full, glossy lips.

He leaned toward her. "What are you thinking about?"

Maddie turned toward him. "Dancing. I'm so glad Marcus asked Sasha to dance. Tonight has turned out...pretty wonderful." Again, the dreamy smile. It reached her eyes as she stared at him and did strange things to his stomach.

"You did a good job planning it."

"Thanks. It does seem like everyone is having a good time. Do you think the auction will go well?"

Jake shrugged. "It usually does. How much did they raise last year?"

Maddie leaned closer to him, face to face, nose to nose. "Three hundred and fifty thousand dollars." Her eyes widened. "Can you believe it?"

"What's the goal this year?"

"We have to top it, of course." She gave a short laugh. "I'll be a failure if we don't top it."

"Let's dance," he said suddenly, standing and holding out his hand. "It won't help to worry about it."

Maddie stared into his eyes for a moment and then nodded. "Okay."

Had she really hesitated? Maybe she wasn't as interested as Jake thought. There was something about her, something he couldn't quite put his finger on, but Maddie was a guarded woman and, he thought, trying to resist this attraction between them.

She let him take her hand though as he led her to the dance floor. It was a fast song and the crowd was really getting into it. They squeezed their way over to Sasha and Marcus, who looked like they were having a great time. Sasha wasn't Marcus's usual type. He usually dated African-American women—models, aspiring actresses, an athlete once, but all curvaceous figures. Sasha was on the short side, really thin and not quite the stellar

74

face he was used to seeing with Marcus. But Marcus had his big grin on, twirling her around as they danced. Interesting.

The crowd became hot and sweaty after three more dances, Jake taking off his suit jacket, Maddie losing the demi-mask and sparkly white wrap that had been around her shoulders most of the night, exposing round, creamy shoulders. The place was really heating up with the music.

At ten o'clock the lead singer announced their last song, a slow one, and said that the auction would follow. Jake had to laugh. The crowd was certainly in the right frame of mind to spend some serious cash.

Maddie gave him a hesitant look. Maybe she didn't want to dance the slow one with him. She had kept him within arm's distance during the fast ones. The thought sent a swirl of confused unease through him. He didn't usually attach himself to a woman for the evening without being on a date. Why did it feel like they *were* on a date? He didn't want to let her go and he most certainly didn't want her to dance with anyone but him. He reached out and grasped her hand, pulling her toward him. "It's the last dance. We can't quit now."

She nodded and let him pull her into his arms, even letting her forehead press lightly against his shoulder for a moment. He felt her take a long breath and knew, instinctively, that she had closed her eyes.

Was she playing some game? Hard to get? He internally shook his head at the thought. Maddie may have her secrets but her heart was pure, her intentions open and honest. He leaned his face toward the pile of elegant curls on top of her head. She sure did smell good, too. His hands were at her waist, but he wanted to move them to her back and pull her closer. He looked around at the other dancers, wondering if anyone would notice. The fabric of her gown was like silk or satin or whatever lingerie was made of, very slippery and silky, very easy for his fingers to skim over. He tightened his hold on her waist, allowing his hands to move slightly around and pull her closer, leaning his head toward her ear, trying to think of something clever to say. He loved it when she smiled at him, immediately understanding where he was coming from.

"You having fun?"

She tilted her head back to look into his eyes and gave him a little nod and that smile he was hoping for.

"You want to go out?" It popped out before he really had thought about it.

"Now? I can't leave. I'll probably be here all night. I have to oversee some of the clean-up when everyone leaves."

Jake groaned internally. He was really messing this up. "I meant some other time. Next weekend, maybe."

"Oh." Several emotions crossed her face then she looked back up at him, leaned up on tiptoe and said quietly in his ear. "I have to tell you something about me, Jake."

His heart sank. She was too good to be true. He should have listened to his misgivings earlier. No one could be so perfect for him. "Oh yeah? What's that?"

Pressing closer to him so that she could whisper it, Jake could hardly concentrate on her next words.

"I'm a widow. Recently."

The pain of it filled her eyes and pierced him like the pain belonged to him, like it had happened to him. "I know. I'm sorry."

"How do you know?"

"Word gets around. We're all pretty close around here." Jake leaned toward her ear. "Are you not ready to go out on a date? Is it too soon?"

Her blue eyes, the color of sapphires, turned confused, as if she hadn't considered the question before. "I don't know." Her gaze dropped from his eyes to his lips, causing a streak of white-hot desire to run through his body. Before he knew what he was doing, he leaned in and brushed his lips against her soft lips. It wasn't long, slow and soft and sweet, but it made his heart pound in his ears and she looked like she'd been bulldozed—dazed and bewildered. It was the most endearing look he'd ever seen. When he leaned toward her to kiss her again she pulled back.

"Wait, there's something else."

Something else? His excitement plummeted.

"I have a son. A two-and-a-half-year-old son that matters more to me than anything in the world."

Jake hadn't heard that. But his head was swimming with the touch and feel of her, and even though he normally wouldn't consider dating a woman with a child, he heard himself say, "I like kids."

He didn't really know if that was true or not. And he'd never had to sell himself, practically beg for a date. The music stopped. He took a bracing breath trying to concentrate on the decorations and ignoring Maddie for a moment to regain control of his spinning brain.

Maddie stepped back. "Thanks for the dance, Jake, and the lovely evening. I just don't know if I'm ready."

She turned and fled, disappeared really, leaving him feeling suddenly, inexplicably, empty and alone.

CHAPTER TEN

The auction began on time. Jake saw Maddie in the front, helping to direct the auctioneer and occasionally holding something up for the audience to get a better view of it for bidding. She had a bright smile pasted on her face—that smile he was coming to recognize, the same smile she'd worn during the dance number at halftime. It was her "nervous but not going to show it" smile. How he knew that about her already, he wasn't sure. He rarely felt like he had figured out the women he dated. This was new. It really felt like they knew each other on some other level that he couldn't really grasp. It was just there.

As the auction continued, Maddie looked more and more nervous. Jake did some quick calculations in his head and thought he knew why. It didn't look like they were going to make their goal of beating last year's numbers. Jake knew something about the pressure to always be better, do better, perform better. He was used to it by now, knew how to use it to his advantage instead of letting it become crippling. But Maddie didn't have the experience and looked ready to crumble. As the last item sold, Jake watched Maddie turn in a slow circle on the stage, her face shocked to see that everything was gone. Jake found himself on his feet, walking up to the stage and whispering to the auctioneer. He shrugged mentally. She was going to be really mad at him, but there just wasn't anything else he wanted to bid on.

~~~~~~~

Maddie watched as Jake spoke to the auctioneer with a deep sense of unease spiraling within her. What was he doing? The crowd was getting restless, looking expectantly at her and then curiously at Jake. She'd been trying to ignore him, block out all the feelings he was making her feel. She wasn't ready for this. What if she dated a man who wouldn't or couldn't love her child? How could she replace a boy's father with a stranger?

What if she fell in love again?

And that kiss…Brandon had never kissed her like that, had he? She couldn't ever remember wanting to dissolve into the floor with Brandon, she'd melted, but not like this, never like this. It was wrong. She couldn't trust it.

The auctioneer was smiling at her and motioning her to come over to him. When she arrived at his side, he turned her toward the crowd and announced in a booming voice. "We saved the best for last, folks. A date with Madeline Goode, our lovely program director."

Maddie's jaw dropped open. Her head jerked from the grinning, sweaty auctioneer to Jake, horror in her eyes. What had he done? He was making a fool out of her!

She would lose her job for this! Dizziness buzzed through her head and nausea rose to her throat. She swayed. Oh no, she was going to faint. But she didn't faint. She never could when she really needed to, blast it. Instead, she just stood there, staring out into the sea of upturned faces, some of the men looking interested, the women's faces reflecting everything from envy to disgust. *God, please. Just this once?* She breathed quickly in and out, trying to hyperventilate. No such luck.

The auctioneer opened the bidding at five hundred dollars. No bidders.

This couldn't be happening. Heat rose to her face as she stared out at the silent, watching crowd. She would drop through the floor at any moment.

Marcus raised his hand and yelled with gusto. "Five hundred!" Maddie let out a breath with a moment's relief. At least there had been one bid and Marcus was a nice guy. Maybe Sasha could go with them.

"Six hundred dollars! Can I get six, can I get six hundred for the beautiful angel we have here?" The auctioneer started his babbling.

Why couldn't people tell she was a fairy, she wondered with a hysterical hiccup coming from her chest.

A nice-looking doctor, older but single—a widow too, if Maddie remembered correctly—raised his hand, smiling kindly at her.

Maddie smiled back. Whew, maybe he would win and she could get off this stage and go and torture Jake with the pepper spray in her purse.

The seven hundred-dollar mark flew by with Greg Foreman from college jumping in, looking determined.

Not him! She might have to refuse. She didn't trust that man. Jake was really going to get it for this. She imagined putting a tube of sore muscle ointment in his shorts before the next game. She almost smiled, thinking about it, feeling a little better. She shot a shy, hopeful glance back toward the doctor.

Sure enough, he countered with eight hundred, Greg came back with nine hundred and then the doctor countered again with a whopping one thousand dollars. The nervousness returned. A thousand dollars? What would they expect on this date for a thousand dollars? This was a nightmare.

A hush fell over the crowd, all eyes on Greg as he stared at Maddie, measuring her worth.

Suddenly Jake's low voice boomed throughout the room. "Twenty thousand dollars." He said it with a small smile and those smoldering gray-green eyes glued on Maddie alone.

The crowd gasped. Several people started to clap and radiate good cheer on the now valuable woman on the stage. From some distant place, like a dream echo, Maddie could hear Sasha's familiar cheering and two-fingered whistle. Maddie could only blink at Jake. Twenty thousand dollars? Twenty thousand dollars! It was more than any other item of the evening. If she'd known he had wanted a date that bad, she would have given in. All he really had to do was give her some time.

But it was for the charity, she reminded herself. He was donating to charity and had probably realized they weren't going to reach their goal and wanted to help. After all, twenty thousand dollars was enough to top it and beat it by about five thousand— very close to her personal goal.

The auctioneer proclaimed Jake Hart the winner at twenty thousand dollars and Maddie found the crowd regarding her with a new kind of respect. She shook more hands and received more smiling congratulations for the success of the auction than she'd had on her wedding day.

Suddenly Jake was beside her, easily countering the ribbing he was receiving for paying so much for a date.

"She's worth every penny," Maddie heard him remark to one older woman, who patted his arm and smiled at him with twinkling eyes. "I think you've been caught, young man, good luck to you."

And then to the men he said such things as, "She wouldn't have me. What else was I to do?"

Finally, he turned to talk to her. "You made your goal?"

Maddie nodded. "I was going to torture you with the pepper spray in my purse at first, but now I'm…in your debt. Thank you, Jake."

Jake started to say something when a tall, beautiful woman glided up to them in a full-length, red-sequined evening gown and grasped his arm. "Jake, I can't believe I didn't realize you were here until just now. How generous of you to date for charity."

"Tiffany…" Jake's face registered surprise and his gaze dropped from her perfect face to her low-cut gown and then quickly back up.

The woman turned to Maddie with a bright smile. "You will have a wonderful time with him, Ms. Goode. I can assure you that Jake Hart certainly knows how to show a woman a good time." She smiled again, but this time her eyes were laced with malice.

"I'm so relieved to hear it." Maddie turned to Jake. "Won't you introduce me?"

"Oh…of course." Jake straightened, still seeming rattled. "Maddie, this is Tiffany Daniels. You might remember her family from the guest list, the owners of Daniels Homes."

Maddie nodded. She did remember three names under Daniels; very wealthy homebuilders in the Midwest. Putting on her most professional demeanor, she held out her hand. "Of course. So nice to put a face with the name. Did you enjoy the evening, Miss Daniels?"

Tiffany's eyes narrowed in the face of Maddie's confidence. "It's been a little slow, my dear, but now that I've found Jake, I'm sure my evening will…pick up."

Maddie glanced at Jake, expecting some joking, confident response or rebuttal to the woman's arrogance, but found instead the man looking tongue-tied.

Was she an ex-girlfriend? Or worse. Maybe he was still seeing Tiffany and was just playing the field, taking out any woman he wanted. He was Jake Hart—famous millionaire basketball star. What was wrong with her, thinking they might have something special?

She was surprised by the degree of the disappointment. It made her heart feel leaden, like she couldn't quite breathe. She realized that she had hoped to spend the last moments of the party with him before the long tear-down began. She wanted to hear why he had done it. Was it only for the charity?

She also realized that she wanted to be with him entirely too much for her own good. She had a son and a good job and she didn't want to jeopardize her responsibilities. She didn't have room for such relationships in her life.

Jake finally spoke as Tiffany grasped his arm to lead him away. "I'll call you to set up our date." He didn't even sound excited anymore.

Maddie's heart sank further despite her internal lecturing. "I hope it meets with your expectations." It was a soft-spoken thrust and it stung, she could see it on his face, making her feel at once guilty and ready to flee, find a place to allow the tears to fall that were threatening to escape. She turned and hurried away. He might buy her time, but as wonderful as he could be, it was going to take a lot more than twenty thousand dollars to win her heart.

CHAPTER ELEVEN

Maddie poured the cereal into Max's plastic bowl, sloshed in some milk and handed him the matching plastic spoon. Groaning, she sat beside his chair and dropped her head into one hand, clutching a cup of steaming coffee with the other. "Eat your breakfast, sweetie," she managed before dropping her head all way to her arm that lay across the table. Wow, had she ever felt this awful?

She'd been out until 3am, home and in bed by four and probably not asleep until four-thirty, her mind refusing to quiet and stop thinking of everything that had happened. It was now 7:22 am, and after attempting to divert Max with cartoons while she laid comatose on the couch, feeling guilty for allowing the television to be the babysitter again, and Max beating her on the head with a musical hammer, she had finally dragged herself into the kitchen to make coffee and breakfast. It wouldn't be so bad if her head wasn't pounding so.

"Good morning." Her dad came in the kitchen wearing his PJs and looking half asleep, as cute as Max with their matching tousled hair. "Got any coffee?"

Maddie lifted her head, squinted at him and motioned to the pot. "Fresh ground and everything," she said, laughing, then groaned and dropped her head back onto her arm.

Simon laughed. "You're not feeling so well, eh, sweetheart?"

Maddie just shook her head. They both looked up suddenly as a loud *thwack* sounded by the window. Max was dipping his spoon down to the bottom of the bowl of floating Os and had discovered that if he flicked the spoon up he could propel cereal around the room. Another *thwack* and a spoonful of Os hit her mother's new mini-blinds, sliding down in sticky, milky streaks to the floor.

"No, Max!" Maddie got up and took the spoon from her grinning son. "No throwing food."

Her dad was laughing, or rather shaking while trying not to. "Dad, don't encourage him. Mom will kill all of us if she sees those blinds."

Maddie got a sponge and began cleaning up the mess. Her dad walked over to her, handing her some water and a couple of painkillers. "You feed Max, I'll get this."

"Thanks, Dad." Maddie sat by Max and tried to feed him.

"No," Max stated, his face in scrunched anger. "I do it, Mom."

"Okay, Max, one more try, but if you flick your cereal around the room, Mommy will have to do it. Understand?"

"Can't you see I'm eating here?" Max said with stoic injustice, gripping his spoon in his fist and digging in.

Maddie's eyes grew round with laughter, her lips suppressed. Looking at her dad, she whispered, "He sounds like he's seventy. Sometimes it's like a grouchy old man has taken over his body."

Her dad smiled back at her while rinsing out the sponge. "Naw, he just knows what he wants. Some people are born like that."

The thought whirled around her cloudy head. She couldn't remember ever being like that. She hardly ever knew what she wanted, from the choices on a menu to the classes in college and the career path she had chosen. Her life had just seemed to happen to her and she'd always just gone along with the flow, rarely stopping to find out for herself what she really wanted. Max *was* different, so confident and self-contained even as a toddler. It was really amazing when she thought about it.

"Where's Mom?"

"Still in bed. She was shopping at Walmart until one in the morning again."

"She sure is a night owl. And with the extra money I've been paying her to watch Max, she's probably shopping more often these days."

"Tell me about it." Her dad grinned and rolled his eyes.

"Dad…"

Her dad sat down across from her, sipping his coffee from a mug with pictures of fishing lures all over it. "Yeah?"

"Did you always know what you wanted?"

Her mom did. She knew that. Her mom never seemed to hesitate in any decision. And she'd heard the story countless times of how her mom had set her mind to winning Simon, and how she'd gotten him. But her dad never talked about wanting much beyond a tool for his workshop out in the garage or a new hunting rifle or fishing pole. He always ordered the same food at the same restaurants and let Gloria decide the rest.

"I knew I wanted to teach. I was lucky that I was able to do that for so many years."

"So you never wanted to be a musician?" Maddie knew her father had been in a band for many years when he was younger. They had even toured the local scene, but she'd never really heard what happened to them.

Simon shrugged. "Life has a way of taking over, you know? I played for ten years or so but we just didn't get any big breaks." He let out a little bark of laughter. "Teaching wasn't bad. Every once in awhile you had that great class that seemed interested in algebra, soaked it right up. And once in a blue moon, you had the student you knew would someday be a rocket scientist or help find the cure for cancer, something really big and that you had played a small part in that. Anyway, the most important thing was you girls and your mother who didn't have a college education and couldn't ever earn much more than minimum wage. A teacher's salary pays a whole lot better than a starving artist." He winked at her with a smile.

"Oh, Dad." Maddie compressed her lips together, feeling tears spring up in her eyes. "I'm sorry, I didn't know you gave it up for us."

Her dad laughed and looked into her eyes with such love. "You don't have anything to be sorry about, Maddie girl. I have no regrets."

"None? Really?"

"Well, maybe buying all that blasted exercise equipment that sits in the garage collecting dust." He grinned big at her and rubbed his round belly. "Now that was a mistake."

His attempt to make her laugh made Maddie smile and swallow back the tears. "Thank you, Dad. If I've never said it before, thank you for letting us tell you what you wanted."

He brushed her off, both embarrassed and pleased. "It's what men do, Maddie. The good ones anyway."

"Yes, I suppose it is." She looked at Max and wondered for the first time when his stubborn desire to feed himself would become something bigger, something that would someday effect his loved ones. Maybe it wasn't so bad, to not know what you wanted, maybe this life flow, this river of change and conflict, the giving and receiving, the getting and the giving, was God's plan for her. And maybe she had a lot to learn.

Max grinned big at her, the cereal in a mush around his lips, his eyes alight with the delight of playing with Os, and she was suddenly just so glad to be alive and seeing it.

Gloria chose that moment to walk into the room, loaded down with her latest packages, wanting to talk about the upcoming Thanksgiving holiday.

Her dad got up, gave Gloria a kiss on the cheek, which her mother ignored, and left for the adjoining family room to flip on the morning news. But as Maddie watched his tall form retreat she looked at him with fresh insight and was so glad that Max got her out of bed early, when only she and her dad were up and wandering about the kitchen.

A half an hour later her dad called from the family room recliner. "Maddie. I think you might want to see this."

Maddie had Max on her lap, giving him little kisses along his cheek and neck, making him laugh and listening to Gloria's harrowing tale of walking into the dark Walmart parking lot at one in the morning, seeing purse snatchers in every shadow. They both got up and hurried into the family room. Her dad never said things like that.

He turned up the sound as the three came in and sat down on the couch, all eyes glued to the television.

The news anchor was proclaiming the latest headlines in a cheery voice. "Halloween seems a smashing success for more than the kids this year as the Racers rake in a record four hundred and twenty-five thousand dollars for charity from their annual Halloween Extravaganza Fundraiser. Let's check in with our reporter, Pat Carson, who covered last night's event. Pat?"

Tape from last night rolled. "Yes Debbie, we're here at the Racers Halloween party, thrown every year by Racers Sports and Entertainment, one of the many charity events they sponsor. One of the Racers coordinators and the woman who planned this event is here to speak with us, Madeline Goode. Ms. Goode, a record amount was raised tonight, are you pleased with the results?"

The microphone was shoved into Maddie's face. Maddie on the couch looked on in horror, barely remembering the interview in all the hoopla of the evening. Had she been coherent? Intelligent? Remotely cute?

The camera flashed to a white, sparkly fairy and the Maddie on the couch couldn't help but gasp. She looked…good…and professional, every hair in place. *Thank you, God!*

"Yes, we are overwhelmed with the support for the many wonderful causes the Racers support. The auction went incredibly well, better than we expected. We are so thankful for the generosity of the guests."

"Especially one of the players, I'm told. Maddie, toward the end of the auction, you yourself were bid on. Did you really wring twenty thousand dollars from Jake Hart for a date? Could it be love?"

Maddie on the couch gasped. Her parents gasped. Her mother turned white and stared at her. Her father's eyes widened as he swiveled in his recliner to stare at her.

Maddie on the TV, the one that seemed in perfect control, laughed with an elegant tinkling sound. "Mr. Hart was very generous. I have no doubt that the charities we sponsor will be worth a date with him."

The reporter even laughed. She was so polished, so professional; she could hardly believe it was really her on the flat screen her father had gotten for Christmas last year.

"Well, Madeline Goode, we wish you well on your date. I'm sure all the female viewers agree with me that it won't be too difficult a sacrifice for the sake of charity."

Maddie on TV laughed, agreeing with her.

Her mother turned toward her first as they went to commercial. "You have a date with one of the basketball players? What's this about bidding on you for a date?"

Oh dear, how was she going to explain this? "Sort of." She held Max tight even though he had tired of the electrified atmosphere of the family room and obviously wanted down to see what he could get into. "Jake knew we weren't going to meet last year's donation and decided at the last minute to auction a date with me. I was shocked, Mom. Appalled at the time. But we did make our goal, so I went along with it."

"Jake? You are going out with Jake Hart? Number 14, Jake Hart?" her dad asked with his eyes lighting up. He was a big fan so she shouldn't be surprised he would be excited by the idea.

"Well, I think so. Don't get too excited, though. It's nothing really. Just a stunt to raise money and attention to the cause. He's very nice..." She thought of Tiffany. "...Sometimes, and I think one date is a small price to pay for a twenty thousand-dollar donation."

"Are you serious?" He shook his head and seemed to be talking to himself. "My Maddie girl is going out with Jake Hart." Her dad couldn't seem to reconcile it in his mathematical brain.

"He has a very big...heart."

Her dad almost choked on his coffee while she turned red.

"Just don't fall in love with him, Maddie. A man like that will *break* your heart," her mother announced. "You don't need to be hurt again, especially right now."

Maddie, with visions of Tiffany grasping Jake's very muscular arm, had to agree, much as she hated to. "I'm sure I can manage one date, Mom, without swooning over him."

Her dad was flipping through the options on the TV, looking for the latest recorded Racer game. "Jake Hart," he mused, finding a game and then fast forwarding until number 14 was playing. "There he is."

Gloria raised her eyebrows at Maddie and tilted her head. "He's not bad looking for such a tall man, is he?"

Maddie wanted to tell her mom to zip it, but instead smiled and said. "No, he's not bad looking...for someone so tall."

Darn the man. He wasn't bad looking at all.

CHAPTER TWELVE

Maddie sat at her desk taking advantage of the brief lull in the afternoon to look up Thanksgiving recipes on the internet. Most companies might slow down between Thanksgiving and New Year's, but Maddie was quickly realizing this was the season when charity work revved up to full throttle. Coming up next was the Thanksgiving dinner for the homeless sponsored by one of the players, who also helped serve the meal. They would be ordering hundreds of pounds of turkey, mashed potatoes and green beans, hiring a company to come in and cook it, another company to set up and tear down, the list went on and on. But there was one thing Maddie knew for sure she absolutely had to squeeze time in for—cooking an old-fashioned turkey dinner for Max. She wasn't about to have tacos on turkey day.

Her phone buzzed just as she spied an exciting title—Death by Turkey—and clicked on the link.

"Yes?" Maddie asked the receptionist.

"Jake Hart is here to see you, Maddie."

"Oh," Maddie's eyes widened. "Give me just a minute and then send him in."

She hadn't heard a word from Jake since the party, and that was almost two weeks ago. She had begun to wonder if she'd dreamed the whole date thing, but her dad kept playing the saved news report over and over, which only left her feeling rejected and miserable. Why hadn't he called? There had only been one away game since the party, so that couldn't be it.

She reached for her purse, added some pink lipstick and a thin coat of gloss without the confidence of a mirror, ran her fingers through her hair, which she had worn long and in loose waves today, and stood up. Smoothing down her skirt, she silently thanked heaven she was wearing her new ivory suit, iridescent black-green-blue satin pumps and an emerald green blouse that she knew made her eyes pop with more of a blue-green hue than blue.

Jake knocked and opened the door a little. "Hi, Maddie," he said with a smile, coming further in the room.

"Jake. Hello. It's so good to see you." She was determined to be professional. Walking over to him, holding out her hand, she felt his strong grasp, looked up into his face and had to remind herself to breathe. Boy, did he look good, smell good. He had that five o'clock shadow thing going on with a perfect square chin, piercing eyes that looked right into her. No…don't think like that. "Please, sit down."

His hand reached toward her face. Maddie stood very still while he touched her cheek and then rubbed his thumb across the corner of her upper lip. "You've, um, got some lipstick smeared there."

Maddie gasped. "Oh." She pulled away, pulled a tissue out of a box as she walked over to the decorative mirror hanging against one wall and hurriedly fixed the mistake, wiping off too much on one side and making the whole thing worse. Blast! She needed to look perfect for this.

Jake looked around the office. "Wow. This place looks great. Did you redecorate it?"

Maddie smiled, compressing her lips together in an attempt to even out the color. She gave up and turned back toward him, genuine happiness bubbling up from inside her about her office. "Yes, I just finished. Do you like it?"

Jake nodded as he plopped down on one of two overstuffed chairs that were facing her desk. The backs, sides and fronts were striped cream and beige with brown leather trim and big brown leather cushions. "It's very comfortable and…homey but…" He shrugged as if unable to come up with a good description.

"Elegant and sophisticated?" Maddie prompted with a sparkle in her eyes. Why did he always bring out the flirt in her?

He did that slow smile thing and she had to remind herself to breathe. He nodded. "Exactly. Looks expensive." He raised his brows in flirting-back challenge.

Maddie laughed. "Oh, not really. I enjoy antiquing and reupholstering, you know, finding great deals and then making them over. As long as the design is sound and of good quality." She shrugged. "Then it's just a matter of pretty trappings. Those chairs cost fifty dollars each at a garage sale."

"Wow. That's amazing. I like it a lot." He didn't say anything for the next minute, a very long minute, while he looked around the room, seeming to study the details, and then his gaze settled on her computer, where there was still the photo of the giant turkey. "You cook too?"

Maddie glanced at the computer screen. "Oh that, well, sometimes. I enjoy it when I have the time. My mother seems to only remember how to cook three meals, so, since I'm determined to have a traditional Thanksgiving dinner for Max, I'm planning to cook it. I'm working on my menu. Do you go home for Thanksgiving?" She knew Jake was originally from Colorado and still had parents there.

"Sometimes, but not this year. We have a game on the Friday after, so it's not worth the travel time. Sure looks good, though."

Was he hinting at an invitation? Maddie could not imagine bringing him home to her parents all day. Their brick ranch house, her mother smoking and pecking Jake with a million personal questions, her dad star-struck. Goodness, she would have to be an idiot to do such a thing.

"Would you like to come? If you don't have other plans, that is?" What was she doing? Of course he would have other plans! Something fancy and probably involving Tiffany or one of his player friends at one of their mansions.

94

"Sure." Jake seemed to jump at the chance. "I was going to go out to eat with some of the team, but I'd much rather have a home-cooked meal." He patted his flat stomach and grinned. "Haven't had one of those in a long time."

Maddie mentally groped for a foothold. Why ignore her for fourteen days and then work in an invitation to Thanksgiving dinner? "It could count as our date," she heard herself saying, giving him an out and wanting to spare herself the embarrassment of never being asked.

"No way. You're not going to get out of it that easy." He grinned at her and Maddie wished, not for the first time, that her bench seat had a back so that she could collapse against it. He had such a beautiful smile, the kind that started at his lips and then radiated from his green eyes. It made her feel warm and happy inside.

"That's why I'm here," he continued. "I wanted to get something on the calendar for us." He pulled a phone out of his sports jacket pocket.

"Oh, I thought maybe you'd had second thoughts."

He looked up at her and frowned. "Of course not. I paid for a date and, for one evening at least, you are all mine. So, what does this weekend look like?"

Maddie had a moment where she had to pull her emotions together before they reached her eyes. She was in such inner turmoil about this date that it was already ruined. Jake spoke of it like a business deal, and yet he *had* asked her out before the auction, hadn't he? Everything about that evening was a little cloudy. And then there was the way he'd held her on the dance floor…and that kiss. She felt more of the inner melting sensation just thinking about it. Now he wanted to come for Thanksgiving and meet her family! What did he really think of her? And worse, she kept telling herself she wasn't ready to date yet, would maybe never be ready to risk falling in love again.

God, get me out of this, *please*?

Maddie moved the mouse around while thinking, bringing up her calendar. She should appear busier than she really was, pretend to have a date…hmmm. "Well, I have Saturday free, but don't you have a home game that evening?" What was wrong with her? Would someone just tape her mouth closed?

Jake shrugged. "The game will be over by around nine. We could go out afterward, unless that's too late?"

Obviously, he didn't have children. The jetsetter life of an NBA player probably meant staying up half the night after a game and sleeping until noon the next day. But instead of mentioning that, Maddie nodded. "Okay, that sounds good." She smiled a little uncertainly. "Do you want me to come to the game or just meet you somewhere after?"

An odd, heated look came into Jake's eyes, but she didn't have a clue what she might have done to get that reaction. "Would you come? I know you don't like basketball very much, but I could get you floor seats and you could ask your friend—Sasha, wasn't it? If you want to."

He remembered Sasha's name. That was impressive. And he seemed so eager for her to watch him play, which was cute in a little boy, reminding her of Max, sort of way. "Okay, that sounds good. I actually might bring my dad this time, though. He would kill me if I had those seats and didn't ask him."

"Your dad's a fan?"

"Oh yeah. For years. He's very excited about our date." She grinned. "My mother, though, thinks you are too tall for me." She laughed, she couldn't help it. They were going to seriously flip out when she told them who was coming for Thanksgiving dinner. "I'm sorry, but you should prepare yourself, they're a little weird."

Jake stood up and came around the desk toward her, an intent look in his eyes. He grasped her hand and pulled her up to stand close to him. "Weird is okay." He pulled her closer, not letting go of her hand, close enough that Maddie couldn't think of anything else but how good he smelled. She inhaled slowly, savoring it, staring at the shadow of beard on his chin.

"Maddie?"

She looked up into his eyes, putty in his hands. "Yes?"

"I'm sorry I didn't call sooner. Truth is, I wanted to, but I was a little afraid."

Maddie swallowed hard, trying to ignore the flutter in her stomach. "Afraid of what?"

Jake moved a hand to her cheek and caressed her jaw with his thumb. "Afraid you would keep saying no."

"I...I didn't say no, exactly, did I?"

"You said you weren't ready to date, and I can understand that, but I'm not very good at waiting. So I kind of tipped the scales in my favor with the auction."

"You didn't do that to meet the goal?"

"That sounded better for the press, but it wasn't the real reason why I did it."

She wanted to ask, what about Tiffany and the other women that he probably dated, but couldn't. No matter how smooth his talk, she didn't have any claims on him. "Well, you didn't have to spend twenty thousand dollars, you know. I would have worn down eventually." She smirked at him, the flirtatious feeling back.

"Like I said, I'm not a very patient man." He leaned in, his gaze locked on her lips.

Maddie *be* good, she warned herself. Don't let him do this. Once again, her body seemed to ignore her brain—willful, disobedient, self-indulgent. It leaned in, breathing deeper in anticipation; she was weak, weak, weak.

A sudden knock on the door had them both rearing back. Jake looked away and Maddie's face grew hot.

Jordan Tyler walked in, all smiles and gratitude toward Jake for saving the auction.

Now You show up.

CHAPTER THIRTEEN

After work, Maddie picked Max up from the daycare he attended three days a week, giving Gloria a break from babysitting. As she was strapping Max into his car seat she felt her phone vibrate inside her purse. She dug one-handed into her bag and held her breath, half-hoping it might be Jake. It was Sasha. She pushed the button and held it to her ear. "Hold on, Sasha, I have to finish getting Max strapped in."

"Okay," she heard Sasha say on the other end, thinking she sounded like she was upset.

Maddie hurried to fasten him in, handed him a picture book to look at for the ride home and slid into the driver's seat. "Hey, I'm here. Is something wrong?"

"I went out with Marcus last night."

"What?" Maddie's jaw dropped open. "Marcus Cornell? The player?"

"Yeah, he called last night…"

"How did he know your number?"

"I gave it to him at the Halloween party."

"You didn't. What about Rob?"

"I didn't think Marcus would really call! He dates models and women way out of my league."

Maddie sighed. "But he did call, and you don't sound very happy. What happened?"

"Well, I sort of went to his house. It's unbelievable. Totally gorgeous. We were alone. We were having so much fun together, talking and laughing—he's so funny and sweet. Then we went swimming in his pool."

"Tell me you didn't sleep with him."

Sasha sniffed. "No! But we kissed. I really screwed up and Rob is never going to forgive me. Should I tell him? I've been waiting all day for you to get off work so I could talk to you. I can't stand the guilt."

Maddie compressed her lips together and took a deep breath. "I think you have to tell him."

Sasha's voice sounded really small. "Yeah, you're right. I guess I might lose him."

"You might. But Sasha, it's not as if he's never done anything to make the relationship difficult. He needs to stick up for you with his parents. Make some decisions on his own and be a man. This might be the thing that will make him decide what he really wants."

"Yeah, to be honest, I don't even know if I want him back."

Maddie sighed. "Well, this may be a good test for the relationship. Why did you do it? Do you have feelings for Marcus or were you just star-struck?"

"I don't know. A little of both, I think. He's so nice to me…and funny. I really like him but I don't know that it would go anywhere." She sniffed. "I'm really confused."

Maddie took a deep breath. "Do you think he will call you? Do you want to see him again?"

"I don't know. A part of me does, but he's probably just playing the field. He dates a *lot*, he even told me that. I think I might really like him but I don't know if he's really interested."

"Sasha, don't beat yourself up. Either way you and Rob need to get to the bottom of your problems. Maybe this will force him to take a hard look at what has been going on."

"You're right. Thanks, Mad, you always see the bright side to everything." A brief pause and then, "So, what's up with you? Anything new?"

"Well, you'll never guess who came to my office today."

"Jake? Did he finally ask you for the date?"

Maddie turned onto a side street that was the shortcut home. "Yes, this weekend. And, he's coming to Thanksgiving."

"You're kidding!"

"No. I really have to cook now. I'm so nervous. Do you think my parents will drive him crazy?"

Sasha laughed. "Probably. But Max will win his heart and that will make up for your mom and dad. Where are you going on your date?"

"I don't know. It's after the game on Saturday. You have to help me decide what to wear."

"I've got a new skirt, short but not too short. You can borrow it. How about those new boots, the tall ones? Those would look great."

Maddie laughed. "I can always depend on you for helping me with the latest in fashion. Hey, come over tonight and bring the skirt, okay? We'll get your mind off things."

"Okay, thanks Maddie."

They hung up and Maddie bit her bottom lip, remembering that she would have let Jake kiss her right there in her office if they hadn't been interrupted. She would not, *could not*, make such a mistake with Jake Hart.

~~~~~~~

The seats on the first row of the floor, just behind the players, were amazing—nicely padded, folding chairs with bigger, better armrests and as close to the action as you could get. Maddie looked over at her dad and couldn't help but smile. He had a goofy grin on his face with the eyes of a five-year-old on Christmas morning. She didn't think he had ever looked so happy.

They sat surrounded by other guests of the players, wives and their children, girlfriends and friends. There were a couple of local celebrities Maddie recognized from the news and the pretty weather woman from Channel 8. Maddie waved to the people she recognized from the party, one man yelling over to her, "You had your date with Jake yet?"

She smiled at the man and yelled back, "This is it."

Several people around her laughed and the doctor groaned, shaking his head. "Make him do better than that."

"I'll try. But it will be hard to convince my dad," she pointed to her dad's ball-capped head, who, when he heard her comment, turned around and waved, "that anything can be better than these seats." Everyone around them laughed and Maddie found she was kind of enjoying being funny and the center of attention. She introduced her dad to the people she knew around them and then settled back to watch the game.

It was different this time, being even closer to the action. Everything was louder, faster, bigger and yes, better than the seats Sasha had won. Maddie could feel the vibrations from the pounding floor come up her feet and into her legs. The crowd was like a roaring, cheering giant centipede that came alive in segments, sweeping up and down across the stadium to the music of the game.

When Jake started to play she smiled to herself, thinking he didn't look as bad in the black socks as the other white guys. At least he had something of a tan.

Over two hours swept by and before she knew it, Maddie was being escorted by one of the security officers to the media room, where Jake was to give a brief statement about their victory after showering and changing. She felt a little awkward and in the way of all the busy people setting up for the post-game press conference, but she took a big breath, raised her chin up and smiled at everyone.

When Jake came into the room, he went straight to her, put his hand on her back, leaned in toward her ear and whispered, "Thanks for putting up with all this. You've got that determined smile on your lips, so I know you're miserable." He gave her a quick kiss on her forehead that was noticed by several of the media persons, but no one had time to take a picture, thank goodness. Maddie sighed, a little dreamy, watching him join some of the other members of the team at a long table in front of the giant Racers logo.

The media peppered them with questions, everyone in good spirits over the win. It didn't take long for Jake to finish and come back over to her. He was dressed in a black suit, looking the epitome of tall, dark and handsome and smelling heavenly. This is a business date, Maddie reminded herself over and over, but the words didn't seem to be sinking in past the thumping of her heart. Just relax and enjoy it, she lectured herself.

"Let's get out of here," Jake said, taking her hand and pulling her along the stadium halls and out into the parking garage, where the temperature felt about twenty degrees colder. Jake helped Maddie into her coat, his hands lingering around her shoulders. "If I haven't said it out loud yet, you look great tonight." He looked her up and down with a wolfish grin.

Maddie smiled and looked away from his scrutiny. "Thanks." Sasha was right as usual. The mini-skirt and boots seemed to be a hit.

He led her over to a sleek black SUV and opened the door for her. She had to climb up to get inside, so opposite from her car where she had to sink down into the old, battered seat. She laughed as she slid across the huge leather seat, leaned back against a molded headrest, complete with speakers and headphone jacks, and then glanced over at the glowing blue monitor on the dash. Sheesh, she hoped Jake hadn't seen her getting out of her beat-up car at work. She took a deep breath, unclasped her fingers and sent up a quick prayer for strength against the glamour. Jake and his world seemed bigger than life. Was that why she was so nervous?

As Jake got in she commented, "Nice SUV. It's so roomy inside."

"Yeah, I wanted a Bugatti but I'm too tall, so I settled for this." He flashed her that teasing grin that made her feel like they had their own little private jokes.

"How did you like the game? Better seats this time?" Jake asked as he pulled out of the parking garage.

"My dad was in absolute heaven. Thank you for the tickets. And yes, the game was really exciting so close to the floor."

"Good. Robinson was on fire tonight."

"Really? Which number is he?"

Jake laughed, "Fifty-one. Tall black guy."

Maddie laughed. "That narrows it down." She paused, then blurted out, "I think I only watched you. I'm afraid I didn't pay very much attention to the other players."

She was cursing herself for being so honest when a pleased look flashed across Jake's face. He reached over and grasped her hand. "That's okay. I wouldn't want you giving that much attention to anyone else." He stopped at a red light, looked over at her and brought her hand to his mouth giving it a small kiss, his perpetual five o'clock shadow rubbing against the smoothness of her hand, making her want to touch his face.

The light turned green, but they didn't notice as they stared into each other's eyes in the dark car with the bluish light from the interior making their faces glow.

She couldn't move, sat frozen, just feeling the moment—
the way her heart pounded in her chest, the way his eyes glowed
with intensity, the way—

A car honked behind them, jerking Jake back into action,
turning his attention back to the road. He lowered her hand but
didn't let go, squeezing it instead, and said, "I knew you would
bring me luck. I like it when you're there." He was quiet for a
second, seeming embarrassed that he was so honest, and then
quickly said, "Would you mind if I go home real quick and
change? I have a condo downtown so it's not far from the
restaurant."

Maddie nodded her head. "I don't mind. But you look
great."

"The new dress code. I have to wear a suit anytime we are
on Racers business, but I sure would like to get into something
more comfortable."

"Okay." Maddie thought about being in his home with him
and felt the need to remind herself who and what he was—who and
what she was.

They pulled into a gated community where Jake waved to
the uniformed security officer, who nodded and opened the
soundless gate. The streets were narrow, immaculate and well lit.
He pulled around to number 614, pushed a button on his steering
column and pulled into a three-car garage. It was dark inside but
Maddie could make out the sports car parked next to them, a
couple of motorcycles and a four-wheeler edged to one side. A ski
boat with matching trailer sat gleaming in the third bay.

She was about to let herself out when Jake appeared beside
her and opened the door. He took her hand, helped her out and led
her to a door at the back of the garage. He seemed to like holding
her hand, because he didn't let go, just turned the lock with his
key, opening it and saying, "This will only take a minute."

"Sure, take your time," Maddie assured him, eager to see
how he lived.

The landing led up a flight of stairs to a pair of elegant French doors and then inside to the main living area. Huge vaulted ceilings with skylights, a giant fireplace that Maddie could easily stand inside of and a deep floor area, tastefully furnished in dark leather sofas and chairs, met her view.

Turning from the room, she remarked, "You have a beautiful home."

"Thanks. I had a decorator come in. Hey, make yourself at home, feel free to poke around and I'll be right back, okay?"

Maddie nodded, watched him walk into the recesses of the house, then turned to study his living room. She walked further into the main living area—lots of black and white, the specialized lighting that gave the room an intimate feel, the obvious thousands spent on electronics. Modern, sleek and masculine—the ultimate bachelor pad.

Wandering into the adjoining kitchen, she marveled at the latest stainless steel appliances, the dark granite countertops and sleek European cabinetry. The dining room looked rarely, if ever, used and more formal than the rest of the condo with a huge chandelier and an ornate dining set. Down the hall was a large guest bathroom done in greens with a glass backsplash, black cabinetry and sleek shower/tub combo with matching glass tiles. Again the impressive lighting above the sink, the clean lines of a modern faucet and sleek cabinetry.

Next, she found his study. It was surprisingly warm and homey compared to the rest of the place, filled with basketball paraphernalia. Awards and trophies were displayed on the built-in bookcases and scattered in elegant ease on low tables. Framed photos of Jake with teammates, the mayor and some celebrities graced the walls like magazine covers. A large framed photo sat on Jake's desk, facing his chair. She couldn't see it, but was curious. Was it his family? Didn't he have a sister with kids of her own making him an uncle? Or a girlfriend? What if it was Tiffany? Had he broken up with her for good? She didn't want to think about why and how she knew so much about his personal life, instead hurrying around the corner of the desk so that she could see it before he returned. As she edged around the desk, a light came on automatically, startling her. She backed up, into a small table, heard something topple and spun around in time to see something made of crystal fall to the wood floor, making a terrible crashing sound.

"Oh no!" she heard herself cry, kneeling down to look at the pieces. She reached for the largest piece and stared at it in horror.

Jake came running into the room, wearing only a pair of dark jeans. "Are you okay?" He stopped short, looking at the broken trophy.

"Jake, I'm so...sorry." Maddie looked up, remorse filling her heart.

Jake knelt down beside her, picked up one of the pieces and grimaced. "A college championship win, 1999. We were the underdogs that year. It was a great final game." He touched her shoulder. "It's okay."

"Can I replace it? Can they make you another one?" Maddie asked in a choked voice.

Jake shrugged. "Maybe, but it's just glass. It was a night when we were on. We played well, got lucky and won." He looked down at the broken piece in her hand. "Maddie, let me see your hand."

Maddie looked down, realizing for the first time the throbbing pain. Sure enough, she had a long cut on her left index finger, blood oozing out onto the piece of glass she still clutched. It had smeared on her skirt and the other hand, making a horrible scene. Her stomach rolled in response.

Jake pulled her gently up. "Let's get you to the sink." He led her through the house to his bedroom, another ultra-modern room with vaulted ceilings and skylights. She held her hand tightly to her chest, trying not to drip on the white carpet, hurrying through the huge length of it, noting the rumpled bed with a giant black fluffy blanket and then into his bathroom with its marble tiled walls, a huge jetted bath and standing, glass-enclosed shower. Turning on the faucet, he held her hand under the water for a minute, washing the area. Maddie blinked at the stinging sensation.

"You okay?"

"Yes," Maddie lied.

He raised her hand to look closely at it. "I don't see any glass in there, that's good. It's pretty deep, though." He looked down into her eyes. "We may have to get this stitched up." He opened a cabinet and pulled out a soft cloth. "Here, let's apply some pressure to it."

She didn't realize she was silently crying until Jake's thumb reached up and traced a tear.

"Does it hurt?"

"A little, but that's not why I'm upset. I just can't believe I destroyed one of your trophies. I'm so sorry."

"What can I do to convince you it doesn't matter?"

Maddie looked up at his face, then her gaze dropped lower to his bare chest. She felt heat steal up into her cheeks and quickly looked back into his eyes.

He smiled a slow, melting smile that said he could read her thoughts. His gaze roved over her face and it felt oddly like the warmth of the sun, like a heated caress that left her skin tingling.

She saw him stare at her lips, like the time in her office, but he was fully clothed in the bright lights of an office that day. Now he was shirtless in the semi-soft light of his private bathroom, a messy bathroom that smelled like him and his cologne.

He took a step forward, cradling her hand between them, guarding it from further injury while reaching around to her back and pressing her closer. She tilted her head back, saw her vision go dark as her eyelids closed, felt him coming nearer, his breath on her face, then felt his mouth against hers.

He tasted good. Cool and heated at the same time, soft lips that knew just how to move across hers. She slid her free hand up his back, feeling his warm, smooth skin, up to his nape and then across one shoulder blade, feeling the well-defined muscle. His kiss made her knees go weak and a heady lightheadedness whirled through her mind. Maybe it was the blood loss, but she was quite sure she'd never been kissed so thoroughly before in her life.

She pulled away, needing air before the floating black dots took over. They were both breathing heavy and Jake looked as wonder-filled as she felt. "Maddie…"

It was as if neither of them knew quite what to say.

Jake was the first to resurface to reality. Looking down at her finger, he said, "I should call Dr. Howe. I think he'll make a house call for us."

Maddie tore her eyes away from his, making herself look down at the offended finger, lifting the cloth and studying the cut. "Do you really think I'll have to have stitches? Don't you have any of that wound glue around?" She had used it on Max a time or two and knew how well it worked.

Jake laughed and led her over to his bed. "We're not gluing your finger together. Now sit down and I will call him. I want him to at least take a look at it."

She nodded and watched him call the doctor, secretly thrilled he had yet to put on a shirt. His body was perfect. She tried to keep herself from audibly sighing when he lifted an arm to rub the back of his neck. He turned a little, showing a huge bicep. She jerked her gaze away, only to return to him when he laughed at something the doctor said, watched again as he turned away from her showing broad shoulders that tapered down to a slim waist. She tried not to stare but the ache of her finger throbbed like a beating heart and staring kept her mind on other things.

He hung up and she quickly averted her eyes.

"He'll be here in about twenty minutes. You need anything?"

She needed him to put his shirt on but she wasn't about to say that out loud.

"Can I get you something? A glass of water? A drink?"

Maddie shook her head. "Oh, no, thank you. I'm fine, really." She bit her lower lip and looked at her finger. "Is our date ruined?"

Jake shook his head. "I don't think so. I'll cancel our dinner reservations and then we'll just hang out here if that's okay. I'm sure we can think of something to…talk about." His eyes turned smoky again, the green more gray, and Maddie had to look away. What if he was just really good at this? What if he spoke like this to the countless groupies that flock to a NBA star? She had to keep her wits somewhat about her and protect herself. After all, she was on an auction date…for charity. It didn't really count, did it?

They moved into the main living area. Jake had donned a dark blue shirt that hung from his shoulders in perfect elegance. He motioned her over to the deep, soft cushions of the couch. He sat close to her, talking in low tones about the game, obviously pleased with the win, making Maddie want to love basketball as much as he did. He had an arm draped over the back of the couch near her shoulders, but not touching. It took effort not to lean into his side and just nestle there.

Just as she thought that the doorbell rang. Great. Time for pain.

Sure enough, it was Dr. Howe. He was an attractive, fortyish man with an easy smile and manner that made Maddie glad he was there. He took a quick look at the cut, brought out a medical bag and before Maddie had time to feel nervous had stitched two stitches, promising no scar to mar the "beauty" of Maddie's hand.

Jake thanked the man, promising something as payment in a low voice that Maddie couldn't hear or make out clearly and then was gone. It was an hour and a half since they'd arrived at Jake's and they'd missed their dinner reservations, but it was still too early to call it a night.

"Do you want to watch a movie?" Jake asked with an apologetic smile after the doctor left.

She wanted to do anything but watch a movie, but politely nodded. "Sure. What do you have in mind?"

He had that look in his eyes that said they were both trying to shove their feelings beneath good behavior. "I have something of a library to choose from."

He motioned Maddie over to a cabinet that pulled out to reveal a huge library of movies. "Hmmm," Maddie heard herself observe. "Any chick flicks?"

Jake laughed. "There might be one or two."

Maddie thumbed through them. Lots of action, adventure, sci-fi and an occasional romantic comedy. "I can't believe you have this! I love this movie." She held up The Cutting Edge with a big grin.

Jake sighed dramatically. "I think that's my little sister's, but okay, since you sustained an injury and all."

"Not to mention the twenty thousand dollars I'm worth," Maddie agreed with a laugh.

He loaded the film into the player and sank back into the cushions of the couch next to her, from all appearances glued to the ice-skating action.

Jake had his ankles crossed, his feet swaying back and forth, laughing at all the appropriate times. Maddie started to get hungry.

"Hey, you want to order a pizza?" she asked.

"I've got a better idea," Jake replied. He made a call and within twenty minutes a man arrived with a three-course steak dinner.

"How did you do that?"

"I have vast connections," he teased.

"It must be nice to have such power," Maddie mused as she tore into the Styrofoam box of salad. "Umm, raspberry vinaigrette dressing, my favorite. How did you know?"

Jake grabbed a box for himself and shrugged, "I studied you before the date."

"You what?"

He passed her a round roll and some butter. "You know, I asked your co-workers. Found out what you liked so I could order for you."

She stared, non-blinking, at him. She couldn't help it. Had he really gone to that much trouble?

"Why?" she asked quietly.

Jake grinned. "I guess I wanted to impress you."

"Well, it worked." Maddie looked thoughtfully at him for a moment and then frowned, blurting out her fear. "Do you do the same thing with all the women you date? Did you study Tiffany?" The words skipped past her brain and popped out, one by one, before she had time to stop them. She inhaled in astonishment, wishing she could take them back.

"Tiffany? Tiffany Daniels?" His face grew closed.

"I'm sorry. That's none of my business." A couple of heartbeats of silence. "I guess I've done a little research too. I thought you might still be dating her."

Jake laid his arm on the back of the couch, reaching toward her but not touching her, waiting for her to look at him. "You are the only woman I have ever studied before a date, Madeleine Goode."

He knew her name was Madeleine. That she went by Maddie as a nickname. Maddie looked quickly down, feeling sudden gladness spring to her eyes and not wanting Jake to see how much she loved what those words meant. She loved the rush of excitement they produced inside her, but what if he was only a really good pretender?

If only she had a safety net and could see across this tightrope to the other side. If only her heart didn't feel so fragile. If only she could be safely ignorant again, not knowing that life could come crashing down at any moment.

If only.

Suddenly, she needed some air.

CHAPTER FOURTEEN

"Mom, can you pass me that stuffing mix?" Maddie asked, pointing toward the box with a wooden spoon. She threw an apron that said "K♥ss the Cook" over her head and tied the strings tightly behind her back.

Her mother's eyes widened. "You haven't put the turkey in yet? It's never going to be ready in time."

Maddie tilted her head and stared at her mother, her eyes widening with annoyance. "Mom, I told you, I'm not stuffing the bird. I'm trying a new recipe and it's been in the oven for over an hour already. I'm making this sausage and mushroom stuffing on the stovetop. It's going to be great."

"Okay." Gloria shook her head. "But you should never try out new recipes on company. You just never know how they're going to turn out."

"Yeah, I know." Maddie *was* a little nervous about all the new things she was trying at once. She wasn't a bad cook, but she wasn't an expert either.

Yesterday, she'd made three pies—pumpkin, pecan and apple. This morning she and Gloria, both edgy about hosting Jake, had gotten up extra early to prepare the rest of the meal and set the table. Maddie had even bought a new tablecloth and centerpiece so that everything would look pretty.

The doorbell rang with unexpected clarity. Maddie and Gloria looked at each other, eyes wide. "It can't be," Maddie whispered in horror. She hadn't even put on her makeup or fixed her hair yet. "He *would* be a half an hour early!"

"I'll go check. You run into the bathroom in case it's him. We can't have him seeing you like this."

Maddie nodded agreement to the plan and made a dash for the bathroom, calling Max in after her, knowing that a closed and locked door would soon produce yells from him as he always somehow found her and wanted her when she was behind a locked door. "Come on, Max. Mommy wants to tell you a story."

Max took her hand and seemed to think it was great fun running into the bathroom with her. He quickly plopped down on the toilet with the lid still open and nearly fell in as Maddie snatched him off, laughing and scolding at the same time. "Put the lid down Max, unless you have to go."

Max decided he did have to go, taking up several minutes to help him with his button and zipper. Maddie made sure he sat low enough to not spray the room since he wasn't tall enough to stand up yet, all the while trying to hear the muffled voices from the living room.

Finally, she was able to pull out her makeup bag and dot on some concealer and powder over it. She was sweating from the heat of the kitchen, which made the makeup turn into orange/brown goo on her cheeks. "Oh…blast," she mumbled, hoping Max hadn't heard, and flipped on the bathroom fan. She rubbed frantically at the streaks, making it worse as the powder turned into horrid little orange balls. She wanted to yell in earnest, but she refrained, taking a cool washcloth to her face instead. With a deep breath, she started over.

She heard a laugh. It *was* Jake. He was here already. Why couldn't he follow simple instructions? Now the whole meal was at risk.

"Tell the story, Mommy," Max reminded.

"Oh, yeah," she muttered. Why had she said that to him? Swiping a pearl pink lip-gloss across her lips, she scrambled for an idea. "Once upon a time there was a giant frog." Eyeliner, a touch of eye shadow in purple and brown to bring out her eyes and some mascara, the application of which had her talking from the corner of her mouth. "And he was so fat he couldn't hop like the other frogs, so…"

She pondered for a minute, trying to make it as silly as possible to get Max to laugh. "So, he put on a girdle." She smiled at the image in her mind and shook out her hair from the pony tail she'd had it up in all morning and finger combed through it.

"What's a girdle?" Max's face scrunched up in cute curiosity.

Maddie laughed. How to explain it? "Umm, kind of like a pair of really tight underwear, so it holds in your stomach." She put her hands at her waist and squeezed to demonstrate.

Max's face registered horror. "Why would frogs wear underwear? Frogs don't wear nothin', Mom."

Maddie shrugged, trying not to giggle while combing Max's hair. "Well, the girdle didn't work anyway, so he bought himself some…giant springs, strapped them on his big, webbed feet, and then he could jump as high as a four-story building."

Max's eyes grew wide, his chin jutting forward. "I want springs like that."

Maddie took him by the hand, giving herself one last look in the mirror, thinking it was the best she could do with the nanoseconds she'd had to work with, and shook her head. "No springs today, Max. Let's go meet Mr. Hart. Remember? I told you a friend is coming for dinner today."

Max patted his round stomach. "Turkey day."

"Yes, let's go check on our turkey."

They came out of the bathroom together, walking down the short hallway and into the living room where Jake stood with her parents, a white box in his hands and a bouquet of beautifully hued fall flowers in her mother's arms.

116

"Maddie, there you are," Gloria said as if she didn't know where Maddie had gone.

Maddie gave her mother a tight smile then went over to Jake and gave him a light hug. "Happy turkey day," she said, smiling into his eyes, not able to suppress the pure pleasure coursing through her just at the sight of him in dark jeans and a perfectly fitting button-up shirt.

"'Appy turkey day!" Max parroted.

Jake squatted down in front of Max and grinned, holding out his large hand, which Max promptly high-fived. "Happy turkey day to you too, Max. Do you like turkey?"

Max patted his little round stomach and nodded, dimples showing. "Mmmmm. Mommy's cooking it." He announced like it was the greatest feat on earth.

Everyone laughed.

Jake held out the box. "I brought you a turkey day present, Max."

Max's eyes grew round as he reached for the box. He tore into it like only a child can and then grinned as he pulled out a stuffed turkey that sang and said funny things like "eat beef" when Max pushed on his stomach.

When Jake stood back up, Maddie looked up at him, feeling her heart swell with warmth. "Thank you, Jake. That was so thoughtful."

"Did you see these beautiful flowers?" Gloria gushed. "I'll just go put them in a vase and check the dinner. Simon, get Jake something to drink. Max, come help Grammy find some water for these gorgeous flowers."

Maddie's dad clapped Jake on the shoulder like they were old friends. "You want a beer?"

"Sure." While he left to get it Jake took Maddie's hand and held it out. "You look pretty," he said, taking in the blue dress and apron she'd forgotten that she was still wearing.

Maddie looked up at him, a shy smile playing across her lips. "You look pretty good yourself." The flirtatious tone to both their remarks made heat steel up Maddie's cheeks.

Her dad came back in on that note, embarrassing her further. Here, she'd been afraid her parents were going to do something stupid and she was the one acting like a star-struck groupie. Her dad handed Jake the drink and motioned to the recliner and the football game playing across the big screen. "You a football fan?" Simon asked.

Jake nodded, taking a sip and sitting on the couch, probably not wanting to take what was obviously her father's chair. "North Carolina's playing today, right?"

The men talked and Maddie waved at Jake and went into the kitchen to hurry dinner along, sighing with relief. It looked as though things might go better than she thought.

The sweet potatoes looked wonderful, bubbling and oozing with brown sugar and butter in the oven next to the turkey. The homemade egg noodles bubbled in chicken broth on the stove. They were still a little tough, but smelled great and would be ready in another fifteen minutes. The mashed potatoes and gravy were the easy part, just heat up in the microwave toward the end, which left the stuffing on the stove and the rolls to bake at the last ten minutes. The marshmallow cranberry salad was in the fridge looking elegant in a beautiful cut-glass bowl.

Maddie's mom edged closer to her, glancing around the corner to make sure they were alone, and rasped out in too loud a whisper, "You didn't tell me he was so handsome. He looks better in person than on TV, doesn't he?"

Maddie grinned, really looking at her mom's face. Gloria was a petite woman, always thin, but now, as she'd gotten older, curvier, which her father assured everyone he liked better, with strawberry blond hair and a round face. "I know. He about took my breath away when I walked into the living room." She reached for her glass of water, took a small sip and stared dreamily off into space.

"I just hope he doesn't break your heart," Gloria whispered.

Maddie patted her mom's arm. "I'm guarding it. Believe me, I'm worried about the same thing."

They set the table, filled the glasses, put the rolls in the oven and set the timer. Maddie wandered back into the living room to check on how Jake was doing.

Jake was sitting on the couch, his long arm stretched out across the back, Max squeezed in next to him, as close as the little boy could get, looking up at him with innate idol worship. Jake had Max's favorite storybook in his hands and was reading it to him in a low voice, pointing at the pictures, smiling and nodding when Max got a picture right. They were so wrapped up in each other that they didn't even notice Maddie at the door, glass suspended in her hand, tears forming.

Razor sharp, the truth sank through layers of physical attraction and infatuation. If she allowed these feelings for Jake to grow, allowed him into her heart and her home, it wouldn't only be her heart that she was risking, but Max's too. How could she possibly put her little boy through more pain? More loss? The agony of loving and losing.

And yet, watching them, so close and comfortable together, she found she couldn't tear Max away. He…*they* deserved friends at least, didn't they? She could resist the attraction. She could build in healthy boundaries for her and Max so that they could enjoy his company without falling in love with him.

"Daddy," Max said, pointing to the dad in the picture. He then looked up at Jake with the most cherubic smile and stated with sweet simplicity, "You can be my new dad."

Oh no, stop! Maddie rushed into the room, not knowing what to say.

Jake smiled at the panicked look on her face. "It's okay," he assured her. He ruffled Max's hair and squeezed him in a tight hug. "Whoever gets to be your dad is one lucky man." He kissed the top of Max's curling hair and then pointed to the mom in the picture. "Who's that?"

"The mommy," Max said with assurance.

"She's not as pretty as your mommy, is she?"

Max looked at Maddie, looked at her from a different perspective than he ever had before, and something flashed across those two-year-old eyes. He shook his head. "'Cause the lady in the story is not my mommy."

Maddie inhaled sharply. Jake smiled a slow, admiring smile. "He's a smart boy."

Maddie blinked back the tears and did that nodding, shaking-her-head thing that she did when she was agreeing and confused. "I can't believe he just said that."

Jake got off the couch, seemingly unaffected by the fact that her father was there, eyes glued to the game. He walked over to her and gave her a kiss square on the mouth.

Maddie reared back. "What was that for?"

"I'm obeying the apron," he said, a mischievous look in his eyes.

Maddie looked down at the "K♥ss the Cook" sign on her chest and laughed, turning pink. Lowering her voice and leaning toward him she teased back, "What if it had said 'Marry the Cook?' Would you have done that too?"

"I'm thinking about it," he said, shocking her. "Maybe I just need a sign."

Maddie didn't know what to say to that. Everything with Jake was too right. She felt like she was swimming with the current when she was with him, so different than it had been with Brandon.

Gloria saved her from answering as she called out, "Dinner's ready."

Her dad took Max's hand and led him into the dining room with a private wink toward Maddie.

Maddie reached for her apron strings to untie them, but Jake stopped her and turned her around. His knuckles brushed against the nape of her neck, sending goose bumps along the column of her spine, as he untied it for her. He slowly did the same at her waist, making them late walking into the dining room.

They gathered around the table, where her father said grace. He was exceptionally eloquent, thanking God for their family, for Maddie and Max living with them, for their guest and Maddie, again, had to fight back tears. What was wrong with her today?

~~~~~~

Jake sat across from Maddie, Max in his high chair beside her, and tried not to stare. Maddie as the housewife, the mother, the cook, the nurturer was even more appealing than the classy woman he saw at work. He couldn't help it. He imagined them married. He imagined himself in the husband and father role. It was something he had never known he wanted…until now. He had never considered what it would be like to have a son. Had never known the jolt of protective joy that Max inspired when he'd cuddled up next to him and asked for a story. Never imagined the pride that would fill him as he filled his plate, knowing that she'd spent hours in the kitchen cooking it for him. He felt dazed, a little confused, like a fish lifted out of a comfortably warm fishbowl and set free into the sea, where there were colors and textures and wants and needs that had yet to be explored, that were core deep, that he hadn't known he had been missing.

This must be what love feels like.

There was a surrendering to it. It was a choice and he suddenly knew that if he dove in, he was all in. There would be no turning back from this admission. The fishbowl would then feel closed and small and mean…without light or color. Like a choice between heaven and earth. He couldn't get away from it. He had to decide right here, right now.

Something must have shown in the look he gave her across the table, because she stopped, her fork suspended toward her mouth, and looked at him with that beautiful half-smile with a question in it.

He stared back, thoughtful, purposeful, knowing the path ahead. He would have to fight to win her heart. It would be a challenge, but he was never so eager to begin a battle. He knew battle. He knew reaching beyond the possible. He knew how to win a prize.

"It's good." His voice came out huskier than he intended. "The food, I mean," he corrected himself, belatedly remembering their audience. "You're a great cook, Maddie."

Maddie compressed her lips together in a look of embarrassed pleasure at the compliment, took a deep breath and laughed a small laugh. "Internet recipes. Thank you."

Simon nodded his agreement and looked to Gloria. "You girls did real good. Jake and Max and I are lucky men today."

Max, with mashed potatoes smeared across his lips, lifted his plastic blue spoon high in the air in spontaneous agreement and they all looked at him and laughed.

After everyone finished, Jake volunteered to help Maddie wash the dishes, hoping to be alone with her in the kitchen.

"Max likes you," she said softly, both pleased and uneasy with it. Jake could tell by the sparkle in her eyes and the tightness in her shoulders.

"I like Max." Jake stepped up behind her at the kitchen sink and wrapped his arms around her. "This is the best Thanksgiving I've ever had. Thank you for inviting me."

She turned her head to look up at him. "Really? You don't get to go home much anymore?"

Jake let his hands glide from her arms to her shoulders and then down to her waist, watching the water from the sink running on the dirty dishes in a hot, steamy flow. "Sometimes I go back…but, you know after you leave home, it's never the same. I guess I'm in that in between time…not really belonging there anymore and not really having a family of my own yet."

Maddie gave him that same half-smile, but this time it was filled with confusion. "You want a family of your own?"

"I didn't know I did…until I met you." He leaned closer, kissing her neck, just behind her ear. She smelled so good, like brown sugar-laden sweet potatoes and perfume.

He felt her take an indrawn breath. "Jake—"

"Yeah…I know."

He turned her and rested his hands at her waist, kissing her temple and then along the side of her cheek and back down and into her hair, feeling the moment razor sharp, not even wanting to kiss her lips yet.

The water made a thick steam that rose up and around them. She trembled in his arms. He whispered in her ear, "I know you're scared but if you want to talk about it, if you want to cry on my shoulder, I want to be there for you."

She lifted her face. She looked into his eyes and for a moment, a flash in time, the blue depths of her eyes were unguarded. He saw clearly her sorrow, a soul bereft, a spirit downtrodden, and it snatched his breath from him.

"You loved him so much, didn't you?"

She pressed her lips together, trying not to cry, and then dropped her head on his chest and nodded. "I thought we would be together forever. I didn't know. I didn't understand what could happen."

"No one could. No one could." He pressed her to him, wanting to ease her pain, wanting to do something…anything.

"I think I'm falling in love with you, Maddie." He paused, letting it sink into both of them. "I know it's too soon. I know it doesn't make sense and I know you don't want it right now. But I'll wait. I'll be here when you're ready."

She lifted her head, the tears now real. "What if I'm never ready?" she said on a breath.

Jake smiled. "Someday you will be. Someday you will be healed enough to take a chance again."

"I don't know…"

"Shall I prove it to you?"

Her eyebrows drew together in a manner that he was recognizing as confused stubbornness. "How?"

"Kiss me."

Her eyes widened.

He reached over and turned off the running faucet, his hand returning to her cheek, wiping off a tear with the pad of his thumb. "*You* kiss *me*."

She was breathing too fast, slowly shaking her head, which made him smile. "You can do it."

She leaned toward him, tentative in the initiative-taking. "How do men risk this?" she asked suddenly, smiling. "Even though you asked for it, I'm afraid you're going to reject me."

Jake laughed out loud and hoped it wouldn't have her parents walking in. "I won't reject you. I can hardly wait."

Taking a deep breath, she leaned in again, up on her tiptoes. Jake barely helped by tilting down his head a little. This was her battle and she needed to conquer it and come to her own conclusions about it.

Her lips felt cool, a little dry and shy. They started to move across his, a slight opening, her mouth reaching out, exploratory, cautious. Jake resisted the urge to take over, only responding in kind.

She placed her hands awkwardly on his upper arms and stretched up a little further toward him. Tilting her head, she tried again, letting go a little more, slanting her lips across his. "Kiss me back," he felt, more than heard her say against his lips, causing him to smile against her mouth.

"I am. This is your kiss. Make it what you want." A couple of heartbeats, and then, "What do you want, Maddie?"

~~~~~~~

It was that question again. Did she know? She should be good, do the right thing and send him packing. But that wasn't what she wanted. She wanted him. She wanted to rush to the altar and marry him already. The basketball star that she never dreamed would notice her. The tall, dark and handsome man that he epitomized and that left her weak in the knees when she watched him move across the court or her office or her home. The sweetness he showed her when he looked at her with compassion and understanding. The man who sat with her son and read him a story…and seemed to love each second of it.

She wanted *him*.

~~~~~~~

He felt the change against his mouth and then the catch in her breath as she allowed the feelings to flow through her and into the kiss. She melted into him, but stayed in control. She explored, tasting him, moving to touch places on his lips and in his mouth that had his head spinning. She contoured her lips in both wide and little movements that tasted him. She completely let go.

He was lost, rocked, spinning in a sensation that he'd never explored before. His heart pounded, his hands grew sweaty and the woman in his arms conquered him like he'd never imagined was possible from just a kiss. She engulfed him until he didn't know where he ended and she began. It was unlike anything he'd ever experienced.

~~~~~~~

Maddie pulled back, holding the back of her hand against her flushed, swollen lips, her eyes wide with disbelief. "What are you doing to me? What have you done?"

He let out a breathy laugh. "I…I'm not sure what I'm doing." But his eyes said differently. His eyes said he would like to kiss her more and more and what that led to.

"I'm not one of those women, Jake. I'm not another star-struck fan that will just let you do anything and then…watch you walk away."

She swallowed, looking up at him, her hand against his rock-solid chest. "I have a son."

Jake nodded, his brow knitted together. "Do you really think that's all I feel for you?" He backed away, turned toward the kitchen cabinets and ran his hand over his face. Then he pierced her with gray-green intensity. "Do you think I run after women like this? Read their sons stories and love their turkey dinner and go to their home and meet their parents, just…just to get her into bed? Is that all you take me for, Maddie?"

There was pain in his eyes and she felt it pierce her, reach slowly down into her heart and twist. "I'm sorry. I don't think that. It's just that…"

When she couldn't finish, he nodded. "I know. You are a widow. You recently lost your husband and you're scared." He stepped closer and she could smell his cologne waft over her. "Tell me, Maddie, what can I do to show you that I'm here for the right reasons. How can I prove myself to you?"

Maddie tilted her head back and stared into his eyes. It would be so easy to give in, but she kind of liked being asked. "Well," she said with a serious tone, "I am looking for a new church. You could visit a few with me? Just on the Sundays when you are in town?" She came into his arms, enjoying the feel of them wrap around her back. "It's hard to go alone."

"Church, huh?" He squeezed her tighter into his chest and leaned down to breathe into her ear. "You *are* good."

Maddie kissed his neck, reveling in the feel of his smooth skin and the wonderful way he always smelled. "Oh no," she assured in a whisper toward his ear, "not good enough." She ran little kisses up to his mouth and then paused just an inch away from his lips. Breathing together for a moment, she laughed on a soft breath. "That's why I need to go to church."

CHAPTER FIFTEEN

Maddie was surprised how quickly Jake had agreed. Even more surprising, he insisted on picking them up that very next Sunday. She glanced down at Max, who was running around the living room, arms spread wide and pretending to be an airplane while reaching into the closet for their coats. Jake would arrive any minute.

Maddie checked her reflection one more time in the living room mirror while she shrugged into her coat. She was just getting Max's hand through his coat sleeves when she heard the doorbell ring. "Hurry, Max." She kissed his cheek as she pulled a fleece cap over his curls and lifted his hood, zipping the coat with practiced speed. "Our ride is here."

She handed Max his mittens, hoping the task would occupy him for a few minutes, and rushed to the door. When she opened the door it was to a white world, the snow still coming down in pretty clumps. The sight of Jake, so bright and early and looking like God's gift to women in dark slacks and a striped, royal blue button-up shirt under a dark wool coat that draped his broad shoulders perfectly, nearly took her breath away.

When she didn't say anything, just stared, he smiled and clapped his gloved hands together. "Shocked I made it?" He looked down, gesturing toward his clothes. "Have I dressed appropriately?"

"Oh, yes," Maddie said in a rush. "I was just so surprised...that is...by all the snow." Maddie stood back for him to enter. "We're nearly ready. Come in for a minute?"

Jake stepped into the living room, his shoulders dusted with snowflakes.

"Max rushed to greet him while Jake squatted down and held out his arms. "Max, my man. Are you ready to go to church?"

Max gave him a big squeeze around the neck and nodded. "Got to go to church!" Max shouted.

Jake laughed. "That we do, Max. That we do."

Maddie turned from slipping into her gloves and grasping her purse. When she saw that Jake was gently trying to coax Max's fingers into his mittens she smiled. "You boys ready?"

Jake looked up from the task and grimaced with a smile. "This is harder than it looks."

Maddie laughed. "You'll get the hang of it with some practice."

"I think I'd like that." Jake said it low, but it had reached Maddie's ears and made a shiver of pleasure race down her back.

Jake scooped Max into his arms, the boy looking thrilled to be so high off the ground. "Shall we?" Jake opened the door for Maddie.

There was his massive, shiny black SUV sitting in her parents' driveway.

Max shouted in glee. "Great big truck!" He grinned even wider when Jake opened the back door and sat him on the huge leather seat.

Maddie trudged through the snow to her car to get the car seat. She pulled and pulled on the door handle, but the door was solidly frozen shut.

"Stay put, Max, I'll be right back." Jake shut the door and trudged through the snow toward Maddie. He gave the door handle a big jerk and with a giant creak the door swung open. Jake grinned victoriously at her. It was such a cute little-boy look, something she had seen on Max's face when he'd thought he had done something wonderful, like go in the potty, that she giggled.

"Why thank you, kind sir. However did you get so strong?"

He must have known she was teasing but looked pleased by the comment all the same. As she stepped forward to grab the seat he leaned in and gave her a quick kiss, then hauled the seat out and carried it back to the truck.

Maddie could only smile and try hard not to feel so happy as she followed him back to the vehicle. Happiness turned to alarm when Jake tried to open the door and found it locked. "Oh no," Maddie said, rushing forward to peer through the dark glass. "Do you have the keys?"

Maddie took the car seat from Jake so that he could search his pockets. "I think I left them on the seat with Max."

"He is probably playing with them and that's how he managed to lock the doors." Jake went around the back and sides, trying all the doors, while Maddie rapped on the glass, shouting in a happy voice, "Max, honey. Do you have the keys?"

She could just barely see Max scoot toward her and stand on the seat, waving the keys at her. "Good, Max. Now, push the buttons. Push every one, okay?"

Max said something back that she couldn't hear and started to look upset. He was probably wondering why she wasn't opening the door. "No, no, Max. Don't cry. We are going to play a game, okay? You push the buttons on the key chain and then Mommy will surprise you when I open the door. Ready? Push the buttons, Max!" She smiled as big as she could and clapped her hands together in fake excitement.

Max dropped the keys.

"Oh, Jake. He dropped the keys."

Jake came up beside her, peering through the window. "Keep talking to him. We have to keep him calm."

Maddie nodded. "Max, go get the keys, sweetie. We can't play the game without the magic keys." He looked ready to argue, then decided to give it another try. He pushed his little body to the edge of the seat, turned over onto his stomach and then slid down to the carpet. Maddie couldn't see him for a couple of minutes and was starting to worry when suddenly his head popped back up and he flashed the keys at her, waving them back and forth.

"Good, Max, great job! Now push those buttons!"

She was hoping and praying he didn't hit the panic button. That would scare him for sure. Just as she thought that thought, Jake said in a bright voice, "Don't push the red button, Max. That's the loser button. Not the red one."

Max looked as if he had just been about to push that very one and backed his hand away. They both watched as his cute little face studied the key fob. Suddenly, there was a loud click and the doors were unlocked. He'd pressed the right button on the first try!

Maddie rushed to open the door and took her gleeful son into her arms. "I won! I won!" he cried over and over.

"Yes, you won!" Maddie agreed, gently prying the keys from his hand. Jake took a deep breath and shook his head, smiling down at the two of them. "That was scary."

Maddie nodded, "Thank heaven he found the button!" She gestured toward the car seat. "Let's get him strapped in, shall we?"

Jake looked so relieved that Maddie couldn't help but laugh as she buckled Max safely inside.

"So, iChurch, huh? Sounds modern," Jake commented as they pulled out of the driveway.

Maddie arranged her dress against the slippery leather of her seat and nodded to him. "I've tried out two other churches recommended to me from my church in Muncie, gone a few weeks to each of them, and they were okay but I want to try a couple more before I make my decision."

Jake reached for her hand across the wide console between them. "Sounds like a good idea. What exactly are you looking for?"

Maddie took a deep breath, thinking about the question. She watched his profile, how chiseled and gorgeous and bigger than life he seemed in the SUV, watched his free hand easily guide the vehicle with the steering wheel as he navigated the Sunday church rush hour and tried to remember what she wanted in a church.

"Well, my parents always attended the same church for as long as I can remember. It was good, very traditional. My sister and I did the Sunday school thing and I was in the church choir. But after I married Brandon and moved to Muncie, I don't know. It was weird. It was like he and I were living different lives sometimes. I worked full-time to put him through college and then I had Max. He was either going to class and studying or, after landing his first big job, working all of the time. Max and I...we sort of found our own church. It became like a family to me."

Jake glanced over at her. "Sounds like you found something you needed."

Maddie nodded. "I did. And I loved the worship. They have a great worship team. It was like being at a concert every Sunday. The people really got into it. They lifted their hands and clapped and, well...worshipped God with such freedom."

She waited with an indrawn breath to hear what Jake would say to that. She had no idea what kind of religious upbringing he may or may not have had.

"Is that weird, do you think?" she asked into the silence.

He seemed to be thinking about it. "Well, when you put it like that. I mean, people cheer and raise their hands and clap for us—a basketball team—and they don't think anything about it." He glanced at her again and she could tell that he was really thinking this through. "And we're just playing with a little orange ball. Just trying to get it to swoosh through a net more times than our opponents. It's great. I'll grant you that. But if I were to really to imagine heaven…seeing God?" He looked at her again, his gray-green eyes piercing in intensity. "I can't imagine that raised hands and clapping would even begin to be enough. I'm no god and they give *me* that."

Maddie blinked back sudden tears. No one had put into words how she felt about it before. "Exactly," she said softly. "That's what we're looking for today."

The church was in a strip mall. They pulled into the packed parking lot and found a spot. Maddie started to unstrap Max from his car seat but Jake stopped her. "Let me get him." He pulled the straps away and gathered her son into his arms. "Come on, Max. Let's go to church!"

Max gave a happy laugh and nestled into Jake's arms like he belonged there while Maddie quickly turned away, trying not to slide on the ice on the pavement in her heels and keep the tears that kept rising up this morning from her eyes.

Together, as if they were a family, they walked to the double glass doors.

The greeters, a heavyset man and a trim, pretty woman greeted them with smiles and programs. Maddie clutched hers, seeing the heads turn in the lobby toward their threesome, knowing that Jake might be recognized. They made their way down a long, carpeted isle to a row of chairs about halfway back and in the center. Jake settled Max securely on his lap and stretched his long arm across the back of Maddie's chair. Within minutes the lights dimmed and the worship team took their positions on the stage.

The leader had longish dark hair and deep eyes. He spoke a little, welcoming them, then began to strum his guitar. He began to sing in a deep baritone about God's glory. The rest of the team stood with their eyes closed as this one man and one acoustic guitar filled the warehouse-like space. His voice was pure. His words grew into a fullness that made Maddie breathe deeper as a peaceful feeling swept through her. Then the band joined in.

~~~~~~~~

Jake watched Maddie's face. Her eyes were closed and her hands were tightly clasped in front of her pretty dress, but he couldn't keep his eyes from her face. She was feeling…something.

Religion had never meant much to Jake. He hadn't been raised in the religion of a church, only the religion of a sport. But something Maddie had said on the drive over had struck him. They were all looking for a touch from God, weren't they? If he did believe in God, and he did, he didn't know exactly why or how, but he had felt Him at times during his life. When he'd signed his first contract with all those colleges vying for him, he'd felt some guidance beyond his father's booming voice. He had felt sure…had some feeling of rightness and peace that he was supposed to go with Georgia Tech. And then, when his girlfriend had decided to abandon him and attend a different college, he had known, somehow, that it was the right decision for both of them.

He may not have entered a church before today, but there had been God moments in his life for as long as he could remember. He didn't doubt the existence of a God who loved him, who watched over him, who knew him since before he was born.

He looked down at Maddie's captivated face and suddenly knew. This music might be the thing that brought Maddie closer to God, but Maddie would be the one who brought him closer to God.

He took a long, deep breath as gratitude filled him. She was the one. For so many reasons…he had found his other half.

With Max dozing against his chest, his freshly shampooed curls tickling his neck, Jake reached over with his other hand and grasped Maddie's hand.

CHAPTER SIXTEEN

The day was bright for mid-December, a blue sky with white clouds, giving a reprieve from the gloomy, overcast weather. Maddie pulled her car into the model home's parking lot and looked for Sasha's red Ford Mustang convertible, Sasha's biggest splurge. As she turned off the engine, Sasha pulled in beside her and waved.

"This neighborhood is great," Sasha stated with a big grin as she got out and locked her car with a chirruping beep.

"I know. I can't believe I'm really doing this." Maddie had worked for the Racers long enough to have saved a respectable four thousand dollars to add to the money left over from Brandon's life insurance. It might just be enough for a down payment on a starter house for Max and her.

As they walked up the sidewalk and into the model home, Maddie asked, "How are things with Rob? You didn't call, so I didn't know if you wanted to talk about it. Did you tell him about Marcus?"

Sasha nodded, hand on the doorknob. "I'll tell you all the details later, but suffice it to say," she turned, tossing her long, dark hair, "he calls me daily and has even hinted at a ring."

"You're kidding?" Maddie placed her hand on the door to keep Sasha from opening it yet. "He wasn't angry?"

"Oh, he was steaming mad. He ranted at me both over the phone and on text until I was ready to slug him. I told him that as far as I was concerned we weren't in a real relationship anyway and he finally conceded that I was right. He said he would like to start over. I guess since someone like a famous basketball player wanted me he decided he would fight for me. For the first time

135

since we've been together, he is actually chasing after me. Can you believe it? Men!"

Maddie shook her head, perplexed. "Do you want him that way? I mean, you know, having to be so goaded into it and all?"

Sasha grinned. "I'm waiting to see how long it lasts and if it survives his parents' house. I talked him into a visit with me included this time. If that doesn't go well," she shrugged, "I may have to end it. I really think this might be our turning point." Sasha pulled the door open. "Come on, let's find you a house."

Maddie had thought a lot about buying an established home—she would probably get more for her money—but she couldn't get away from wanting something fresh and new, a new beginning where she and Max could make their own memories, so she'd decided to visit some builders.

The office was spacious and neat, with a well-lit room displaying floor plans and a community map. "Look," Sasha whispered, pointing. "It has a neighborhood pool!"

Maddie nodded, pointing at another spot on the map. "And a park. Max would love that."

A woman came over to them, petite and well dressed, with brown hair and glasses. "Hello." She held out her hand with a big smile. "I'm Rebecca Slater."

Maddie shook her hand, a little nervous. "I'm Maddie Goode and this is my friend, Sasha."

"Welcome to Meadow Grove. What can I help you with today?"

"I'm looking into building a home. We would like to see the models."

Rebecca swept an arm toward the floor plans on the wall. "Wonderful. We have twelve lots left. Which model would you like to see?"

"I can probably afford one of the smaller homes, but I would like to see them all."

"Let's look at the lots available first and then I will show you the models." Rebecca led them over to the center of the room.

The three crowded around a square glass case in the middle of the floor. Inside was a replica of the community, little cardboard houses lining the streets, green paint designating the hilly property from the flat and blue paint for the fishing pond and swimming pool. Rebecca pointed out the remaining lots. One was within close proximity to the park and within walking distance to the pool. Maddie looked at Sasha and grinned.

"What style of home are you looking for?"

"It's for me and my son, Max. I would like a two-story, maybe something with vaulted ceilings and an open floor plan on the first floor."

"Oh, yes. We have just what you're looking for," gushed Rebecca. "Come see the Commodore."

They followed the saleswoman back to the wall with the oversized floor plans and tried to imagine them as carpeted, decorated homes.

"I think I like the Ecuador," Maddie said at last. "Can I see both, though?"

"Just follow me," Rebecca said in a happy voice. "You're going to love the models. Everyone does."

The first home was a small ranch, but tastefully decorated. Maddie nodded her way through the tour, thinking she could do better.

The second had an odd layout that she didn't like, but the third was, as Rebecca assured, very similar to the Ecuador, and Maddie loved it. The entry gave way into a huge family room with vaulted ceilings. The dining area and spacious kitchen were separated by a long counter with granite countertops and barstools. Maddie loved the idea of having Max sit at the counter doing his homework one day or eating a snack while she was cooking in the kitchen. There was a nice-sized powder room and a laundry/mud room. Then they headed up the stairs.

The stairway led to a bonus room that overlooked the family room below. A short hallway led to a jack-and-jill bathroom with two medium-sized bedrooms on either side. Maddie noted that one could easily be turned into an office.

The upstairs seemed perfect with the three bedrooms, two bathrooms and lots of closet space. The master bedroom's closet was big enough to be a room all on its own.

"You'll have room for all those shoes we've been buying," Sasha teased, peeking into the closet.

"We've been buying? If my credit card bill is any indication, I'd say you've been talking me into them, and I've been buying." But she grinned while she said it. The house was perfect.

She was just about to ask the price when her cell phone rang. The number on the screen didn't look familiar.

"Excuse me," she murmured, stepping into the huge closet and hearing Rebecca say she would let them look around by themselves for a while and meet them back in the office when they were finished.

Maddie saw Sasha plop down on the huge bed as she said "hello" into the receiver.

"Is this Madeline Goode?"

"Yes."

"My name is Sabrina Bridgestone."

"Yes?" Maddie questioned when the woman stopped talking.

She heard a deep breath and then the rush of words. "I need to speak with you concerning your husband. Concerning Brandon."

Maddie adjusted the phone on her ear. "What is this about?"

"What it's about is too complicated for a phone call. We need to meet."

"Who are you?" Maddie demanded, a feeling of deep unease spreading from her stomach. "My husband…is no longer living."

"I know that," the woman snapped. "I know that." This time it was said low and sad. "I knew your husband. Knew him very well. Better than you know, and we need to talk."

"Who are you? Is this some kind of sick joke?"

"Listen. I didn't want you to ever know about this, about Brandon and me, but something's happened. Something I have to warn you about. Can you meet me today? Anywhere, you name the place and I'll be there."

Brandon and me. The phrase spiraled through her mind. Brandon and her? A tight sickness gripped her chest. "You have to give me more information to go on than that. I won't believe some cryptic woman that's calling me out of nowhere."

"Brandon had a birthmark on his right hip, down low. Now will you see me? I don't want to have to come to your house. I'm trying to leave Max out of this."

A deep chill crept through her body at the mention of Max, and she saw that her hand was shaking. The phone at her ear shook. Her legs shook so that she had to sink down the bare wall of the closet onto the carpet. Finally, she managed to speak in a quivering voice. "Are you telling me that…you had an affair with my husband? My dead husband?" Her voice rose and Sasha came into the closet, eyes wide with horror.

139

"That's the least of it, sweetheart. Believe me, I wouldn't call you to tell you that, not now. Not when he's gone."

Maddie pushed the disconnect button on her phone and dropped it onto the carpet. Saying nothing, seeing nothing, she stood up and walked out of the closet, out of the model home, out of the office, ignoring the waving Rebecca, and got into her car.

Once there, she just sat and stared. It couldn't be true. Brandon wouldn't have, couldn't have had an affair. The woman must be a lunatic.

A few moments later, Sasha rapped on the window. Maddie rolled it down. "Yes?" she asked as if nothing was wrong.

"Maddie. She called back." Sasha held out the phone.

Maddie shook her head. "She's crazy. I'm not talking to a crazy woman."

Sasha leaned into the window and whispered, the phone held tight against her chest. "She told me what she told you. Mad, how could she know about Max and the birthmark? She may be telling the truth."

Maddie shook her head, not bothering to whisper. "I don't know, but she's a kook. I'm not discussing my husband with an insane woman." Her voice rose until Sasha leaned closer and said, "Shhh. Okay. Can I find out what she wants?"

"Sure, you talk to her."

The wind had picked up since they'd been inside the model homes, the sky turning a leaden gray in the west. Sasha hurried around to the passenger side of Maddie's car and got in.

"I'm back," Sasha said into the phone, turning it on speaker. "You're going to have to tell me what you want. Maddie won't talk to you."

"You tell her she'd better listen. I'm being generous here. Giving her a big warning that she will thank me for later. Now, I'm

140

not saying anything else on the phone. You get Maddie to the restaurant LoLa's on 86th Street in one hour. I'll be the tall redhead. You can't miss me." The strange woman hung up the phone.

Sasha turned to Maddie's frozen form. "We have to meet her. One hour at LoLa's."

Maddie started to shake her head.

Sasha put a hand on her forearm and squeezed gently. "If she's crazy, she's crazy. If she's not, then you need to know what she has to say. It's more than just blowing the whistle on Brandon. I don't know what it is, but Maddie, it's more than some affair."

"More than an affair?" Maddie turned to Sasha with stricken eyes. "How could anything be worse? It can't be true! I would have known. There would have been signs. Sasha, my husband did not cheat on me."

"Come on." Sasha started to get out of the car. "I'm driving you. We'll pick up your car later."

Maddie shook her head. "All right, we'll go see the crazy woman, but I don't want to leave my car. Just go and I'll follow you over there. Is LoLa's even open for lunch? I thought it was a bar."

Sasha shrugged. "If not, she said we won't be able to miss her. Guess she'll be in the parking lot."

"Did she say any more about what she looks like?" Maddie asked, as new horrid thoughts entered her mind. "Is she beautiful, do you think?"

Sasha shrugged. "We'll know soon enough. Stop torturing yourself."

Maddie shook her head. "You're right. I don't want to know. Just hand me a lip-gloss." She might as well look her best

141

when meeting her husband's mistress. God help her, she didn't know how to feel.

Sasha dug in her bright Prada bag, then held out the gloss. "Here." She held out another tube. "Add some eyeliner, you look like a ghost."

Maddie stared at herself in the visor mirror. She did look a fright; big, shocked eyes with shadows beneath them, pale cheeks and her trembling lips. So opposite from the excited face she'd seen in the bathroom mirror of the model home. Suddenly, she looked at Sasha. "You don't think she's crazy, do you?"

Sasha took a deep breath and grasped Maddie's arm. "I don't know what she is, but I think you should find out and I won't let you go through this alone. I'm sticking with you."

Maddie nodded. "Okay, let's go."

Sasha sped to LoLa's at a hell-bent rate, Maddie trying hard to stay behind her and not think about anything.

They pulled into the strip mall parking lot where the restaurant was located. Maddie took one more glance in the mirror, decided she couldn't improve on her light makeup and windblown hair and got out of the car. She didn't realize how nervous she was until her knees buckled and Sasha had to come around and help support her.

The place was dimly lit and beautifully decorated in art deco style—metal stars glowing with multi-colored lights hanging against a gold stucco wall. Along the bar, amber and orange lights dropped from the ceiling in long, cone-shaped glass. Seating groups of low, overstuffed chairs in reds and purples were scattered around, making intimate settings for private parties.

But neither Maddie nor Sasha saw a redhead.

After walking around the place twice and deciding that Sabrina must not be there, they found a low, round table with no one around and settled in to wait.

Maddie sipped her water, her palms sweating so much that she almost dropped the glass twice. Finally, after ten minutes of strained silence with Sasha, a tall, gorgeous woman walked in and stood blinking in the low light.

CHAPTER SEVENTEEN

Maddie knew the second Sabrina found them in the corner. She paused, stared at Maddie intently and then, with a determined look on her face and narrowed eyes, strode over toward them.

"How does she know who I am?" Maddie asked in stunned bewilderment. "Did you tell her what we look like?"

Sasha shook her head. "No, do you think Brandon showed her a picture of you?"

"Oh, Sasha. I think I'm going to throw up or faint or something." She pressed her fingers against her forehead and tried to breathe.

"Pull it together. Remember, no matter what, you were Brandon's wife. He loved you. Be confident, condescending even."

"Condescending?" The woman stood before them as Maddie pasted on her best version of condescension and knew it wasn't working. It just wasn't in her.

"Maddie?" the woman asked with crisp confidence. "Thank you for coming."

Maddie introduced Sasha in a surreal daze. How did one behave toward one's husband's mistress?

"I'm glad you have a friend with you. You're going to need the support." With that proclamation she sat down and settled herself, waving to the waiter and ordering a drink.

Maddie didn't know what to say, just stared at the willowy beauty. She reminded her of a redhead she had seen on one of those reality dating shows.

"How do you know Brandon?" Sasha asked, her own brand of condescension coming across more like hatred, her eyes narrowed, lips pressed together in a line of menace.

The woman took a small breath. "You should be glad I called. It will give Maddie an important heads-up to what is going on. Listen, I'm not supposed to be talking about this to anyone. I may lose my job anyway, but if this got out..." She paused, thin, perfect eyebrows raised. "If they find out what I'm doing right now I will be fired immediately...but I figured I owed you that much." She suddenly looked ready to tear up. "Before it all crashes down on top of you."

Maddie's voice caught, but she managed, "What...what are you talking about?"

The drink came and Sabrina took a long swallow, tossing back a long, auburn curl.

"I worked with Brandon, was his boss's boss, really. I am vice-president of loan servicing. Brandon, as you know, was a loan officer. About a month after Brandon started working for us, we...noticed each other. I'm sorry Maddie, but we began an affair and it lasted until he died."

Maddie just sat and stared. She was sorry? This woman and Brandon? Mental images of them together bombarded her mind. No, she couldn't think of it. Couldn't imagine the whys and wheres and hows. There would be time for the anguishing thoughts later.

"But that's not it, is it?" Sasha cut in. "You wouldn't call the wife of a dead man just to torture her with this knowledge after he's gone, would you?"

Sabrina shook her head. "No. Of course I would not do that. I'm only telling you that so that you'll understand the rest." She took another long sip of her drink. "You will be getting a call from a private detective soon. Anytime now."

"A private detective?" Maddie gasped.

"Over the last few months, the bank has had several customers default on their loans, very large loans that were recently procured. Last month the bank hired a forensic accountant and conducted a thorough investigation of our accounts. They found the loans were taken out by people who never existed."

"What does this have to do with me?"

The woman held up her hand. "Let me explain. Upon further investigation and handwriting comparisons, we discovered that the loans were approved by your husband. He was taking out loans, either spending the money or wiring it to banks overseas, and then taking out other loans to make the payments. It worked undetected for eight months, but after he died...well, no one was paying off the loans and we slowly realized something was terribly wrong."

Maddie just sat and stared. They had to have the wrong person. Her husband would have never done such a thing. She actually felt relieved—for a minute.

"I realize this comes as a shock, but Maddie, your husband embezzled over a half-million dollars."

"No." Maddie shook her head, her hand a waving stop sign. "You need to go back to your investigation. Brandon would have never done such a thing."

Sabrina leaned forward. "And I bet you thought he would have never cheated on you either."

Maddie looked at the woman, thoughts catching up with themselves, unable to make sense of anything.

"Don't be stupid. I didn't risk so much for you to ignore me. He did. He was leading a double life. I am under investigation too. They know I approved many of the larger loans and somehow they discovered we were having an affair. Brandon spent a lot of money on me, we had our own apartment, he...he bought me things. We took lots of trips together. He told me it was an inheritance and that you knew nothing about it. I regret that I let him convince me. But I was in love with him."

"You were in love with him." Maddie voice sounded dead. Her whole being felt numbingly dead. "Why would he do this to me?"

Sabrina shook her head. "I realize it will take some time for this to sink in, but I have plenty of proof and I'll get it to you if you need it. The important thing is that the bank doesn't decide to make a criminal case out of this. Brandon's dead, they can't get him. They are trying to track down and recover the money in accounts outside the US, but this bank is aggressive. They are now investigating you and me to see if we were accomplices, or at least 'willfully blind' as they say in a case like this.

"Were you?" Sasha asked. "You said you approved many of the false loans."

Sabrina shook her head and looked straight into Sasha's eyes. "I didn't know anything about it. I find it hard to believe that I didn't. I thought he told me everything." Looking at Maddie, she gave her a small, sad smile. "I'm sure you didn't know anything, but you'll have to convince the private detectives. We don't want them to prosecute either of us in a criminal case. We can't have this going to court. You would probably lose your fancy job with the Racers." A brief pause. "You could even lose Max."

Maddie just stared, terror-numb.

Sasha growled, "Don't you dare bring Max into this. She's innocent and nothing will take Max away from her."

The woman shrugged one shoulder. "There's one more thing."

"There's more?" Sasha asked incredulously.

Sabrina nodded. "I don't think Brandon died of a car accident. I think he…committed suicide. I think he knew that he was in too deep, that he couldn't keep it going much longer and panicked."

"How could you say that? He lost control. He drove off an overpass on the highway." Maddie gritted her teeth. "His body was unrecognizable from the fire."

"Yes. Perfect wasn't it?" Sabrina tapped her French-manicured fingernails on the table. "I've thought about this a lot. The guardrail on the bridge would have made it a very unlikely accident. He went over the side just before the rail began, angled right for the ravine. And I know something else. He had been researching explosives before the accident. I think he had a bomb in the car to make sure…to make sure he died."

The pretty lights in the room, lights she'd so admired when they had first walked into LoLa's, started to blur. The room tilted to the right, then slid forward. Maddie closed her eyes tight. She found she couldn't breathe very well and heard her breath coming in short gasps, but didn't know they were coming from her. Sasha grasped her on the shoulder. "Maddie. Maddie, get a grip on yourself. Look at me, Maddie."

Maddie turned as if in slow motion to her friends familiar face and said in a little girl's voice that sounded as if it were coming from a long way away, "It's not true, is it, Sasha? It can't be true."

Sabrina downed her drink and stood up. Looking at Maddie, she handed her a card. "If there's anything…well. Goodbye."

They watched her go, both too stunned for words.

~~~~~~~~

Maddie's grip on the steering wheel left finger indentations on the leather cover she'd bought to conceal the paint-chipped original, weaving in and out of the traffic, trying to get home to Max, the only solid thing left in her life.

"I can't do this!" she yelled into the empty space of the car. Then she looked up and yelled at God. "I can't do this. Do you hear me? It's too much. I can't…" Angry tears started to fill her eyes so that she couldn't see. She dashed them away with the back of her hand, determined not to cry. "It's not fair. What have I ever done to deserve this? I've always tried to be good, do the right thing."

Maddie turned onto the quiet, tree-lined side street that led to her parents' house. It was growing dark and this street, curvy and dense with woods on either side, had always felt a little creepy at night. She pressed on the brake and just sat, staring. "What am I going to do?"

A car came up behind her, slowing down, obviously wondering what she was doing stopped in the middle of the road. Stepping on the gas, she quickly gathered some speed. She turned the corner and saw her driveway. A black car was sitting in front of her parents' house. It was her in-laws.

"Oh, come on," she groaned.

Maddie pulled in behind the black car, remembering the first time she'd met Lydia and Robert Goode. Brandon had brought her home with him from college during Christmas break. She later learned that he had planned to ask her to marry him in front of his whole family on Christmas Eve but that the days with his parents had been so stiff and uncomfortable, had gone so badly, that he'd waited, angry at his parents for not thinking Maddie was a good match for him, angry at her for being so shy and insecure that she wouldn't stand up to them, angry period. He'd proposed the following weekend, and Maddie had sensed a determination behind the proposal that had little to do with her. But she'd been young and inexperienced and very much in love with the most handsome boy on campus, so she'd happily agreed to become Mrs. Brandon Goode. Now, she had to wonder if she ever really knew him. How could he have lived two lives right in front of her? Why hadn't she seen any signs? There must be something terribly wrong with her, with her judgment of people, to have had such a horrendous thing happen.

His parents in the driveway might mean they knew of the investigation, she realized, getting out of her car. They would never drive all this way just to visit her and Max. Suddenly, she was intensely glad that she knew. Hearing it from Robert and Lydia would have been worse. They would have somehow blamed her. They were the kind of parents that if Brandon had gotten into trouble at school they would blindly take his side and blame the other party. Brandon could do no wrong.

When she walked in she saw that her parents were sitting in the living room with the stiff-faced Goodes, who were sitting far apart, on either end of the couch. Lydia sat straight up, her back not touching the back of the green upholstery, her hands knotted together in her lap. Robert was red-faced and tense, clutching the iced tea her mother had apparently given him.

"Oh, Maddie, you're home." Gloria rose and gave Maddie her seat, dragging in a dining room chair and saying, "I've been calling you for the last twenty minutes. Your cell phone must be dead."

Maddie frowned. She was quite sure the battery hadn't died. Nodding to her in-laws, she found herself numb again, as if watching the scene from outside her body. "Robert, Lydia, what a nice surprise. It's so good to see you. Have you seen Max?"

Max ran into the room at the sound of his name being called. "Mommy, you're home," he cried out in delight, propelling himself into Maddie's legs. Seeing his adorable face, the face that looked so much like Brandon's, and thinking that someone could take him away from her made sudden tears spring to her eyes. She picked him up and gave him a big hug, hiding her face in his curly hair.

"Max, did you say hello to Grandma and Grandpa?" She looked at her in-laws, her cheek pressed against Max's. Max looked over to Maddie's parents and said, "Hi, Grammy. Hi, Poppy." Her dad waved at him and gave him a funny face, sticking out his tongue and making Max giggle.

150

"No, sweetheart. I meant your other grandma and grandpa. You remember Grandpa Robert and Grandma Lydia, don't you?"

Max shook his head and stared at the strangers with wide eyes.

"Of course he doesn't remember us, Maddie," Lydia scolded. "You never bring him to visit. You can't expect the child to know us."

Maddie didn't remind her that she was a single parent, working full-time and trying to give Max a stable routine. She didn't mention that it would be easier for them to come to Indianapolis, but that they hadn't, had only even called twice since Brandon's death.

Then the truth suddenly filled her. Those were excuses. If she loved these people, nothing would have kept her away from their love and support during such a difficult time. She had needed them to lean on and maybe…maybe they had needed her too.

"You're right. I'm sorry. I should have come more often." She found herself saying instead, "I'm so glad you're here now." She looked down at her precious son, remembering that Max was the only thing they had left of their son too. "Max, can you show your grandparents what's in your pockets? I know you have some treasures in there somewhere."

Max eagerly scrambled down and ran over to his grandparents. He was a quintessential packrat and Maddie knew there would be something in there to give them all a moment's relief. Digging into first the right one and then the left one, he pulled out a plastic ring that was too big for his finger, a toy car, some plastic snakes and frogs and a yo-yo. With adorably pudgy hands, Max carefully spread out his goods on the cushion between them. Maddie watched as they responded, their faces changing from harshness to delight, as he held out first one toy and then another for them to admire. When Max came to the yo-yo, Robert said, "I used to have a little skill with a yo-yo. Can I see that, Max?" Max looked doubtful for a second, studying the big

151

outstretched hand suspiciously, and then looked up and into his grandfather's eyes. He seemed to deem him trustworthy and dropped the yo-yo into Robert's hand.

Carefully, as if the little toy were made of precious material instead of plastic, Robert slipped the loop around his middle finger and held out his arm. Max watched in wide-eyed amazement as Robert made the yo-yo go up and down, up and down.

"Teach me, Grandpa," Max demanded, making them all laugh. Robert pulled him over to his lap and placed the ring around Max's chubby finger, showing him how to curl his fingers around the yo-yo in his palm, facing the floor. Together they let go, watching the toy head for the floor, then Robert gave Max's hand a little lift and the yo-yo came back into Max's hand. Max laughed out loud, yelling, "Do it again. Do it again, Grandpa!" Which they did, several times.

Watching them, Maddie wondered if maybe they *had* come just to visit and see Max, but that thought was quickly burst when Lydia said, "Maddie, we need to talk to you." She stopped for a second and seemed to gather herself. "It might be best if it were in private."

Maddie glanced at her parents—her mom's face filled with worry, her dad looking curious. "My parents know everything there is to know about my life to this point. I think they should stay. And Max won't understand. He's fine."

"But you don't understand. This is of a nature to be quite embarrassing."

Maddie nodded. "I'm sure we're all going to have a moment's shame while this comes out."

Lydia gasped. "You know? Has the private investigator been here too?"

"Private investigator?" her dad piped in. "What's going on, Maddie?"

Maddie started and then stopped. Started again, looking down at her clasped hands in her lap, not knowing how to break the news to her parents. They had loved Brandon almost as much as she had. "Someone called me today. Her name is Sabrina Bridgestone and she demanded I meet with her. That's where I've been for the last couple of hours." She looked up at her mom, pain radiating from her chest. "Brandon was having an affair with her."

Her mother gasped. "An affair? Brandon?"

Maddie nodded, looking at the stunned faces of her in-laws, knowing they hadn't been told this part of the story. "She was also Brandon's boss. She told me Brandon embezzled over a half a million dollars from the bank." She rushed through the rest, "I didn't believe it, I still can't quite believe it, the news is still so new to me that I haven't had time to piece it together. But she told me the bank is investigating and that they will want to question me, just like they questioned her."

Brandon's parents sat and stared at her with blanched faces. Her parents sat there and stared at her with shock in their eyes. Why was she so calm? It was as if it was happening to someone else and she was relating a story about a stranger. When no one said anything, she asked her in-laws, "What were you told?"

"He couldn't have had an affair. Not Brandon. I don't believe it," his mother exclaimed.

"You didn't believe the embezzlement either, and they showed us some pretty strong evidence," Robert reminded her. "Maybe this woman demanded a lot of money. Maybe that's why he did it." He looked around the room, bewildered. "I just can't make sense of it."

Maddie's parents found their tongues at the same time. "Is that where you went today? To meet his mistress?" her mother asked. Her dad's face turned red. "I want to see that proof. When did he do this? How did he do it?"

"Maybe it was the pressure of being the only breadwinner," his mother said as if on a side note.

Maddie had taken the heat before, silently, when Brandon's mother had made little biting comments about her giving up her job and staying home with Max. Lydia had worked all her life and Maddie wondered if she wasn't envious, but there was no excuse for it this time. Maddie exploded, "Brandon never complained about me staying home with Max. It was more cost effective than working and paying a babysitter to raise our son." Her voice lowered. "I didn't see one dime of that stolen money. Your precious son didn't bring it home to his wife and son, not that I would have wanted him to, but still, he spent it on himself and his mistress. Don't ever blame me for this again, do you understand, Lydia? Never again."

Lydia looked as if she'd been slapped, then she started to cry. "I'm sorry, Maddie. I just can't accept it. There must have been something…"

Maddie knew the feeling but she was too angry at the moment to comfort anyone. She was grieving all over again. She got up and got Max a cup of milk to have a moment to collect herself and then sat back down, trying to answer all their questions to the best of her ability. Lydia and Robert filled in some missing blanks. They had been shown loan applications with their son's signature of approval on it. They had been assured that the identities of the people requesting the loans were fake. Brandon hadn't even bothered to try and write differently for each one. The police had also verified that they were reopening the accident case and investigating whether to reclassify it as a suicide.

Maddie had to excuse herself again. She stood in the dark kitchen and pressed on her temples, her head pounding like a migraine was coming on. When would they call? She was ready to get it over with and show up at the bank, but she had no idea who to talk to. The waiting, the pretending for Max that everything was normal again, the anger that was building inside her every time she pictured Brandon with that—

She took a long breath. No. She couldn't let herself think like that. She had to be strong—for Max.

Jake's face flashed across her mind. Her face flooded with heat. What would he think of her now?

CHAPTER EIGHTEEN

Maddie couldn't believe she was sitting at her desk trying to work as if everything was normal. Her emotions swung the gamut from horrified to depressed to mad as a hornet and jumpy at every sound, waiting for the investigator to call or show up. She wished Brandon was alive so she that she could strangle him to death.

How could she have been so stupid? How could she not have seen? Her mind replayed the last year of Brandon's life over and over, trying to put the pieces together. There had been sudden business trips, long weekends where she had been alone with Max, waiting for her loving husband to walk through the door. But they'd been so excited about this job, his first real professional job that made good money. She'd been happy to make the sacrifice. It was for them, for her and Max, he'd always assured her, and their future.

She was so lost in thought, staring at her computer monitor, that she didn't even hear her office phone ringing until it had stopped and started ringing again.

"Hello. This is Maddie Goode," she answered automatically.

"Maddie. Oh good, you're there." It was Jake.

"Jake?" Oh no, what was she going to say to Jake? She couldn't tell him about Brandon. It was too shocking and excruciating and…humiliating. What would he think of her? Of the fool she'd been? She had ignored a text he'd sent a few days ago. He'd been preoccupied too, though, with two away games, which had given her some time.

"Hey, I just wanted to call and thank you for Thanksgiving dinner. And I really liked that church."

"Oh, sure. No problem. I'm glad you liked it." Her voice sounded as dead as she felt inside.

"Maddie? Is everything okay? I know I've busy but I've thought of you every day. I hope you're not angry."

"Um, no. I understand. Everything's fine. What are you up to?" She tried to sound normal, but knew she was failing miserably.

"I'm at home." There was a pause and then, "I'd like to take you out again. You know, a real dinner date this time. Would you like to go out this weekend?"

Maddie panicked. "I can't." She shook her head. "I'm sorry but...Jake, I can't see you anymore."

There was a stunned silence on the other end that made her heart ache. She had to be strong and she didn't want to argue with him, so she plunged ahead, burning any bridge that might tempt her later. "I don't..." She took a deep breath. "I have decided that I don't want a man in my life right now."

"I don't believe you." His voice was raw. "Maddie, what has happened?"

"I can't tell you anything that's going to make sense to you. You should forget you ever met me, okay? I'm not worth it. Listen, I wish the best for you but I'm just not the one for you. Goodbye, Jake." It was hard, but she closed her eyes and slowly hung up the phone.

~~~~~~~

Jake stood in his jeans and socks, hearing the click but not believing it. Anger and confusion coursed through him, making his head pound. Something had happened, he was sure of it. Something was terribly wrong. Hitting the "end" button, he tossed the phone on the bed, went to his closet and threw on the first shirt he grasped. She wasn't going to get off that easy.

157

He drove over to the offices, growing angrier and angrier in the SUV. He parked, tires screeching and echoing in the parking garage, and hurried up the marble stairs to the glass doors. The receptionist's face lit up with a big smile as he came out of the elevator. He didn't even slow down, just turned down the hall and went to Maddie's office. He burst through the door, finding her sitting at her desk staring with a blank look on her face at the computer monitor.

She jerked at the noise and turned toward him. For an instant he saw relief, then she became closed and determined.

"Jake."

"What's going on, Maddie? Tell me the truth this time."

Maddie sighed and motioned to a chair. She got up, poured Jake a cup of coffee from her own little coffee station set up on an antique buffet against the back wall of her office, putting two creams in and stirring it for him. Handing him the delicate cup, she took a deep breath and sat down. "Let me ask you a question," she began, more serious than he had ever seen her.

"Okay." He felt his guard rise, knowing that whatever she was about to say she was convinced and resolute.

"When you decided you wanted to become an NBA player, I mean really decided that nothing else would do and that you would sacrifice anything to have it, what was that moment like?"

"Maddie, what's going on?" He sat the coffee down and stared at her.

"Just go with this, okay? I'm getting to it."

Jake's eyebrows knitted together as he thought back. "There were different stages to it, I guess. First my dad encouraged me, played ball with me all the time, signed me up for every team and workshop available. But at some point it started to become my dream."

"Was there a moment? A crossroads, I mean? Where you had to decide if it was worth all the work and sacrifice and the letting go of other paths in life, other choices?"

Jake nodded. "I guess there was. In college. I was playing pretty good ball, but one day the coach and I had a talk, one on one, and he made me see that I was going to have to work a lot harder, become single-mindedly focused on my goal if I was going to have a chance to succeed. I decided then that I wanted it. And I played better. That was really the beginning of my training for the NBA."

Maddie nodded, folding her hands together on top of her pretty desk. "All my life I've pretty much gone with the flow. I went to college because that's what everyone did. But I didn't really know what I wanted to do or be. The only thing I ever remember daydreaming about as a little girl was being a wife and a mother." She shrugged. "We all know those things aren't enough in today's world. So I tried to think of what I wanted to do as a career, but I didn't feel passionate about anything besides being a singer, and I didn't think that would make a living. Then I met Brandon and got married and after having Max I really felt like my life was perfect...my dreams had come true."

She took a long breath, her hands clasped so tight her fingers turned white. "But I was wrong. It was all a lie, more than you know. I still have Max and I have a job that I really like, which I am so thankful for." She paused, obviously trying to put into words what she wanted to express to him. "Jake, I really like you. But I can't go back to that place of floating around, never making conscious choices. Like the day you decided to become an NBA player, well, I've decided to take charge of my life. I'm going to find out who I am and what I want. I'm going to make decisions, hard decisions, for myself and Max. I have to do this right now and I can't have you or any other man in my life for a while...maybe never."

Jake tried to grasp it. He understood her point, but everything inside him screamed that she was wrong. She could find all that out with him. He wouldn't stop her from that. And he was sure that something had happened to cause this change in her. Something she didn't want to tell him.

He could only nod, a hollow, gnawing pain gripping his heart. He stood, knowing he was going to have to wait it out, knowing he couldn't change her mind. "I can't say I'm happy about it, but I understand what you're saying. I hope…" He stopped and expelled a breath, his lips compressed, holding back the bleak emptiness that would start the minute he left this room. "I hope it all works out the way you want it to, Maddie."

~~~~~~~

Maddie choked back the clog in her throat. She'd gotten through. She'd hurt him, but she could tell that he really knew what she was talking about. It was hard, this letting go of him, but she had to know why her decisions so far had brought her to this place in life and if her judgment, her heart, could ever be trusted again.

CHAPTER NINETEEN

Jake walked off the basketball court, shoulders drooped, a growing, gnawing pit in his stomach. They'd lost, again, and worse, his performance seemed headed for a true slump. Less than six rebounds and no points, he couldn't really remember, which was terrifying enough, considering he had memorized every game's stats for the last two years. It was getting pathetic, and if he didn't find a way to climb out he was headed off the starters and on to the bench.

He jogged into the locker room with the others, listened to the coach's lecture while wiping a towel against his forehead and neck and then letting it lay along the back of his neck, trying to put into words what was wrong.

"Hart, you better get your head back in the game. You're a professional, not a teenager with love-life problems."

A few of his teammates guffawed, hurriedly stopping when Jake leveled his direct stare on them. "No excuses. Get back into the game or you're going on the bench. One more chance."

"Yes, sir." Jake nodded briskly. He'd do it or die trying.

After everyone had showered and dressed, Marcus came over to talk to him. "Let's go out, man. Get your mind off that Maddie girl and onto some new horizons."

It sounded depressing, but he found himself nodding, stuffing gear into his duffel bag, thinking he had to try something. All he knew for sure was that he didn't want to go home, couldn't go into that silent, empty house and try to fill the hours doing anything but picturing her determined and strained face.

They went to the new club in town owned by one of their friends. The place was dimly lit and had a Vegas feel with smoke machines, music that pulsed with synchronized lighting and lounging beds. Jake laughed as he stretched out on the bed they'd been shown to, pushing aside the gauzy drapes, kicking off his shoes. Marcus bounced down next to him, a bottle of champagne in each hand. It didn't take long for four women, full of sensual smiles, cat's eyes assessing, purring compliments into their ears, to take up residence on the giant, swinging bed.

Tabitha, black hair with smoky blue eyes, squeezed herself on one side of Jake, while Lisa, a shapely, quick-witted blond, pressed against his other arm. After a couple of drinks, he lifted his arm and placed it around her creamy shoulders.

The women tried to get him to dance, but he steadfastly refused. He had one goal for the evening—drink heavily so that he would sleep most of the day tomorrow. Then Monday would come and he would get his head back on and straighten out his game. Maddie was a thing of the past. Tonight he would lounge with beautiful women and forget her.

The words slurred in his head, repeating themselves. Forget her. Forget Maddie. For—get—her.

As he was thinking that, Tabitha reached up and pulled his head down to hers. Before he really understood, he found her kissing him, deep and hot. He let his eyelids fall shut, allowing the kiss to wash over him, but his insides recoiled with the feeling that it was wrong. She felt wrong, she tasted wrong, she breathed wrong—it was all wrong.

Pulling back, he wiped the back of his hand across his mouth and must have looked at her hard, because she stared a moment, lips compressed, eyes narrowed and then turned away and sat up, angry. Lisa had watched the ordeal.

"Give me a try, sweetheart. Maybe cold-blooded girls like Tabi aren't your type. Maybe you like warmth and softness."

Jake looked at her, knowing he shouldn't, but there was something more appealing about Lisa and he shrugged. "Let's dance first."

"Really?" Lisa gave him a shrug and a small smile. "Who knew? The man likes foreplay."

They went out onto the dance floor, where the current song was dying away. At the end of the song a stage came down out of the ceiling, unfolding like butterfly wings with a middle and two side sections. Lights began to dance as eerie music filled the space around them. A snow machine whirled, showering brilliant, iridescent white flakes through the colored lights, catching on clothes and eyelashes, making everyone croon in delight.

Jake and Lisa stared in growing fascination as a slight woman came out onto the stage. She looked like a shadow waif, with no light to see her face. The audience was spellbound by the sight of her and the rainbow snowflakes that held no cold. When she reached the middle of the stage she turned, her back to the audience. They held their breath, waiting for what might happen next.

Jake found he couldn't tear his eyes away from the figure on the stage. She was cold, he sensed, and afraid, holding her slim shoulders erect, waiting…waiting…for something.

The music began, building to the opening, and suddenly she turned, a spotlight lighting her to glowing brightness. She was almost too bright to look at, wearing a white shirt that tied at her waist, white leather pants with leather insets of butterflies and colorful wings scattered across her thigh and down one side. Jake's gaze traveled up the column of her throat, noting the extra long, thick, dark waves of hair that tantalized and teased her throat and shoulders, but her face was too bright to make out from where he stood.

They all stood mesmerized by the music and her brightness when she opened her mouth and began to sing. Her voice had a lilting but raw quality that captured them into silence, stillness, rapt attention. The room grew stone silent, except for the quiet whir of the snow machine as the single notes of a piano echoing behind the power of her raspy, breathy persuasion.

Jake studied her face, feeling an uneasy grip take hold of him. His breathing quickened. He knew this woman, knew the way she held her arms, tight and still against her sides, all the strength within her bottled, held and then releasing in a slow resonance that exploded from her throat. It couldn't be. It could not be Madeline Goode on that stage. He stared at her face, trying to see past the stage makeup, the thick, glittering eyelashes, the bright red lips, the too-white light, making her face seem unearthly. Her body contained the sound, became a living instrument, so like her and yet so unlike her. She didn't move around on the stage, she didn't gyrate and call attention to herself. She just closed her eyes, opened her mouth and unleashed total rule over them.

He found himself breathless.

The others around him had begun to sway and dance, but most of them still had their gaze locked onto her face, most couldn't tear themselves back to the women and men that a moment ago had so enthralled them.

An electric guitar solo began, like classical and rock blended, growing more and more rocky until it suddenly faded away. The woman stood, soaking it in, only her hips swaying, making Jake feel shaky. It *was* Maddie. The real Maddie. This was what she had been talking about.

~~~~~~~

Maddie took a deep breath as the last strains of the song faded into deep silence. Had it been horrible? Did they hate her? She stood, seeing nothing but the blackness of the room and shadow forms, knowing that they were staring at her, but not knowing anything else.

Sudden applause broke out. It grew and grew into echoing clatter, filling the room and her with a feeling of elation. They liked it. As they clapped longer and longer, she found tears streaming down her cheeks. They really liked it, but more, she had so loved singing it.

164

When she turned to leave the stage there was an immediate demand from the crowd that she come back and sing more. She wished she could, but Rick, one of the owners of the club and one of the players for the Racers, had given her this opportunity out of a fluke, and it was the only song she'd had time to prepare. He had heard her singing in the parking garage, getting in her car after work, something she had begun doing in her free time. The echo of the parking garage had pulled at her, and without thought, she had belted out an old favorite, Fleetwood Mac's Landslide, deciding not to care if anyone was around to hear. Rick had clapped behind her, asked her if she sang on stage, which she promptly denied, the school choir and church choir being her only experience. He'd laughed and said, "You should, girl. You should."

Then he'd given her this opportunity. One song, showcased with all the lights and a million-dollar sound system that he assured her would make her successful at his new club. He'd been excited. Wouldn't take no for an answer. Asking her, "What do have to lose, Maddie?"

Her sanity. Her privacy. Her pride. She shook her head as he pressed his card into her clammy hand. He turned, ignoring her fear, telling her the time to show up and to "dress to kill," a task that Sasha had risen to with typical aplomb.

The next four days seemed like an eternity and yet a minute. Sick with nerves, afraid she would throw up on stage, Maddie drove to the club feeling like a fraud that was about to be exposed. But this was what she'd wanted, wasn't it? This finding out who she was and what she loved. She hadn't sung anything but lullabies in so long that she'd forgotten. Forgotten the lost hours in her bedroom with the removable finial from her headboard gripped in her hand, staring at the mirror and singing with quiet force, trying to keep her parents from hearing, trying to keep the scary power in her voice from escaping control.

But not tonight. After the first few terror-filled moments, she let go. Out of her mouth had come a sound she didn't even know she was capable of making, and she wasn't sure but she thought it was pretty good.

Rick met her in the makeshift dressing room. She could hear the DJ start up again as he came in and shut the door behind him. He had a giant grin across his face, teeth glowing white in the dim lights, eyes excited. "That was great. You got some real talent. You know that? It's about to turn into a mob out there, they want you back so bad." He walked over to her and lifted her chin with his long, basketball handling fingers. "Where you been hiding this great big voice, Maddie girl?"

She blushed, fighting the knot in her throat. "I…I don't know."

"Well, it's all out there now. They want you back. I'm gonna make you a star, okay? You're gonna come back next Saturday and sing a longer set, okay?"

Maddie was trembling, everything moving too fast. "I'll think about it."

Rick pulled three hundred-dollar bills out of his pocket and pressed them into her palm. "Three hundred per song. And I'll look into getting you a band for live gigs. I'll call you about that, we'll audition them together."

He kept rambling, but Maddie no longer heard a word he said. Three hundred dollars per song? For doing something that was so wonderful? It was unbelievable. She would do it for free. She had thought she *was* doing it for free. She looked down at her hand, not knowing if it was right to take it.

Rick must have seen the look on her face because he laughed and patted her on the shoulder. "Don't you feel bad about taking that money. I get paid twice that for each dribble I make down the court, and I gotta say," he shook his head back and forth, "you got more talent in your little pinkie finger than I ever had."

Maddie shook her head, eyes glowing. "That's not true. I can't believe this is happening."

"Get used to it. Now, come on out here and greet some of your new fans."

166

~~~~~~~~~~

Maddie's intercom buzzed. The receptionist's voice sounded hesitant and overly curious at the same time as she announced a Mr. Jackson was here to see her. Maddie's heart began to race. This was it. The investigator was finally here.

She answered the knock on her door and let the man in. He was wearing a black suit that had "FBI" written all over it and a somber demeanor that had Maddie quaking in her black patent leather high-heels. With shaking hands, she poured him a cup of coffee, spilling some on the freshly varnished wood of the sideboard she'd refinished. She took a small breath and reminded herself that she was glad he was here, glad to finally get this over with. With a small smile she handed him the coffee, smoothed down her skirt and sat, ramrod stiff on her chair, her hands folded in her lap.

"Nice office," the man commented, looking around. "They must pay pretty well around here."

The accusation was obvious. Maddie bristled. "They do. It's a wonderful organization."

He took a sip, staring her in the eyes, trying to stare her down. Maddie forced herself not to look away. Finally, with a small nod and a slight up-turn to the corners of his lips, Mr. Jackson looked down to sit his coffee cup on the low table between the chairs and pulled out a small recorder. "I'd like to record your answers, if you don't mind."

He said it like she didn't have a choice and clicked on the record button, rattling off the name of the case into the small microphone.

She had debated the idea of getting an attorney, but had decided to wait and see what move they were going to make. After all, she had nothing to hide. The person who had hid everything so well was in the grave.

167

"Madeline Goode, is it true that you were married to Brandon Goode?"

"Yes," Maddie stated simply, determined to keep her answers short and to the point.

"How long were you married?"

"Six years."

"Were you aware that your husband had a mistress?"

He was watching her reaction very carefully. "I learned about the woman a short time ago."

"Really? How so?"

"She called me to tell me."

The man nodded his head, eyes shrewd. "How did you take the news?"

Maddie gave him a tight smile. "Like any wife would. I was devastated. Is my reaction to my husband having a mistress really relevant to the case, Mr. Jackson? I'm glad to cooperate with this investigation, but please, keep your personal questions relevant."

He looked at her with a degree more of interest. "Did the woman also tell you about your husband's crime against his employer?"

Maddie nodded. "She said there was an investigation. That someone had embezzled money from the bank and that they thought it was Brandon."

"And what did you think of that, Mrs. Goode?"

"I was shocked. If it's true, then it appears my husband was living a double life."

"And you had no idea? No signs of a mistress and lots of extra money?"

"If Brandon stole the money, he didn't bring it home. We lived modestly on one income. He must have spent it all on his mistress." She let some of the bitterness creep into her tone and upbraided herself for saying so much, but her response seemed to placate the detective.

"So for the record. Madeline Goode, did you have any knowledge of your husband's embezzlement of funds from First Old Bank of Indiana?"

"No. None."

"Would you be willing to take a polygraph test to prove that?"

"Yes. Anytime."

The man clicked off his recorder. Another tight smile and then he finished his coffee. "I believe you. Which is lucky for you. But this isn't over. We'll contact you when the bank makes it decision."

"What sort of decision? Mr. Jackson, do I need an attorney?"

He shrugged. "It couldn't hurt, but I would wait to see what they decide. With the perpetrator dead, they may be forced to cut their losses, drop the case and not press charges. And then there's always the mistress. It's harder to believe that she had no knowledge of this."

"Yes," Maddie agreed, eyes narrowed. "It is." She reached out for the coffee cup in the detective's hand. "Have a nice day, Mr. Jackson."

He gave her another searching look. "Likewise." And then he walked from the room.

Maddie took a deep breath and collapsed back into one of the chairs facing her desk, closing her eyes, telling her heartbeat to return to normal.

CHAPTER TWENTY

"Maddie, Jake Hart on line two for you," the receptionist buzzed in shortly after Mr. Jackson left.

Her heart gave a lurch at the sound of his name. Jake—on the phone. She had been trying not to think of him, trying to ignore the pull on her heart every time the image of his face came into her mind. Why would he call?

"Hello?"

"Hi, Maddie."

His voice reached down into her and made her stomach quiver with a familiar jolt. "Hi," she managed softly.

"I want to ask you a favor."

She regrouped. Maybe this wasn't the call she thought, half-hoped it was. "Oh. Okay."

"There's a game in New York this weekend. They want to set up a meet-and-greet with me and a couple of the other guys. I really don't know how these things are managed and I was wondering…would you be able to come and help out?"

"Oh." It was business. "Of course. As long as I can get Max squared away. Overnight, then?"

"Yeah. They'll put you up with the team, I'm sure. It's a nice hotel. Do you have a pen? It's American, flight 427, leaving Saturday at 10:30 am. We should be back Sunday evening."

Maddie grabbed a pen and jotted down the details. "Got it. Do you have a contact name for the other team? This is with the Kicks, right?" She amazed herself that the name of the team flew off her tongue so easily. She was really starting to learn this game.

It was kind of strange to have a meet-and-greet in the opposing team's city, but you never knew about publicity stunts in this business.

"This is more of a celebrity thing with more than NBA players. I'll get a name for you. I'm sure they'll fill you in once you get there."

"Sounds good." A long pause. "How are you, Jake?"

Another pause. "I'm okay. My game's been a little rough lately. I'm hoping this trip will turn me around."

"Yeah, I kind of heard about that. Sounds like a lot of pressure."

"Nothing I haven't been through before."

He sounded distant and...lonely. She wanted to fix it, but stopped herself. "Okay, then. I guess I'll see you on the flight."

"That'll be nice. Thanks for doing this, Maddie."

"Sure. It's my job."

"Well, see you soon."

"Bye, Jake."

She hung up the phone, brought up her calendar and stared at the monitor. She didn't have any gigs on the schedule for this weekend. She was kind of glad. Rick was entirely too pushy, wanting eight songs for the next performance. The pressure to learn so many new songs and find a band was going to take a lot of time, time away from Max, and it weighed heavy on her mind. She was going to have to set boundaries with this new endeavor. Max and her job had to come first.

~~~~~~~

Indianapolis International Airport was bustling with travelers early Saturday morning as Maddie struggled to get her heavy suitcase and bulging carry-on off the shuttle bus. She pulled the handle of the large suitcase up, hearing it lock into place, secured the carry-on on top of it, and rolled it toward the main doors. Please God, let it be under 50 pounds. It was going to be close but she just couldn't decide what to wear, so she'd packed lots of options, including everything from a slinky dress to business clothes and even some lingerie. Heaven knew she wouldn't need that, but she liked wearing it and getting out of mommy mode when she traveled.

For the flight she had decided on something comfortable but stylish—black knee-length boots, a brightly printed wrap dress and her cream-colored dress coat with black buttons, which she shrugged off and folded across her arm. After a short line, she had her bags checked and turned toward the escalators and the security lines, hoping the TSA agents would be merciful and she wouldn't have to get into the "naked machine." Everything went well and soon her gaze was scanning the overhead screens, telling her that she had quite a hike to get to her gate.

By the time she made the gate, she was breathing fast and sweating. Where was everybody? Was she late? She looked in panic at the clock and saw that no, she was plenty early. Strange, the team must have already boarded.

A pleasant-looking woman stood at the airline counter and when she saw Maddie, she smiled broadly and motioned her over. "Ms. Goode? We are ready to board you."

Maddie nodded and dug into her handbag for her ticket. "Yes, I'm Maddie Goode. Where's the team?"

The woman cocked her head to one side with an overly bright smile, blinking rapidly. "Follow me, please." Maddie nearly laughed aloud as she turned her back, thinking she looked like a Stepford Wife.

The tunnel to the plane was narrow and dim, reminding Maddie that she didn't particularly care for closed spaces. She sent up a quick prayer for their safety on the flight and then turned toward the long, narrow cabin of the plane.

It was empty.

"Where..." she began.

The Stepford woman turned, smiled and motioned her to follow. "In first class, dear."

Oh. Of course. She'd never flown in first class before. It seemed a waste that the team took up the entire plane just to use the first class section. Maybe they weren't all here yet.

A red curtain separated the cabins. The airline attendant pulled it aside and then squeezed back so that Maddie could pass through. "Enjoy your flight," she said with warmth.

Maddie struggled to get her carry-on around the woman and stepped inside.

It took her a minute. Took a moment for her brain to explain what her eyes were seeing. Every seat was covered with snow-white roses. Petals, half-closed stemmed flowers to full-blown blooms covered every first-class seat. They were scattered across the floor like snowflakes, like a church isle at a wedding, like a virginal runner of pure white—the soft petals were strewn as if they were as easy to come by as snow itself. As if they were common, but they weren't common, they were extraordinary. She looked across the immense show of lavishness to the only other being in the space—Jake.

Jake stood at the far front of the plane, holding a huge bouquet of red roses in his hands, looking at her with something in his eyes that she'd never seen in a man's face before...so intense, so hopeful, soulful, remorseful, wanting...so wanting.

She compressed her lips together, trying to hold back the emotion, trying to be sane and normal and know how to handle this extravagant love show.

"What have you done?" she whisper-gasped.

"Decided not to let you go. Not without a fight, anyway."

She slowly shook her head back and forth. "Why? Why me?"

Jake walked up to her, gently put the roses down on the nearest chair and clasped her hands in his. "Because I don't want to live without you."

"Jake..."

"I know. I know all the reasons you keep telling yourself that this won't work. But for the next two days I want you to let me show you why it will. Just give me this weekend, Maddie. Give me this one chance."

What could she say? Why was it that when she was trying so hard to grow up and be responsible and think of Max and guarding her heart and his, that she had to meet someone like this man, who was so much stronger and surer and capable of blowing her reasonableness into the far corners of the earth, like so many rose petals on a summer's breeze. She was trying so hard to do what was right...this wasn't fair. She didn't want to fight this.

"There's no game, then?"

Jake smiled a kind smile, patient and waiting for her to catch up. "There's no game in New York. There is only you and me."

"But where are we going? What are we going to do?"

"It's a surprise."

Maddie didn't like surprises. Had always been the kind of child to ferret the identity of her Christmas and birthday presents

175

out of her loved ones before unwrapping the gift. She was the kind of mom that had gotten the ultrasound to learn that Max was a boy. Had prepared her heart for whatever was coming so that she could…well, be prepared. But here, in the deep gray-green eyes of this man, were many surprises and she found that she couldn't spoil his joy by demanding to know them.

"I don't like surprises."

"You'll have to trust me then. Can you do that?"

"I…"

"It's a choice. And only you can make it. If you can't put your trust in me then we'll never have a chance. Will you take this chance?"

If she turned her back on this, Jake would let her go. She saw that. Or, she could take the risky road, follow her gut and her heart, and learn this man and let him discover her. The thought of that thrilled her far more than the roses.

"Okay."

Two hours later, Maddie peered out the window to see the New York City skyline. She'd been to the city once before, as a high school student coming by bus, but she'd never seen it from the air.

Jake squeezed her hand, looking down over her shoulder. "I've only been here for games. I can't wait to really experience the city with you."

In that moment, with his quiet declaration, she decided to suspend all her fears and fully enjoy every minute of it with him.

They landed at JFK Airport, a huge, sprawling edifice that seemed never ending, and waited for their luggage. Jake's eyes grew big and round as Maddie grasped her huge upright and heaved it off the belt.

Jake laughed, grasping the handle to the luggage and the carry-on, hefting his one and only bag on his other shoulder. "What did you pack? Your entire closet?"

Maddie shrugged, her boots clicking across the floor as they made their way to the doors and the street. "I wasn't sure what was going to be expected of me, so I brought a little of everything. It's a good thing now! I'll have lots of options for this weekend. I even brought my bikini." She gave him a sideways glance, teasing anticipation in her eyes.

He chuckled. "I might be able to find a reason for that," he said in a low, husky voice.

A limousine awaited them, their names drawn with unfamiliar handwriting on a square white card, just like in the movies. Maddie couldn't help her excited laughter as they fell in, Jake reaching for a bottle of champagne and pouring them both a glass.

"To New York." Maddie lifted her glass, her gaze roving over Jake's face as if she hadn't really looked at him in weeks, which she hadn't.

"To New York. And second chances." His eyes held hers as they tilted their glasses and took a long, cool swallow.

CHAPTER TWENTY-ONE

It had snowed the day before and all of New York City—the streets, the trees and buildings—were cloaked in white, like a winter wonderland of huge proportions. Fashionable people in blacks and grays with an occasional splash of color bustled with the energy of the dealmakers and breakers of the world. With excitement and anticipation, feeling a bit overwhelmed, Maddie tried to capture it all from the comfortable seat of the limo.

The Hotel Grand took up an entire end of a block, towering over them as they were helped from the limo. Maddie stood on the sidewalk, steam from a manhole rising beside her, feeling like she was in a movie, staring up and up toward the top of the building, seeing flags and then higher up, balconies with fancy cornices and iron work on the building's corners. Jake grinned at her reaction, then placed his hand at the small of her back, guiding her inside, nodding to the doorman to follow with their luggage.

The entrance stole her breath. The lobby was decorated in gold—gold walls, shining gold pillars, enormous, cone-shaped bronze and gold flowerpots, twice the height of Jake, filled with tall, delicate white flowers. Light gray to pewter colored chairs formed intimate seating groups where world travelers could read a newspaper or just sit and people-watch. The carpet was thick and plush in bronze, gold and green. A marble fountain lent the relaxing sound of cascading water and stood to the side of the long, golden reception desk. As she looked up, wall after wall of glass went on as far as she could see.

Jake checked them in, explaining in a warm rush in Maddie's ear that they would share a suite but that it had two bedrooms. They rode the elevator up to the 48th floor to their suite.

When Jake opened the door Maddie stepped inside, delight filling her. It was like a beautiful apartment of their own. A full kitchen, an intimate dining area which opened into a living room, complete with a giant flat-screen television. Two simple but elegant modern-style bedrooms were parallel with a huge bathroom connecting them. It was all done in shades of cream, brown and blue, from teal to royal, with accent pillows and vases in bronze. The huge marble tub was chocolate with bronze flecks, complete with jets, the towels aquamarine and so thick she couldn't help touching one.

Jake caught her doing that and laughed. "Do you like it?"

"It's wonderful."

He held out his hand. "Come see the balcony."

She took hold of it, realizing how much she had missed this handholding thing he liked to do, letting herself be led onto their own private balcony overlooking the busy 42nd Street. There were wrought-iron chairs, but they ignored them, walking instead to the railing and looking out over the city decorated for Christmas.

"I still can't quite believe you did this," she said softly, looking into his eyes.

"This is only the beginning." He brought her hand to his lips and kissed the back of her fingers, slowly pulling her closer to him, his eyes locked with hers. She held her breath waiting, thinking he would kiss her.

They stayed like that for what seemed an eternity, each straining toward the other, Maddie not wanting to make the first move in this precarious place where she was letting down her guard. He made a low noise from his throat, low and soft and masculine, and then let go of her hand and pulled her into his arms.

The kiss was different from the other ones, like he'd made a decision, like he was coming from a different, certain place. She might be unsure, but he was very sure of what he wanted. She could feel it in the confident way he was claiming her for his own.

She determined to let go, did so by degrees, letting her body meld against his, letting her mind free-float, allowing only the sensation of his mouth against hers to overtake her. He smelled good, he tasted good, like the champagne they'd been drinking mixed with something tangerine, a fruit from the fruit bowl in the room perhaps, or a mint she'd not seem him take, some thoughtful planning-ahead thing. She allowed her hands to wander where they wanted, feeling the hard muscle of his shoulders beneath his coat. He felt very solid, very real.

Would he break her heart like Brandon? The thought inserted itself like a poisonous dart.

He pulled back suddenly, breathing hard. "Maddie, you kiss like no other."

Maddie felt instant heat fill her cheeks. No one had ever said anything like that to her before. "It must have something to do with whom I am kissing," she said, ignoring her fear.

He pulled her into his side, looking out over the city. "We should change for dinner soon. I have reservations."

"Oh. How much time do we have?" Maddie thought through the contents of her suitcase.

"About an hour. Did you bring a dress?"

Maddie laughed. "A few. A cocktail dress and a black mini-skirt. Will one of those work?"

Jake laughed. "I forgot you had enough luggage for a week. Probably the cocktail dress. We're going to the Babbo."

"Good thing I pack for anything," she said, grinning, thinking that she was quick to contribute to her own capitulation.

They arrived at the restaurant, Maddie wearing a designer dress in sapphire blue, with ornate beading in the middle of the neckline, negating the need for a necklace. She had diamond-drop earrings and a sapphire bracelet on one wrist, completing the elegant look. Her one splash of decadence was, of course, the shoes. Delicate, high-heeled, silver sandals with straps that wrapped around her ankles, they made her legs look longer than anything else she owned.

Jake walked out of his bedroom just as she was smoothing down the back of the skirt and turning, looking at her back in the mirror. A slow grin broke out onto his face. "Wow. You look amazing."

Maddie stood still, a little uncomfortable under the intense gaze of those smoky eyes. He looked good too. Something about the way a suit coat hung from such broad shoulders always reminded her of a male model, and bigger than life.

They slipped into their coats and then Jake said, "Shall we?" He held out his hand.

She nodded, taking it in hers, feeling his warm fingers wrap around with just the right amount of pressure—a perfect fit.

They rode to the restaurant in a cab. Jake pulled her close to his side as they leaned together toward one window to sightsee. They arrived, both a little breathless from the close contact, Maddie ready to make the evening one to remember.

Maddie ordered black spaghetti with jumbo lump crab, throwing inhibition to the wind, while Jake had the ribeye steak. She talked and laughed, recognizing how easy the conversation was between them. She felt like she'd known him forever.

"Tell me about your husband," he said suddenly. "I want to know this past I'm fighting."

At the mention of Brandon, Maddie's heart sank. Was it time to tell him? It might ruin their trip and yet, she had to tell him sometime.

"He seemed perfect," she said succinctly, not knowing a better phrase for her life. "We were happy. I was…grateful, every day, that I had my life."

181

"He died in an accident, right?" Jeff asked.

She shrugged trying to be nonchalant but failing, feeling the weight of the question, drowning in it for a moment and then rising to the challenge. She was determined that it wouldn't destroy anything else in her life...that it wouldn't ruin this.

"I don't know. I thought I knew everything about him. But I didn't. Jake, I recently learned that he was living a double life with a mistress. He financed it by embezzling money from his job at a bank." She took a deep breath. "And...they think he might have killed himself and made it look like an accident." She looked down at her plate, her appetite gone. "He wasn't the man I thought he was at all. Our entire life was a lie."

Jake reached across the table and grasped her hand. "Maddie. Why didn't you tell me? When did you find this out?"

"The weekend after we went to church together. His mistress called me and told me everything."

"And you didn't call me? You must have been...devastated. You should have called me. I would have—"

"There was nothing you could have done, Jake. I needed to be alone and sort out my life, my emotions. That's why I had to break it off. I didn't know if I could ever love or trust a man again." She stared up at him, hoping he could understand.

Jake squeezed her hand. "I'm not that man. I'll never be that man. Anything you want to know, I'll tell you. Anything. The things I barely admit to myself...I'll tell you those things so you'll know me. The good, the bad and the ugly. You can know me better than I know myself. I promise you that."

Maddie turned her head, unable to look into such intensity. She stared at the elegantly dressed men and woman, successful, confident—she was sure nothing like this had ever happened to any of them. "I'm not sure if I believe you, but if you're willing to do that for me...then I want try. I want to really know you, Jake."

A mix of fear and exhilaration thudded in her chest in time with her racing heart. Who knew if he would really be so open with her? She only knew one thing for certain. If she didn't take this chance, this honest attempt by a man she was deeply attracted to, falling in love with, then she never would. She would live the rest of her life in a lonely shadow of what might have been.

A pleased look full of hope crossed his face. "Ask away. Anything."

She smiled, a little excited to have such freedom, such permission. She twirled some spaghetti onto her fork and took a bite then raised her brows at him, thinking of her first question. "Who are you, really? Strip away the basketball. Strip away the NBA star. What is left?"

He laughed and took a big swallow of water. "You're not messing around, are you? That's a tough one, and I'm not sure I know the answer but I'll try." He blew out a breath. "I wanted to please my father. He wanted me to be an NBA player from the first time I showed a glimmer of talent and I went along with it, but it wasn't long before I loved it. A big part of the real me is basketball, or at least athletics—the thrill of beating the odds, of being the best, and pushing my physical body to limits I didn't know were possible. I'm competitive. I like to win."

"What would you do if you didn't have the game? Or maybe I should ask, what will you do when you retire?"

"I've given that some thought. I'm from Colorado and I miss the mountains. I think I'd like to do some ranching out west somewhere." He grinned and shrugged, glancing away. "I haven't said this out loud to anyone but I think I'd like to breed race horses." He laughed at himself. "I don't know much about it, really. I don't even know for sure if I would like it, but I read about it. I buy Horse and Hound and all those magazines, watch racing movies."

"That sounds exciting," Maddie encouraged. "And expensive."

"That leads to another confession. I…uh…haven't been very trusting of women either. I guess I've been thinking of them as gold diggers and I thought that of you at first."

Maddie nodded. "I can understand why you would think of women as a whole like that. You're famous and wealthy."

Jake coughed into his hand and took another drink. "Full disclosure, right? That is what I said."

Maddie laughed. "Is it very painful?"

"Just wait, your turn is coming." He took another big bite, looking to swallow it almost whole, and plunged in. "I'm going to tell you something that only one other person on the planet knows about—my accountant. I, uh, don't really have to worry about making money after I retire."

Maddie's brows came together. "Have you had investments or something?"

Jake let out a bark of laughter. "Something like that. I took a chance several years ago. Bought some stock from a computer company."

"Microsoft?" Maddie asked.

"No, the underdog at the time."

Maddie's jaw dropped. "Apple?"

"Yeah. With that and my other investments, turns out I'm worth about half a billion dollars."

Maddie felt her breath leave in a gush of air. She couldn't even wrap her mind around that amount of money. "Wow. That's…incredible." It made her feel uneasy. Who was she to be with a man like this? But she reminded herself that he was opening up about everything in his heart…and she was the one he had chosen to do that with.

"Your turn." He grinned with a teasing light in his eyes, digging back into his meal. "Besides Max, what do you love, Maddie?"

Maddie smiled a small smile. "I guess that's only fair. For me it's singing." She hadn't meant to bring it up. It was private and yet more public than it had ever been. But the look of pride and pleasure that came to his face when she said it made her glad she'd taken the risk.

"I know." Jake surprised her. "I was there when you sang." He laughed and it sounded a little harsh. "I was trying to forget you. We'd gone to Rick's club and lo and behold, just as I was getting good and tanked so I could sleep a night without missing you, I look up on stage and like everyone in the room...I was spellbound. I didn't know."

"I didn't know either."

"How could you not know you had such talent?"

"I never really let myself sing. Not like that night. Something happened, I don't know what, but I just let go, and there it was. It was so much fun. Better than fun. I can't describe how wonderful that night was."

"You were phenomenal."

"I was terrified." She took another bite. "But I'm so thankful now. Even if I don't sing on a stage much, I'll never forget it."

"Of course you'll keep singing on stage. It's who you are."

No one had ever said it like that before and she realized that it was true, in part at least—even if she only sang sporadically throughout her life, it was a part of who she was.

"Maddie, listen. You said some things in your office about how you couldn't have a man in your life right now because you have to find out who you are, and I'm guessing the news about

185

Brandon really threw you into a tailspin—which is something I want to talk about some more later. But right now, I want you to know that I won't hinder that process. I want to encourage it. I want to be that person who…helps it grow. I think we can be that for each other if you'll let us." He grasped her hand again and it felt so right, so real, so true what he said.

She couldn't get away from it—from him. She knew what she wanted now and nothing was going to stop her from letting it happen.

CHAPTER TWENTY-TWO

They'd gone to the BB King Blues Club after dinner to listen to some live R&B. Jake was recognized by one of the bouncers and even though he was from Indiana, one of New York's biggest rivals, the man asked for his autograph. They were shown to a VIP table toward the front and were able to see the stage incredibly well, even making out the singer's facial expressions in the bright stage lights.

Jake had his arm stretched across the back of the booth seat, his hand brushing Maddie's far shoulder. Maddie closed her eyes in contentment, letting the crooning music wash over her— loving it, wanting to experience the song, this singer's heart wrenching past all their perspectives into an audience's heart, discovering each other like shy lovers touching for the first time. Like her and Jake and this night.

They left a little early, both wanting to be alone together. They walked the few blocks back to their hotel, admiring the lights of the city, holding hands, their breath making frosty clouds in the air.

~~~~~~~

Back in their suite, Jake helped Maddie out of her coat. He shrugged out of his and then wrapped his arms around her waist. Leaning back, she gazed up into his eyes. "Tonight was incredible. Thank you."

He leaned down to kiss her, starting at just below her ear then moving along her cheek to the center of her lips. She let her mind go. He felt her breathing quicken on his cheek, heat shooting through his body. He made a low sound from his throat and pulled her against him. "You are exquisite, Maddie."

187

She sighed, looking up at him with eyes filled with desire, a purr in her throat making her teasing words raspy. "Such big words for a jock."

He laughed and kissed her again, long and deep, his hands gripping her waist, telling himself to try and keep them anchored there and not go any further. He broke away, his breath coming short and fast. "I don't want to go back to my house and live even one more day without you. Let's get married."

Maddie took a quick indrawn breath and then did that nodding/shaking her head at the same time thing that Jake loved so much. "Are you asking me to marry you? Now?" She gave a squeak of laughter. "This isn't Vegas and we agreed to take things slow!"

He gripped her shoulders. "Do you love me?"

"Yes. I love you."

"And I love you. Why date? Let's commit, right now. Maddie, be my wife."

She became very still, as pale as a marble statue.

Jake waited, silent but straining in the dim room, desperate to hear her answer.

"Have faith in me," Jake said quietly into the moment.

She nodded her head, closing and then opening her wide blue eyes to look into his.

"Is that a yes?" He held his breath.

She took a deep breath. "I...yes."

Exhilaration, pure joy like a rising tide, filled him. He pulled her into his arms to kiss her.

"I'll take you ring shopping tomorrow. We'll go to Tiffany's."

"I don't need a fancy ring." She looked almost as eager as he felt.

"I'll charter a plane, then. We can be in Vegas by morning."

"Are you serious?" Maddie burst out laughing. "Or just crazy? Jake, we don't have to rush."

"I want to make it real. We can have another wedding, a big wedding later."

"I don't need a big wedding. I already had that."

Jake got down on one knee. "Then what's stopping us?" He took her hands into his and saw tears gather in her eyes. "I want to hold these hands for the rest of my life. Let's do it. Right now."

"Okay." Her voice was barely audible. He wondered if he was pressing her too hard, but he didn't care. They would have the rest of their lives to learn everything about each other and work through the ups and downs of any marriage. He had never been so sure of anything in his life.

He gave her one long kiss and then backed up and grinned at her. "Change into something comfortable and pack. I have some phone calls to make."

~~~~~~~

Early the next morning, Maddie climbed into the private plane in something of a daze. After catching a few hours of fitful sleep they had risen early, packed up and checked out of the hotel. They were told that the first available plane could be fueled up and ready by 8am, meaning that they would arrive in Las Vegas around 11 am, which would be 8:00 Vegas time. Jake said that would work out perfectly as the courthouse opened at 8:00. They could go straight there to get their wedding license. He assured Maddie that he had it all worked out and she was just to relax and enjoy their wedding day.

A wedding! It still hadn't sunk in. Was this really happening? Was she about to become Mrs. Jake Hart? She could hardly fathom it.

They settled into the plush leather chairs; the cabin roomy and luxurious. There were glossy wood tables that folded out in front of them, a couple of computer monitors, a big screen, built-in TV for inflight movies, and a long side cabinet, softly lit and reflecting beverages and food items behind its glass doors.

"You think you can get some more sleep?" Jake asked after take off.

Maddie shook her head. "I'm too excited to sleep."

Jake put his arm around her and pulled her close. "Me too," he said, kissing the top of her head. "Want to watch a movie?"

"Sure."

Hours later they landed and were picked up by a limousine and ushered to the courthouse where there was already a line forming outside the marriage license office.

Jake took a call while they stood in line, Maddie listening in. "Really. Okay, well, it's not what I wanted but it will have to do. I'll call you back with our decision." He hung up the phone and looked at Maddie.

"Looks like we have two options."

Maddie raised her brows.

"There is one time available time at the Venetian," he cracked a half-smile. "A gondola wedding at the Venetian. Or there is…" He took a big breath and looked to be holding in laughter. "The Little White Wedding Chapel."

"Isn't that the chapel Britney Spears got married in?"

Jake nodded. "I think so. And Michael Jordan."

"Oh, well, another basketball great. We have to get married there." Maddie leaned into his side with laughter.

"Uh, yeah, I thought so too but I just found out that the only officiator there today is, um, Elvis." Jake raised his brows. "How do you feel about Elvis walking you down the aisle, Maddie Goode?"

"Elvis?" Maddie let out a hoot of laughter. "I *have* always been a fan."

"Really? The gondola would be more romantic. I thought you might want to choose that."

Maddie shook her head. "We'll have a small romantic wedding later, for our family and friends. Let's do Vegas right."

A big grin spread across Jake's face. She was already surprising him. "I love you."

After a little paperwork, a couple of questions and showing their IDs they had the wedding license in hand and took the limo to the Aria resort, where Jake had booked them a Sky Suite. Jake opened the door for her and stood aside while Maddie stepped in. She couldn't help but gasp as the suite turned on by itself. The floor-to-ceiling curtains automatically opened and the lights came softly on to reveal a gorgeous space. The suite was two-story, the focal point a huge, winding staircase to one side. There was a deep sitting area that faced a giant screen television with a rectangular marble fireplace beneath it, complete with flickering fire. Next there was a stylish dining room with a long, elegant bar and up the stairs a contemporary bedroom and huge bathroom with a round stone bathtub.

"It's amazing." She turned to Jake, who had been following her while inspecting the rooms. "I can't believe we are really here."

"Come see the view." Jake led her back downstairs to the wall of windows. Below them was a view of the city, the other hotels, the shops and restaurants and people far below. In the distance she could see the hazy forms of the mountains.

"It's gorgeous."

Just as she was about to reach up to kiss him there was a knock on the door. "Who could that be?"

Jake put his finger to his lips and smiled. "I have a few surprises. Stay here."

Maddie watched as he made his way to the door, wondering what he was up to. They had an appointment at the chapel at 4:00 and had decided to freshen up and change beforehand.

A man gave Jake a huge white box with a pink gauzy ribbon wrapped around it. Jake tipped him, nodding his thanks, and brought it over to the coffee table. "I think this is for you," he said with a mischievous smile.

Maddie gave him an excited look, came over and sat down in front of it. "What have you done?"

"Open it."

Taking the ribbon in hand she pulled on it, untying the bow. With an indrawn breath she lifted the box lid and moved aside the thick tissue paper. "Oh, Jake." She stood as she lifted the dress from the box and held it out. "My wedding dress?"

"I hope you like it." His voice was deep with sincerity.

Maddie held it up to her and squealed. "I love it!" It was tea length, white and silver with a fitted top that was strapless, a sweetheart neckline and a full, fluffy skirt. She had never seen anything like it. The top had a subtle animal print and the skirt was silver beneath, with a white tulle overskirt that was shirred and looked a bit like feathers. It was so unique. So exactly her. How had he known?

"It's Robert Cavalli. Sasha told me he is one of your favorite designers and he has a store around the corner from the

Aria. She gave me your size and a lot of other information about you."

"You called Sasha? She doesn't know, does she?" Maddie clutched the dress to her chest.

"I told her I wanted to buy you a dress, that's all."

"I love it. Thank you. But what will you wear?"

"I ordered a tux. It should be here any time."

"You thought of everything."

"Almost. It's nearly noon and I'm getting hungry." He came over and drew her into his arms, cupping her cheek with his hand, rubbing his thumb across her cheekbone. Maddie felt the familiar melting as she looked up into his eyes. "Why don't we go down for some lunch, and then I've booked us a massage. After that we should have plenty of time to dress for the ceremony."

She found it hard to think of food when he looked at her like that. She was thinking about after the ceremony. Tonight they would truly become one. Good thing she had brought that lingerie after all.

After a light lunch (she wanted to be able to fit into that dress!), a hot stone massage, mani-pedi and a facial, she felt like a pampered princess as she slipped into the Cavalli dress. She managed to get the side zipper up and though it was tight, she thought it looked amazing. She slipped into her silver sandals that she'd worn the night before and turned in front of the mirror. Had it only been yesterday that she was in New York? It seemed like a lifetime ago, and yet there was still so much to come. She'd sent an email to her co-workers explaining that she was taking a personal day on Monday, called her mom to check on Max and tell her she was needed one more day—one more day and one more night. She shivered in anticipation and some apprehension. It had been so long since she'd been with a man and she and Jake had only kissed. It would all be new.

She looked at the bathroom clock and put the finishing touches on her hair. It was time to go!

Jake stood at the bottom of the stairs, looking up at her, eyes full of admiration and love, as she came down the stairs, the dress floating up and down with her steps. He had on a black tuxedo, his hair freshly trimmed, his arm outstretched. "Maddie. You take my breath away."

She took his hand and smiled up at him. "I can't believe this is happening. Are we overdressed for Elvis?"

Jake laughed. "You can never overdress for Elvis."

CHAPTER TWENTY-THREE

Jake could barely tear his gaze away from Maddie as they rode in the limo to the Little White Wedding Chapel. Her makeup was light except for her lips—which were red and full. Her blue eyes sparkled like sapphires, glowing with excitement and happiness. And she was about to be his—for the rest of their lives.

As they pulled into the parking lot, Maddie hooted with laughter. "Look! They have a drive-up window! Do people really get married like that?"

Jake leaned across her, smelling her delicate perfume, and looked out the window. "I suppose they do, but don't get any wild ideas. I want to see you walk down the aisle," he said with a smile, leaning nearer to her throat and kissing her beneath her ear.

The limo pulled up to the entrance of the pretty white building decorated for Christmas. They got out and Jake took Maddie's hand. He paused on the steps toward the front door.

"Are you sure about this? I don't want to feel like I pressured you into a fast wedding."

She looked up at him, the sunlight making her skin creamy and rose kissed. Her lips curved into a smile, her eyes searching his. "I'm sure. Are you having second thoughts?"

"No way." He leaned down and breathed into her ear. "I'm the happiest man on the planet right now."

She squeezed his arm and leaned closer. "Me too. Happiest woman, that is."

"Okay then. Let's get married."

They made their way into the chapel and where a smiling, middle-aged woman greeted them.

"Oh my goodness, don't the two of you look fabulous! We haven't had such a beautiful couple in a long time. Come right this way and we'll get you your flowers and boutonniere. You have Elvis, right? To walk you down the aisle? Our main Elvis is sick with the flu but don't you worry, everyone seems to be coming down with it but we have a great back-up. He used to perform in a very popular lounge right here on the Strip. You chose your songs when you called, right? He plays one while walking you down the aisle and then he plays one when you light the unity candle. They'll take lots of pictures so don't you worry about that either. I just know they're going to want to record you two, why just look at how stunning you look together…"

She continued rattling off details, barely pausing for a response. Jake winked at Maddie, who had her lips clamped together, trying not to laugh.

"Here we are, then." The woman handed Maddie a big bouquet of white roses and handed Jake a white rose for his lapel. "Now, we'll just give you a minute to pin that on and take a breath and then Jake, we'll have you go up to the altar to stand. Do you have any guests?"

They both shook their heads, Jake feeling a stab of guilt. His parents would not be happy when they heard about this. He could just see his father's face, demanding answers, and his mother's crushed expression. Maddie's parents were going to be let down, too. A plan to rectify that started to surface in his mind but he pushed it aside. They would deal with all that later.

Maddie finished pinning on the boutonniere and stood back to judge its placement. Her eyes started to glass over. "You can't do that yet," Jake said with a gentle smile. "We haven't gotten to part where you cry."

Maddie let out a shaky laugh and blinked the tears back. She took a deep breath, her chest rising and falling against the outline of the top of the dress—a dress that looked amazing on her. "It's just that…"

She took another shaky breath. "I can't believe I found you."

Jake leaned down to kiss her, saying, "I'm the lucky one."

"Whoa, whoa, whoa!" A man in an Elvis costume came around the corner, hands waving. "None of that yet, young man." He laughed in an Elvis voice. "Now, you take yourself off to the altar there and I'll see to this ravishing young thing."

Jake gave the man a steady stare but turned toward the small room and walked down the aisle toward the altar, hearing Maddie giggle at their officiator as he said, "He ain't nothin' but a hound dog."

~~~~~~

It was like a dream—a strange, yet wonderful dream. Maddie felt like she had been transported to some other world while Elvis took hold of her arm with one hand and his large microphone with the other. With a jolt, he began to sing, Can't Help Falling in Love. He took a firm grasp of Maddie's hand, put it in the crook of his arm and started them down the aisle. Maddie pressed her lips together to keep from laughing, feeling intense happiness—despite the circumstances—swell from her heart and to her eyes. She stared at Jake, the white and red decorated chapel flashing by as they walked, so small and pretty with its short, white painted pews and baskets overflowing with flowers. It didn't take long to reach Jake. Elvis deposited her hand into his and then finished the song with waving arm motions, his heavy thighs moving up and down as if doing sumo squats—yes, they had gotten fat Elvis—but his voice was deep and sounded just like the old records her dad used to play.

Jake's eyes were full of mirth. He took her hands into his and squeezed lightly. "I can't believe you picked the Elvis wedding over the gondola," he whispered in mock horror.

197

"What can I say?" Maddie shrugged a bare shoulder. "I'm a fan."

They both laughed.

"Shhhh!" Elvis took his place in front of them. "Now, Jake, Maddie, continue to hold hands, just like you're doing there, and gaze lovingly into each other's eyes."

Maddie's chest quivered with laughter.

"This is a special occasion and one not to be entered into lightly." He looked up at the nonexistent crowd. "Any objections? No? Good." He looked down at an open book. "Jake Hart, do you take Maddie to be your wedded wife? Do you promise to love and protect her, cherish her and comfort her, in sickness and health, rich or poor, forsaking all others for as long as you both shall live?"

Jake's face grew serious at the words and his gray-green eyes darkened. "I do."

"And Maddie, dear, dear lovely Madeline Faith Goode." Elvis looked down with serious eyes beneath his big sunglasses. "Do you promise to love and cherish, comfort and care for, in sickness and health, rich or poor, forsaking all others for as long as you both shall live?"

Maddie looked back into Jake's eyes, took a big breath and nodded. "I do."

"The rings."

Oh no. They didn't have any rings, did they? Jake had thought of everything but that. Just as she thought it, she saw him take two rings from his pocket. He pressed one, a silver band that must have been for him, into her palm. Maddie's brows rose, shock filling her, as he positioned the other ring, a huge diamond engagement ring, round with stones all around it and running halfway up the sides of the band, over her left ring finger.

"Wow, that's a blinder," Elvis remarked in a genuinely awed voice.

Maddie felt her breath catch as Jake slid it further down her finger. It was the most gorgeous ring she'd ever seen.

Elvis cleared his throat. "Repeat after me. With this ring, I thee wed."

Jake slid it into place and gripped her fingers. "With this ring, I thee wed." He leaned toward her and whispered. "I hope you like it. Sasha sent me some photos."

Maddie just stared at him and then at the ring, unable to speak. He'd told Sasha? She couldn't think about that now. Elvis was giving her directions.

"Madeline, put Jake's ring on his ring finger please and say, with this ring, I thee wed."

She took the simple band, thinking she should get him something nicer later, and slid it down his long, basketball-playing finger. He had such long fingers, such elegant hands. The way he could handle that orange basketball, flipping it and tipping it into the basket. Just the thought of it made her flush with warmth. Those hands would be all over her soon.

She felt faint and tried to shake herself out of it. "With this ring, I thee wed."

Elvis leaned toward her. "I didn't think you were going to get that out, pretty lady."

Maddie laughed. It was—truly—like a dream, a funny, out of body, wonderful dream.

"You may now light the unity candle."

He started singing Love Me Tender while Maddie and Jake lit their individual candles and then held them together over the larger candle that sat on a marble stand. Maddie watched as the flames melded, became one and ignited the wick of the larger candle, thinking the song was right—all her dreams were being fulfilled in this moment and she would always love him. Always.

They sat close together in the limo on the way back to the hotel. Her skin flushed every time she thought about what was to come. She and Brandon had not waited until their wedding night, having been college sweethearts for two years before marrying and not really thinking it was that big of a deal. But now, she realized, it was a big deal. Having that moment to look forward to—coming together for the first time as husband and wife—made it so much more than a physical act. And she was nervous.

They sipped champagne, kissing until Jake's lips were almost as red as hers.

"Here, let me wipe that off before we get out." Maddie pulled a tissue from her sparkly clutch and wiped Jake's mouth with it, laughing.

Jake's eyes were heated. "I hope you're not hungry."

Maddie shook her head, the champagne making it feel light and weightless. "I'm not hungry."

They made their way to the elevators, everyone staring, some people recognizing Jake and saying his name. She saw a few people pull out their phones and take pictures. Once inside the elevator, Jake pulled her to him and kissed her again, long and deep, their breathing becoming ragged.

They rushed to their room, laughing. Jake threw open the door and then turned and lifted her into his arms, carrying her over the threshold.

The room turned on by itself—the lights came up, the fire started—and Maddie gasped from his arms. The room was filled with flowers and balloons.

Before she could protest he carried her up the stairs and to the bedroom. She shrieked with delight.

"Now, to undress my bride." He lowered her feet to the floor and lowered his lips back to hers.

Maddie took a shattered breath.

She'd never been so happy in all her life. And this was just the beginning. Jake Hart was so much more than a NBA star and all-around wonderful guy—he was now and forever her husband.

~~~~~~~

It was nine o'clock Monday night when Jake pulled into Maddie's parents' driveway to drop her off.

"You're sure you are okay with this?" Maddie asked, feeling bad.

"I don't like it, but I understand. You want to talk to them alone."

Maddie leaned over to kiss him, saying, "My parents will never understand that we ran off to Vegas to get married and it was so...special and romantic that I don't want anyone sullying it with questions and judgments."

"But you'll tell them we're engaged?"

"Yes, we'll just tell everyone we're engaged for a little while. We need to ease Max into this." She gave him a quick kiss. "They will really think I've lost it if I tell them everything at once."

Jake got out and opened the back to pull out Maddie's luggage. He wanted to take her home now, go in there and scoop up Max and take them both home, but she was right. They could announce their engagement and then plan a small wedding for immediate family, slipping in moments to be together as often as possible. He told himself it was the right thing to do, but it wasn't easy. "I'll call you tomorrow."

Maddie nodded, both excitement and apprehension in her eyes. "My parents are going to be shocked."

"But happy, I hope?"

"I think so."

Jake helped Maddie to the door with her luggage, letting Maddie go inside alone.

Driving home, he thought about the plans they'd made on the plane. His schedule was incredibly busy for the next weeks, so they had decided to wait until February, when there was a break in the schedule, right around Valentine's Day, for their second wedding. Jake wanted his parents and sister there. He wondered what their reaction to all this was going to be. His father would say it was too early, that they didn't know each other well enough, and his mother would likely be upset about the quick and simple nature of it. Her only son getting married had always been something she had looked forward to, talking about it when he had dated Jessica for two years in college. His sister, Valerie, would be great— thrilled with the romance of it. Jake grinned, thinking of her face when he told her. She would love Maddie.

He thought he would invite some of his teammates, but the likelihood of very many of them making it was slim. Most had families of their own and plans for those small breaks in the schedule, but there was Marcus, he would probably come.

Maddie was inviting her parents, her sister from college and Sasha, who already thought they were engaged.

He walked into his condo and stood in his living room, looking at it with new eyes, the eyes of a husband and father. God help him, he was suddenly, literally overnight, a father. Would he be any good at it?

As his gaze roamed over the bachelor pad, the art deco style so different from Maddie's office—the glass, the art, the breakables—he came to a quick realization. "This will never work." They were going to have to move. He was faintly surprised that he didn't mind. He imagined the three of them in a nice house up in Carmel, where many of his teammates lived with their families.

He would call his realtor first thing in the morning.

CHAPTER TWENTY-FOUR

The weather was dark, foreboding for a December morning. The wind gushed against Maddie's small car on the highway, making her grip the wheel with white knuckles. She passed semi trucks, feeling their pull and the wind try to drag her into the sides of their vehicles. Maddie slowed down and switched the radio channel to the morning news. The weather was just wrapping up, saying that a snowstorm was brewing.

"And now, for a story from Muncie, Indiana. First Old Bank of Indiana has just announced a criminal suit against bank vice-president Sabrina Bridgestone for the embezzlement of $655,000. The bank explained in a statement that the prime perpetrator, Brandon Goode, allegedly committed suicide six months ago after learning that he couldn't keep the crime going. They wouldn't comment on the man's wife, Madeline Goode of Indianapolis, but said that they were still investigating. The bank is determined to make an example of those left behind, issuing a statement of retribution to the full letter of the law."

Maddie jerked the steering wheel back to the left, realizing that she had almost run into the side of a mini-van. "What?" She inhaled the cold air of the car, trying to focus on the road. A criminal investigation? Sabrina arrested?

She switched lanes, trying to get off the highway, finally able to pull onto a side street. She stopped the car and leaned over the steering wheel, her stomach rolling. It hadn't ended. It wasn't going to end. She was going to have to get an attorney.

Maddie reached for her cell phone, wanting to call Jake, wanting to lean on him, but she stared at the phone instead, thinking what if he wouldn't want her now? She hadn't even had a chance to talk to him more about Brandon yet. She hadn't told him she had been questioned or that they might still call her into question. Dear God! What if she went to prison for this? She would lose everything. She could lose Max!

~~~~~~~~~~

Gloria clutched Max to her on the couch, not wanting to believe what she had just seen on the news. She had asked Maddie if she could keep Max with her today, knowing how much she and Simon were going to miss having their daughter and grandson living with them after Maddie married Jake, and wanting to spend the full day playing with him. Max had crawled up into her lap after breakfast and was sucking on his thumb, snuggled against her chest, his favorite blanket pulled up over him. She'd just felt his forehead, wondering if he was feeling well, when the perky news reporter, standing in front of the bank her son-in-law had worked for, began speaking.

Her heart lurched as they flashed a giant-sized photo of Brandon and then switched to footage of the woman Jake had been having the affair with. Outrage grew inside her seeing the tall redhead for the first time. She was glad to see the police handcuff her and haul her away in the squad car. When she heard the reporter say that the case had become a criminal case and that the wife, Madeline Goode, was also under investigation, she gently slid Max off her lap. "Grammy is going to make a phone call, Max. I'll be right back." She handed him a book and one of his favorite stuffed animals before hurrying for the phone.

Just as she reached for it the doorbell rang. Putting the phone back down, her heart hammering inside her chest, she wrapped her robe more securely across her chest and opened the door. Three men in black suits stood staring at her.

"Yes?" she asked through the crack in the storm door.

The man in front flashed his badge. "FBI, ma'am. Is this the house where Madeline Goode resides?"

"Yes. She's my daughter. But she isn't here. She is at work."

"We have a search warrant, ma'am. We need to come in and search the house."

"I would like to see that warrant." Gloria opened the door a little wider. "And your badge. I'm not letting strangers into my house without being sure you are who you say you are."

The man pulled out his badge and let her study it. He unfolded a piece of paper and handed it over through the crack. Gloria stood there trying to decipher the legalese, making the men stand out in the cold as long as possible. Max climbed down from the couch and hugged Gloria's leg, staring wide-eyed at the agents.

Finally, Gloria stepped back. "I'll show you to Maddie's room." Gloria opened the door to her daughter's room, the room she'd grown up in as a little girl and felt tears threaten her eyes. "I don't know what you expect to find among her things," Gloria commented, shaking her head. "Aside from her work clothes, she doesn't have much."

One of the agents nodded his head once. "Does she store other things elsewhere? A storage unit, perhaps?"

Gloria wanted to curse at herself for opening her mouth. "Yes. She has a storage unit. Mostly furniture, I think."

"We'll need the location and key."

"I don't have a key and, like I said, Maddie is at work."

"You might want to give her a call and ask her to come home immediately. The more she cooperates in this investigation, the better things will go for her."

"She didn't do anything wrong. Except marry a fraud."

The man stared at her while another, younger-looking man stepped forward. "That call? This shouldn't take long."

"Well, don't make a mess of it. There's no reason to trash the room you know. Just take your time." She lectured them like they were little boys.

"Come along, Max. Grammy will get you a snack while she talks on the phone."

"Cookies!" Max exclaimed. It was a distraction that usually worked.

In the kitchen, Gloria got Max settled and picked back up the phone, her hand shaking. How was she going to tell her daughter that the FBI was in her bedroom?

~~~~~~~

Jake was sitting in his living room, killing time before he was due for practice, his feet propped up on the coffee table, swaying back and forth, excited to begin the day and hear back from his realtor. He picked up the remote, took a big spoonful of cereal and crunched down on it as he clicked through the channels. The news was recapping when he heard the name "Brandon Goode." Everything in him stopped as he sat up and turned up the sound. "Yes, Steve, reports are that the man responsible for the embezzlement is dead—committed suicide, some suspect, because he knew he couldn't keep the scam going."

"Who, then, is the criminal case against, Angie?"

Angie, the cute reporter, standing outside of a courthouse, replied in clipped tones. "Well Steve, apparently there is a mistress and a wife involved. Sabrina Bridgestone, the girlfriend of the deceased and fellow bank employee has been arrested and is now out on bail waiting a court date. The wife, Madeline Goode, is still under investigation. No word yet as to an arrest."

"Sounds like a movie I saw once. And right here in Indiana."

"Yes, Steve. We'll be watching this case very closely for further developments."

"Thank you, Angie."

Jake sat frozen as the news moved on to more mundane stories, his body locked in shock, his cereal growing soggy. He looked at the phone, wanting to call her, but changed his mind. She would freak out when she heard about this and he wanted to be there in person for her. She was going to need him.

~~~~~~

When Maddie arrived at the Founders Level, it was to find the police already there waiting for her. Two uniformed officers stood with her boss, Jordan, as she walked out of the elevator. Her face felt like chalk, ready to break off into white chunks of humiliation, and her steps faltered as she imagined them cuffing her right here in front of everyone.

"Maddie, the police have some questions about your husband," Jordan said softly. "Let's go into your office."

Maddie nodded, leading the way, her knees knocking together, her jaw hurting from holding her mouth so tightly closed. Her cell phone started ringing from her purse. "Excuse me," she said, answering it. She walked to the far corner of her office, Jordan talking to the police in loud tones to give her a little privacy.

"Hi, Mom. Is Max okay?"

"Yes. He's fine. That's not why I'm calling. Maddie, something terrible has happened."

"I know." Maddie said low into the phone.

Her mother didn't appear to be listening. "The FBI is here. They're searching your room."

"What?"

"I just watched the morning news and heard they arrested Brandon's mistress. They said the case had been turned over to the authorities, then the doorbell rang and there they were with a search warrant wanting to look through your things. They're in your room right now. Maddie, are you listening? They are investigating you! They want the keys to the storage unit!"

"Okay, Mom. I gave dad a key, see if you can find it. The police are here now. I need to go."

"Need to go? I'm coming down there."

"No." The last thing she needed was her hysterical mother in the middle of this mess. "I need you to keep Max safe and calm. I don't know when I'll be home, but I will call you as soon as I know something. It'll be okay, Mom. I didn't do anything wrong."

"I know you didn't, honey. But I'm afraid they won't believe it. They want someone to blame. Maddie, how can you be so calm? You could be going to jail like that Sabrina woman!"

"No. That's not going to happen." She didn't tell Gloria that she wasn't calm on the inside, that she was afraid she just might be going to jail today. "I need to go. I'll call you soon."

She hung up and walked back toward the men, offering coffee from her freshly brewed pot that she had programmed to have ready when she walked through the door. The men declined.

They sat down, which Maddie thought must be a good sign. If they were going to arrest her, they would have done so already, in front of everyone, wouldn't they?

"I heard about the investigation. On the news on the way over," she blurted out. "That was my mother on the phone. She saw the morning news and called to tell me. I think I need to call an attorney before I answer any questions, gentlemen."

One of the officers nodded. "We're not here to arrest you, Mrs. Goode, but that might be wise."

"If you're not here to arrest me then what do you want?"

"We'd like you to come down to the police station. Just answer some questions, make a formal statement, perhaps take the polygraph test that you agreed to. We are prosecuting Sabrina Bridgestone and need your side of the story."

"So I'm not under investigation? I'm not a suspect?"

"We're not at liberty to comment on that, ma'am. But we're not here to arrest you, only request your presence for some questioning."

"Do I have to leave now?"

The other policemen nodded. "That would be best, ma'am."

"But I need some time. I need to find an attorney."

Jordan spoke up. "I know of someone, Maddie. First-rate in criminal law. A friend of mine." He turned to the policemen. "This woman couldn't possibly be guilty of any crime. In the time I've known her, she is the most honest, dependable person I know. She has a sterling character. She is one of the best people I have ever had the privilege of working with. I would be happy to be a character witness in her defense if it comes to that."

"That will be something to discuss with her attorney, Mr. Tyler." The policemen stood. "We really need you to come with us now, ma'am. But we'll give you a few minutes to call someone."

Jake burst into the room.

"What's going on? Maddie, are you okay?"

"Who are you?" asked one of the officers.

"I'm her husband. Anything that has to do with her has to do with me."

Jordan turned to Maddie. "You're married?" The shock on his face took her aback. Nodding her head, Maddie gave him a pleading look. "Just recently. We haven't told anyone yet."

Jake looked ready to throttle someone.

Maddie spoke in a calm voice. "These men are here about the embezzlement case concerning Brandon. They want me to go to the police station and answer some questions."

Jordan quickly added, "They are giving her a few minutes to call an attorney. I've recommended a friend of mine, Reginald Walters. I'll just go into my office and get his number."

Jake turned to the police. "She doesn't have to go with you if you aren't placing her under arrest, does she?"

One of the men shook his head. "But it will go better for her if she cooperates. Are you Jake Hart, a player for the Racers?"

"Yes." Jake sounded short and irritated, looking ready to slug him if he gushed about being a fan, or asked for an autograph. The man backed down. "We'll just give you two a minute." He gestured to the other officers and the three left to wait in the lobby.

"I saw it on the news and came as quick as I could."

Maddie let herself be gathered up into his arms. "I'm scared," she whispered. "What if they don't believe me?"

"They will. There is no evidence that you knew anything about this. You're doing great. Just stay calm and confident."

Maddie took a deep breath, nodded and pulled back to look into his eyes. "I hate to get you involved in this, but I'm so glad you came."

"I'm your husband, remember."

"Jake, we can't tell anyone that. I want to keep your name out of this. What if it gets in the news…it will sully your career, your name."

"We share the same name. The sooner we get that out there, the better."

Maddie shook her head. "No," she stated with quiet force, "we have to keep you out of this."

"Maddie, listen to me. Your problems are now my problems. I will stand by you in this. That's all that matters."

Jordan entered the office. "Sorry, didn't mean to interrupt. Congratulations, you two. I had no idea…"

The shock on his face made Maddie's face heat. "We only just got married over the weekend. Please, Jordan, don't tell anyone just yet. I want to keep this quiet until this mess is over. We were planning a wedding for family and friends in a few weeks to make it public but now," she looked at Jake, "we have to wait until this is over."

Jordan nodded, his lips pressed into a grim line. "Jake, she's right. This could have ripple effects on your career. Let's keep this under wraps until the case is over and Maddie's name is cleared."

It was the wrong thing to say. Jake walked over and leaned into Jordan's face. "She is my wife and she is innocent. Nothing is going to change that."

Jordan took a step back, hands raised. "Okay, okay." He shrugged. "We'll just do the best we can with it then."

"I'll convince him," Maddie insisted. This wasn't how she'd imagined starting their lives together.

CHAPTER TWENTY-FIVE

Maddie sat in the passenger seat, watching the buildings go by in a blur, clutching her handbag in her lap, sending up silent prayers, prayers that made no sense but in every sentence contained the phrase, *help me, please God, help me get through this.*

Jake reached over and took her hand. "You okay?" He had insisted on driving her even though both she and Jordan had tried to talk him out of it.

She looked over at him, feeling a rush of love and gratitude. "I'll just be glad when it's over."

She'd called her mom when they first got into the car and learned that the agents searching her room had taken only her diary as evidence. Her diary. She felt a hot blush wash over her face, thinking of her private thoughts written on those pages. This was getting more awful by the moment. "I wonder what evidence they have. I mean, against Sabrina. They must have found something pretty substantial to arrest her like they have."

"He had an apartment, right?"

Maddie nodded. "I don't know what happened to it after he died, though. Sabrina must have packed up his things, taken them to her house or destroyed them." She remembered her own time of packing up their small apartment, going through his things, cherishing them, not wanted to get rid of it all, saving things for Max. Anger filled her. She would have to go to the storage unit she was renting and go through it all again, look for clues that her life was not as it seemed. How was she to reconcile all of this with her son when he got older and started asking questions? He barely remembered Brandon, a fact that Maddie had been determined to change as Max grew older. She had wanted Max to remember his dad, now she didn't know. Maybe he shouldn't know much beyond

213

staring at a picture. But someday he would ask, someday she would have to explain all of this to her son.

"I'm really nervous about the polygraph. What if it's inaccurate? What if I'm one of the those people that it can't read correctly?"

"It won't be. Just be as calm as possible and answer the questions. Maddie, it's obvious you didn't know anything, they'll see that."

Maddie sighed as they pulled into the little cement block police station. "I hope you're right."

The place was quiet, not like on television where it was full of people being arrested and officers busy solving crimes. She could hear the loud click-clack of her high-heels as they followed Officer St. Morgan into a small office. He spoke with someone, made a quick phone call, all in a blur of action that Maddie barely noticed, and then nodded. "Follow me, Mrs. Goode." Looking to Jake, he said, "You'll have to wait here, or in the lobby." He looked distractedly around. "There's coffee around here somewhere, just help yourself."

Maddie followed him down a long hall with a shiny linoleum floor that reminded her of her grade school into what could only be an interrogation room. This, she thought in a moment of hysteria, looked like TV.

There were two cheap metal chairs and a long, narrow table. The officer motioned to a chair. "If you'll have a seat, Mrs. Goode, someone is coming to hook up the polygraph."

"Has my attorney arrived yet?"

The man shook his head. "Not to my knowledge."

"I would like to wait until he gets here."

"Just don't let him talk you out of doing this test. If you pass, this process should go much easier for you."

Maddie thought that he was probably right. What harm could it do to take the test anyway? She wasn't guilty of anything.

A woman in uniform came in. She was stern faced and big, her gun belt so tight that Maddie wondered how she was able to sit down. The woman saw Maddie look at it, stared at Maddie's pearl pink suit and curled her top lip to one side, smacking on a piece of chewing gum.

Maddie felt her heart speed up. Was this the person who was going to administer the test?

It looked like it. The officers said something quietly to each other that Maddie couldn't quite make out and then the woman said, "I'm Officer Lambert. If you'll hold your arms out I will strap this on you."

Maddie shrugged out of her jacket, her white blouse feeling too thin, and held out her arms. She roughly wrapped two rubber tubes around Maddie's chest. "That's a little too tight," Maddie stated helplessly.

"Oh, well, we wouldn't want that, now would we?" Great. The woman hated her.

She loosened it, just barely. Maddie took a deep breath and grimaced.

Next the officer strapped on a blood-pressure cuff, also tight, but Maddie resisted the urge to comment, and attached two metal plates with wires to her fingers. Maddie sat down, feeling like a science experiment.

Officer Lambert plopped down on the chair opposite Maddie, her thighs squeezing between the armrests. She squirmed in the chair to get comfortable, making it squeak in protest.

Maddie kept her eyes on the woman's face and started praying her *please help me* litany again.

215

"We'll start with some questions to gauge your normal readings. Just answer yes or no."

Maddie nodded, taking a deep breath, pretending she was in a play and just acting a part.

"Is your name Madeline Faith Goode?"

"Yes." The woman stared at the laptop screen, jotting down notes on a pad of paper.

"Were you married to Brandon Andrew Goode for six years?"

"Yes."

"Have you ever stolen anything in your life?"

The question jolted her. Had she? Her mind raced back to the time when as a teenager she took twenty dollars from her dad's dresser, but she'd paid it right back. Did that count?

"Have you ever stolen anything, Mrs. Goode?"

"Ah. Yes," she answered, wanting more than anything to be honest. The woman didn't look too pleased with that answer, but Maddie tried to ignore her.

"Did your husband die in a car accident?"

Were these trick questions? Did anyone know if it was an accident or a suicide? "Yes," she said, sinking inside. It was hard to tell how these results were going to be with such questions.

"Did you know your husband was having an affair with Sabrina Bridgestone?"

Maddie got mad. This was not a yes or no question. "I found out a few weeks ago," she stated, feeling the blood pressure cuff grip her.

"Please, keep your answers to yes or no, ma'am."

"How am I supposed to do that with these questions? I didn't know during our marriage, which would be a no. But I do know now and learned about it about a little while ago, which would be a yes. Please, be more specific."

The woman pressed her lips together and scribbled something cryptic on her notepad. Maddie tried to calm down.

"Did you know that your husband was embezzling money from the bank *during your marriage*?"

Maddie shook her head. "No."

The door suddenly burst open and an older man, glasses askew, looking like he'd just run a marathon in a three-piece suit, rushed into the room. "She doesn't have to answer that," he bellowed. "I'm her attorney and I want a stop to this test immediately."

He turned to Maddie and thrust out his hand. "Sorry to be late. I was in court. I'm Reginald Walters, your attorney. Whatever you do, don't answer any more questions! Get this apparatus off of her."

Officer Lambert smiled at the man. "She assented to it and we got what we needed, anyway." She walked over and stripped Maddie of the gear while her attorney looked on, mad and flustered.

"I would like a moment alone with my client before any more of this investigation takes place."

The officer rolled her eyes as she snapped closed the computer and left the room saying, "Of course you would."

Reginald walked over to Maddie and shook her hand. "Okay, Mrs. Goode, let's get the story. The real story."

He sat down across from her, dug into his attaché case for a notebook, pen poised over it.

Maddie looked at him in a daze, not knowing where to begin or what this stranger wanted. She didn't even know if she liked him.

"Just a quick version of events as you know them," he encouraged.

"I was married to Brandon for six years. We had just celebrated our anniversary when he died. About two years ago Brandon took a job at First Old Bank of Indiana. He was very excited. We both were. He seemed to be doing well there. Then, he had a car accident and died very suddenly. I was shocked…devastated. I moved back to Indianapolis with my son to live with my parents."

"Looking back on it, did you see any signs that would point you to Brandon's double life?"

Maddie shook her head. "I've thought and thought about this. He went on lots of business trips, over-the-weekend kinds of trips, but it was a new job. I didn't know what to expect and so I just thought that was a normal part of the job."

"So there weren't any new purchases—clothes, cars, gifts for you and Max?"

A new suit flashed in Maddie's mind. "He wore a lot of nice business clothes. I thought they must be expensive but Brandon said his parents bought them for him, for his new job."

"Nothing else? No big-ticket items?"

Maddie shook her head. "We were working hard to get out of debt, our student loans and car bills, so that we could save for a house. We were very careful with our money. We spent only what we had to on necessities."

"Okay," Mr. Walters finished. "When did you learn of the embezzlement?"

"Sabrina Bridgestone called me a few weeks ago. She wouldn't say what it was she wanted on the phone so I agreed to meet with her. We met at LoLa's and I had my best friend with me, Sasha Lang. She can testify to any of this. Sabrina walked in and told us that she had been Brandon's mistress, that they'd had an apartment together and that the bank suspected Brandon had been embezzling over a half a million dollars."

"Did she mention that she was also under investigation?"

"Yes, I think so. She mentioned that she was Brandon's boss and that some of the larger loans had required her signature."

"Do you believe she didn't know?"

Maddie shrugged, shaking her head slowly back and forth. "I don't know," she said in a small voice. "She was in the right position to know a lot more than I did. They worked together and shared an apartment, she…she said Brandon told her everything…" Her voice cracked and she cleared her throat, taking a quivering breath. "I thought the same thing. I thought we were perfectly happy. If he could deceive me then I think he could deceive her."

The attorney stood. "Thank you, Mrs. Goode. I'm going to find out the results of the polygraph and we'll take it from there. Just wait here."

Maddie stopped him, touching his arm. "Do you believe me? Do you think I'm innocent?"

"Of course." He didn't even blink.

Maddie took a deep breath. "Thank you."

CHAPTER TWENTY-SIX

Maddie finally came into the office, where Jake had been waiting for nearly two hours, the corners of her mouth quivering, her face devoid of color. As soon as she opened the door, Jake knew something was terribly wrong. "What is it?" He hung up his cell phone and went over to her, grasping her upper arms.

Maddie turned her face up and choked up. "I failed the polygraph. I think they might arrest me. They're talking to my attorney now. Oh Jake, I can't breathe."

Jake guided her to a chair then filled a Styrofoam cup with water from the water cooler and took it over to her. With a hand firmly on her hands he sat beside her. "What do you think happened? Did you have trouble with the test?"

Maddie shook her head. "The questions were so strange. I couldn't answer just yes or no to a couple of the important ones. And the examiner hated me. I could tell. She wanted me to fail."

Jake found that hard to believe. Why would anyone want this sweet woman to fail a polygraph? But he didn't say that. "What is your attorney saying?"

"He said the test wouldn't be admissible in court, that I was coerced to take it before he could arrive, and told me that it is a false positive. He gave the police a formal statement and told them to make their decision. If they arrest me, I may have to stay here awhile before I can arrange bail."

Jake got up and began pacing the small rectangular room. "This is ridiculous. They can't have one shred of evidence."

Maddie lifted her head. "They have my diary," she said suddenly, panic in her eyes. "They've had that since this morning."

Jake squatted down in front of her. "Why would that matter, Maddie? You didn't know anything...did you?" It was his first moment of doubt.

"No. But I haven't read that far back, I couldn't bear to read it since he died." She clenched her fist together. "I can't remember...what I wrote. I always write every little thought in my head. What if there is something that makes it look like I knew something?"

"You're over-thinking it. It's going to be okay," Jake stressed, hoping he was right. "I hear someone coming."

He stood next to her chair, wishing he could guard her from this, wishing he could deflect it like he did in a game and turn it around to their advantage.

Mr. Walters walked in. He had a smile on his face. "They've decided to let you go home, Maddie."

She took a sudden breath of relief. "It's over, then?"

He shook his head. "Not quite. They are still reviewing all of the evidence and if they find something new that incriminates you, you could still be charged."

"What about the polygraph? How could that have turned out to be positive that I was lying?"

"I've reviewed the questions that were asked and spoke to the examiner. She admitted that they were rushing to get you tested before I showed up, that she might have asked inconclusive questions. It would never hold up in court."

Maddie sagged back against the chair, looking as if a weight had been rolled off her shoulders. "That's wonderful news. Thank you so much, Mr. Walters."

He nodded at her, looking pleased with himself. "You will have to testify during the court proceedings against Sabrina

Bridgestone. The state's attorney's office will no doubt contact you as a witness. It won't be over for some time yet."

"As long as I'm not the one they are prosecuting, I can handle it."

"Can I take her home now?" Jake asked, wanting to get her as far from the situation as possible.

"Certainly. I'll keep in touch."

They shook hands and then Jake handed Maddie her handbag, leading her toward the front doors with his hand at the small of her back.

As soon as he pushed the doors open to the cold December air, he knew he'd made a mistake. A big one.

Cameras flashed in their eyes. Microphones were shoved into their faces. Questions were shouted out like barking orders.

Maddie stepped back instinctively, her back coming flush with his chest, the top of her head fitting perfectly under his chin. "What?" he heard her say.

"Jake, is it true that you and Maddie Goode are married? Did you have a ceremony in Las Vegas?" an attractive blond woman, her mic reading *Insider Tonight*, shouted at him.

Maddie gasped. "Oh no."

Jake grasped her upper arm and whispered into her ear. "Let me handle this."

"Maddie, did you know about your husband's involvement in the embezzlement of over half a million dollars from First Old Bank of Indiana?"

Maddie, like most first-time victims of the paparazzi, just blinked into the bright white lights.

Jake started them down the stairs, his body leaning over her, protecting her. "Please, no questions. Let us pass." Jake was big enough to make it happen. One cameraman stepped into the path, getting a close-up of their faces, and Jake decided to plow into him. Looking the other way as if he didn't notice him, he walked his nearly seven-foot frame right into the guy, knocking him to one side, the camera flying to the pavement.

After that, the sea of people parted, letting them through, but the questions continued to rain down upon them, some shockingly intimate.

"Is it true that you ran off and got married in the Little White Wedding Chapel with an Elvis impersonator walking you down the aisle? Isn't that same chapel that Britney Spears was married in?"

"Sources say there were wedding night photos? How do feel about those pictures leaking out?"

Jake looked up at that question, startled. They *had* taken some racy shots, knowing that they weren't going to live together right away and for fun. Had they confiscated Maddie's phone as well as her diary? "If that shows up anywhere you'll regret it," he warned, opening Maddie's side of the car door and striding around the front of his vehicle to get into the driver's side. He started the engine, took a deep breath and gunned it.

They followed them on foot and with their cameras until Jake turned out of the parking lot and really stepped on the gas. He couldn't get away fast enough.

Maddie stared at him in wide-eyed shock. "How could they possibly know about those photos?

Jake looked at her. "Did they take your phone?"

"No, I have it right here." She dug into her purse and pulled it out.

"We need to delete all of those photos."

223

Maddie nodded, beginning to scan through her photo library. "I only have three but…" She flashed one toward him that showed them both from the waist up and Jake groaned. Maddie panicked. "If these get out! How could anyone get ahold of these?"

"I don't know. Did you write about them in the diary?"

She sucked in a big breath. "Yes, that and more. Oh, I feel sick. I told you I write down every little thought I have. I wrote down everything, every detail of our wedding night. How you looked and…smelled. Jake, you have to pull over. I really think I'm going to be sick."

Jake turned into his community, only to discover more reporters hanging outside the gate. "Pull it together for a little while longer, sweetheart. Look."

She covered her mouth with her hand. "Where have they all come from?"

Jake frowned, seeing several of the tabloids represented in the crowd. "I have a feeling we're going to have to get used to it, for a while anyway.

"I'm sorry, Jake. I didn't know. I'll never write in a diary again."

He squeezed her hand. "Just look confident. We'll get through this."

He drove through the crowd, doors locked, windows up tight, going as fast as he dared. They couldn't follow them into the community, but they would have gotten a shot of them going into it together and piece together some story. It wasn't going to be pretty.

His phone rang as they walked through the door to his condo. He dug it out of his pocket, seeing that it was his coach.

"Jake, we have to talk."

"I know. Now's not a good time, though."

"Now is the only time. The owners are here. Everyone is upset here. You need to get over here now."

Jake rubbed the muscle along his right shoulder, feeling a headache coming on. "Okay, I'll be right there." He hung up the phone.

"The Racers?"

"Yeah. My coach."

"I understand. I'm going with you. I need to get my car. I need to go home to Max."

"But you're coming back, right? You and Max are still coming over tonight? We were going to tell him."

"Jake. Maybe we should let things cool down first. This is all so crazy, so unpredictable…"

Jake blew out a big breath, the disappointment weighing on his shoulders like a heavy blanket. "Yeah, you're probably right. I'll have to settle for calling you later."

They drove to the stadium, where they found a few more reporters. Jake dropped Maddie by her car, made sure she wasn't accosted before she drove away, and then headed inside to face the music.

Jordan met Jake at the doors of the Racers offices. "They're in Rodney's office, all of them. Be careful, man."

Jake gave a high nod. "Thanks for the heads-up."

He walked into Rodney Hillman's office, the president of the multimillion-dollar organization that was professional basketball. An ominous atmosphere thickened the air as he shook hands with the stern-faced men—his coach, the team's managers and the owner of the team. They were all there.

"Have a seat, Jake. Drink?"

"No thanks." Jake sat.

"This is a delicate situation, Jake. We like Maddie. We understand that you've developed a relationship with her, but to be blunt, we can't have this business of hers muddy our name, your name."

"Maddie's innocent. She had nothing to do with what her husband did."

"I believe that," Rodney continued. "We all do. That's not the problem. In the public eye, you know as well as we do that she'll be guilty until proven innocent. It's the way things work, whether we like to think the country runs better than that or not."

"What do you want from me?" Jake looked around the room, staring each man in the eye. "We're married. Nothing's going to change that."

"You're married! Damn it man, who knows about this?"

Apparently Jordan had been true to his word and not said anything. Should he tell them what just happened at the police station? At his own house? About the diary? It was much worse than they thought, and it would all come out in the next couple of days anyway.

"The press already knows. I just got back from taking Maddie to the police station. There was a pack of them there."

Rodney took a long puff from his cigar and leaned back in his chair, eye squinting at Jake. "It'll be all over the six o'clock news."

Jake sat up in his chair. "What's the big deal? Maddie didn't do anything wrong. Anybody that knows her knows that's true. Her name will be cleared and everyone will forget all about it. We got married over the weekend, so what?"

"Your game has slipped since you met her. Your head's not right," his coach commented, adding fuel to the fire.

Jake shrugged. "For a game or two. I played my best when we were dating and she was there. It just took her a while to come around. I'll play great now. Now that she's mine."

One of the men chuckled. "Sounds like true love, all right."

"We'll lay low. Dodge the press until this is over. You should put out a statement supporting her, telling the world that we know she's innocent. Do you realize what her husband did to her?"

"Do you realize what marrying a woman with that kind of baggage can do to you? At least tell me you got a prenup, man." This was spoken by one of the team managers.

"I don't need advice as to how to run my personal affairs. This is really none of your business," Jake shot back, about to stand.

Rodney smiled without humor. "Unfortunately, Jake, that's not entirely true. We own you. You signed a contract that says you won't do anything embarrassing to the team image. This is damned embarrassing."

"What do you want?"

"Separate. Temporarily, at least. Give it some time. Heck son, you hardly know the girl."

Jake envisioned his fist in the man's face, but took a deep breath instead. "That's not acceptable. We are planning a second wedding for family and friends in a few weeks. We didn't want it to get out that we're already married—she has a son and our families would have been disappointed to miss it, so we've been saying we are engaged. It's all planned."

"Well, unplan it. You don't own your life, we do. And it would be best if you remembered that fact."

Jake stood. "This conversation is over."

"You think about it, Jake. We can always trade you."

"Yeah, you do that." Jake stalked from the room.

He was seeing red as he walked to his car in the parking garage. He was almost looking forward to the intimate details of the diary coming out. Expect for the parts that were going to make him look like a lovesick idiot to his teammates, he might even laugh about it.

~~~~~~~

Maddie drove home, tears dripping down her face, ignoring the constant ringing of her cell phone. She just couldn't talk about it anymore. She needed a break.

Glancing at the screen, she saw that it was Sasha and changed her mind. Sasha was always good for her.

"Okay, what exactly is going on?" Sasha demanded without preamble.

"Oh, Sasha. Thank heaven you're back in town. I can't talk about it on the phone. Can you meet me right now? I need to see you."

"Of course. I'll meet you at Moe's in fifteen minutes.

"Okay." Maddie hung up, knowing she wasn't ready to face her parents just yet.

CHAPTER TWENTY-SEVEN

M̲oe's, the bar and grill where Sasha and she always met, was quiet, thank goodness. Maddie slid into a booth, deep and private, the darkness of the room suiting her mood, the blaring of the big screens drowning out any confessions. Sasha was quickly recognizable as soon as Maddie caught a glimpse of someone walking in wearing a plaid skirt, dark tights and boots.

She slid into the seat, folded her hands together and leaned her chin on them, looking at Maddie with deeply compassionate eyes. "Okay, tell me everything."

Maddie started with the New York trip, telling her how Jake had asked her to go on business and then all the roses in the plane.

"Oh my gosh. I've never heard of anything so romantic. You didn't call me? How could you not have called me?"

"I haven't had time. Really. So much has happened in the last few days. And you were out of town at Rob's parents'. You have to tell me how that went."

"Oh no, not yet. Your life is much more interesting than mine right now. How did he propose? Was the wedding wonderful? I only know that much because Jake called to get advice." She quirked a brow. "But it seems everyone knows about it now. It's all over the news."

"It was wonderful and so spontaneous. I guess it was naïve of us to think we could keep the marriage a secret for a while."

"But so romantic."

"Yes, so perfect. Now…being connected with me is so bad for him. The Racers aren't happy."

"You don't think he regrets it, do you?"

Maddie shook her head. "I don't think so. But a part of me wouldn't blame him if he did. I don't understand how he can want someone with all of this…" She stopped, tearing up. "This baggage?"

Sasha reached across the table and laid her hand over Maddie's. "Stop. Stop that right now. You're the best person I know. You had nothing to do with Brandon's bad decisions. Nothing, do you hear me?"

"Don't make me cry," Maddie choked out. "I don't want it to be like this. The beginning of our lives together shouldn't be so awful. Sasha, a part of me says I should discourage this marriage. For him. For his career."

"He's a grown man. You don't have to save him, Maddie."

"I don't?"

"Life is life. If he sticks with you through this, he'll stick with you through anything. He is obviously crazy about you."

Maddie's cell phone rang. She pulled it out of her purse and looked at the screen. "It's my boss, Jordan. I should take this."

Sasha nodded, taking a drink and ordering a plate of wings from the hovering waitress.

"Hello?"

"Maddie, oh good, I've reached you."

"Hi, Jordan. How are you?"

"I'm scrambling here. Listen. I was just called into a meeting with the owners. Maddie…they've asked me to fire you."

Maddie expelled all the air in her lungs. "What?" She swallowed hard. "Why?" As if she didn't know.

"They don't like the negative publicity. They said they won't allow this criminal case to be associated with the team and sully the Racers name."

She felt her heart sink to her feet. She loved that job. The first real career job she'd ever had, and she'd enjoyed the challenges of it. "I understand," she said instead.

"They've given you six months' severance pay. It's very generous."

"Yes, it is. Thank you, Jordan. For calling and telling me. I would have hated to hear it from anyone else."

"I'm upset, Maddie. You don't deserve this. But there was nothing I could do. I'm sorry. Really sorry. You were great at your job."

"Thank you. I mean that, Jordan. Should I come in tomorrow for my things?"

"You can come in sometime to clean out your office, but there's no hurry. We won't replace you anytime soon."

"Okay. I'll just come in tomorrow and pack up. I don't want to let it drag out."

"I understand." A long pause ensued. "Maddie, for what it's worth, I know you are completely innocent. I know you'll get through this."

"You're a good friend, Jordan. Thank you."

"Oh, one more thing. Jake was in the office before me. He left really angry. I don't know what they said to him, except that many of the higher-ups were there. They apparently had quite a confrontation with Jake."

Maddie's heart sank even further, if that was possible. "Thanks for telling me. Jake will probably try to brush it off and not tell me the full story. Thank you for everything, Jordan. You've been a great boss. The best."

"Well, okay then. I'll let you go. You take care, Maddie."

"You too."

They hung up.

"Don't tell me they've fired you," Sasha stated, wide-eyed. "What kind of monsters are they?"

"Monsters worried I'll screw up the Racers name, that's what. And Jake's name. I think they're putting a lot of pressure on him."

"It's not fair. You've done nothing wrong. I bet you could sue them."

Maddie shook her head. "I'm trying to stay out of the courtroom, not get in it."

Her phone rang again. "Oh, no," she cried as she glanced at the screen. "It's Rick. The player that has me sing at his club."

"Oh, that's right! In the midst of everything I forgot to ask how that is going."

Maddie held up a finger. "Let me get this and then I'll tell you all about it. It'll be good to talk about something positive."

"Hey, Rick, how are you?"

"Hey, girl. Great. Great. You're famous!" He said it like it was a great thing, and Maddie had to smile.

"Infamous, you mean?"

"No, Maddie girl. This is a good thing in the music industry. I've had three calls since the afternoon news, one from a talent scout."

"You're kidding."

"No. Tony Baron from Distilled Rock Records. You gotta sing next weekend!"

232

"There is no possible way I can sing next weekend. My life is falling apart and it's going to get worse before it gets better. You don't know the half of it."

He chuckled into the phone. "Maybe I do. Maybe I've got connections everywhere. Listen, Maddie. In this business, entertainment I mean, getting your name out there is everything. Everything. Now come on, hon, sing us a short set on Saturday, let this guy come and take a listen and I'll do the rest. All you got to do is sing."

Maddie took a sip of her soda, deep in thought. Why not? How could anything possibly get worse that it already was? "Okay, just three songs."

"Great. I'll see you at eight on Saturday for rehearsal. Oh, and I found a band. I think you're going to really like them. This piano player is really something."

"You're so crazy." She grinned into the phone. "But I'm going to trust you."

"There you go. Go with your gut. It won't let you down and neither will I."

"See ya."

"Yeah. See ya Saturday."

She hung up and looked at Sasha, slack-jawed. "I give up. I'm not in control of my life and at this point, I really don't think I ever was."

Sasha shook her head. "What did he say?"

Maddie laughed. "A talent scout wants to see me. From a record company. They want to hear me sing."

"Maddie!" Sasha's eyes were as wide as saucers. "This could be your big break!"

"Big break? I don't deserve a big break! I've only been singing for a few weeks."

Sasha made a noise in her throat. "What about all of the years in high school choir and the musicals. They were always begging you to do the solos and you always chickened out and took the supporting roles." Sasha pointed her finger into Maddie's face. "And what about all those years at church? Weren't you in the church choir since, like, age five? And the Christmas and Easter pageants you begged me to come to? Just because you haven't been trying to make it in the music business doesn't mean you haven't been preparing for this moment your whole life."

Maddie clamped her lips together and stared at her best friend. "I guess you're right." She let out a little laugh and looked down at her plate, trying to still the excitement within her. Then she looked back up at Sasha. "What would I ever do without you?"

Sasha shuddered and shook her head, her dark, straight hair waving back and forth. "It doesn't even bear thinking of."

"Okay, enough about me. What's going on with you? How was the trip to Rob's parents'?"

Sasha frowned, looking down at her plate. "I broke it off. After two days at their house, I could just tell." She pressed her lips together and shook her head. "It's never going to work with us. His parents hate me, and he…he did try harder, but it just wasn't enough. I want someone…crazy about me. Not someone who makes me feel like a second-class citizen. It was pretty awful."

"So you flew home early? Just left?"

"Yep. And I feel really good about it." She nodded, her lips pressed into a smile. "Free, in fact."

"Wow. I thought it would be harder than this. You two have been dating since college."

"I know. So did I. I think that was part of the problem. I didn't realize how stifled the whole thing had gotten to be. It was just familiar, so we both kept it going, not realizing there are lots of better options out there. I'm really excited about dating. There are so many hot men in the world, you know?"

Maddie laughed. "What about Marcus? Is he one of those hot men?"

Sasha turned her head slightly and looked sideways at Maddie, a sly grin on her face. "Absolutely. And he called. While I was on the plane flying home."

"No way."

"Yes way."

"What did he say?"

"He said he wanted to see me again. We have a date this weekend." She paused, stretched out her hand across the table. "But listen, Maddie, if you need me this weekend, I'll postpone it."

"Are you crazy? With the schedule these players have during the season, you have to take the dates when you can get them, believe me, I know. Go. Have a great time." Maddie let out a big breath. "Isn't life bizarre? How did we end up dating NBA players? And I married one! Remember when we went to the game and joked about getting Jake's phone number? And now? I still can't believe it."

"Yeah. I still can't believe you stole my man," Sasha teased, grinning.

"I couldn't help it. He pursued me!"

"Whatever. Miss Beautiful shows up dressed to the nines to work everyday, damsel in distress..." Sasha put the back of her hand against her forehead and looked up with a Southern belle imitation. "Why, I just cain't find my interview, mister big, strong basketball player."

They both laughed. "Gosh, I hope I wasn't that stupid." Maddie rolled her eyes.

"Too bad I'm just not the damsel-in-distress type." Sasha crinkled her nose.

Maddie looked lovingly at her friend. "No. You're the sweep-him-off-his-feet-and-make-him-wonder-what-hit-him type. I think you've forgotten that about yourself."

Sasha let out a short laugh. "Maybe so. Thanks, Maddie."

Maddie wiped the BBQ sauce off her fingers and reached for her purse. "I'm so glad I have you, Sasha. Look at me, laughing and joking and having a good time, and I thought I might be going to jail this week. You are my best friend."

"You're not going to jail, so stop talking like that." Sasha took a deep breath. "You're my best friend, too. Don't forget that after you're married this time."

Maddie shook her head. "I won't. I promise."

CHAPTER TWENTY-EIGHT

They had decided to go on a double date. Marcus had spoken to Jake at practice during the week and mentioned taking the girls out to a local seafood restaurant after the home game. Jake had agreed, thinking at the time to take Maddie's mind off the trial that was a few weeks away, though now he was wondering if it was such a good idea. They were still being hounded by the press, making his coach increasingly short-tempered and the whole team on edge. They'd lost again tonight, even though Jake had played better than he had in weeks, but still, everyone was feeling the pressure.

He walked over to Maddie after the game and gave her a quick kiss. "How's it going?"

Maddie looked up at him, people filing out of the stadium all around them, many looking their way. "Everyone keeps staring at us. More than usual. It's disconcerting."

"Just act normal. As soon as this trial is over, they'll move on to something else."

"We can only hope."

Sasha came up to them. "Where's Marcus? I'm starving."

"He was still showering when I left, but he should be here any second," Jake told her.

"Oh, there he is." Sasha pointed, then walked over to him, a provocative smile on her lips. Jake and Maddie watched as Marcus leaned down, whispered something into her ear, smiling broadly and making Sasha laugh, and then kissed her in front of everyone.

Maddie giggled. "What are they doing?"

Jake half-smiled. "Probably trying to take some of the heat off of us, if I know Marcus. He's a master at tactics like that in the game."

"Defense?"

"Yeah. Something like that." Jake took her hand. "Let's get out of here."

The four left the stadium, glad to see that there weren't any paparazzi lingering around. On the way to the cars, Marcus asked Maddie, "Have they decided whether or not to drop the case? I heard they can still go after you."

"Marcus. Don't ask her like that, she'll start crying." Sasha glared at him.

"Oh. Sorry." He grinned big. "You can take 'em, Maddie. You'd have that jury eating out of your sweet little hand."

Maddie shook her head. "Thanks, but I hope it won't come to that. From what my attorney says, unless some new evidence that comes out in this trial with Sabrina, he doesn't think they will go after me. I just have to get through testifying at her trial and pray that goes well."

"You don't have to defend the mistress, do you?" Marcus asked.

"No. Not really. My attorney has been prepping me all week. I basically have to answer questions about her. How we met, what she told me, any signs I might have seen that Brandon was embezzling and had a mistress. At this trial they won't be questioning me directly about any involvement they might suspect I had. But they still could if the bank isn't satisfied with the outcome of this trial. I will be so glad when this is over."

Jake didn't mention that he had spoken to the judge to request the court date be moved up as quickly as possible on the calendar. Sometimes it did pay off to know people in high places. He'd done it for Maddie, but now, if this thing didn't end soon, if

Maddie actually had to defend herself, he might be seriously looking at being traded. This was affecting his career more than anyone knew. His coaches, the owners, they were all breathing down his neck, putting constant pressure on him that Maddie was a bad deal all around.

Worse, he'd spoken to his parents on the phone last night. They were hearing stories in Colorado and demanding explanations. His father was livid. Told him to get his head back where it belonged, on his career and not chasing after a problematic woman. When he told them they were planning to have a wedding on Valentine's Day his father had gone ballistic and his mother had started crying. Things were beginning so rocky in this marriage and his parents were so against Maddie without even knowing her that Jake had begun to think maybe they should cancel the second wedding, postpone moving in together until this whole mess had cleared up.

"I don't know how you're dealing with the pressure," Sasha said, opening the car door for herself.

"It's not easy."

Jake and Maddie walked over to Jake's SUV. "We'll see you there," Maddie said, waving and getting into the car.

They followed Marcus to the restaurant. Jake was quiet, thinking. He could feel Maddie's troubled gaze upon him.

After a couple of minutes she blurted out, "Are you okay?"

"I should be asking you that."

"I'm okay now. When I'm with you."

He looked at her and smiled, but it felt strained.

Maddie turned back toward the car ahead and said in a small voice, "I'm sorry."

"Don't say that."

"You shouldn't have to be dealing with all of this."

"We'll get through it."

Maddie sighed. "I hope so."

At the restaurant they ordered, the four of them laughing and small-talking. Jake noticed that Sasha was very comfortable with Marcus and Marcus had an openness about him that Jake hadn't seen with just anyone. He laughed at Sasha's humor, he responded to her thoughts on a matter, he looked at her, really looked at her, and once Jake saw something in his eyes, something admiring and he thought, maybe Sasha was the one for him. Maybe they'd both found love through a radio show contest.

The main course was cleared away and Jake excused himself to go into the men's room. As he was washing his hands, a young man came up to him, grinning from ear to ear.

"Are you Jake Hart?"

Jake nodded. "Yeah."

"Wow. This is my lucky night."

Thinking the man wanted an autograph, Jake said, "Sorry, man, I don't have a pen on me."

"Oh, I don't want your autograph. I'm a reporter for *Current Stars* magazine." He gave Jake a sly look. "How would you like to get your side of the story into print?"

Jake shook his head. "No thanks."

The man looked suddenly angry. "Come on. I'll print whatever you want. For instance, did you really get married in Vegas? And then those photos, wow. Those were something."

Jake felt the blood rush to head and stared in unbelief at the man. "You've seen photos?"

"They're online. Listen, they are insinuating that your wife is an embezzler and a gold digger and that she has you duped. If you want a rebuttal…well, this is your chance."

Jake took a long breath. He shook the water off his hands, grabbed the paper towel and wiped his hands, trying to control to urge to slug the man's overeager, smug face. He didn't know how to reply—no glib, funny comeback, he only heard himself state, "Madeline Goode is none of those things." He turned and strode from the room, the man's voice following him down the hall. "Are you saying she isn't your wife? Are you getting the marriage annulled or something?"

Jake made his way to the table, breaking into a sweat, wondering what had just happened. She was Madeline Hart now, legally, and he hadn't meant to insinuate anything different. "Did you pay, Marcus? Let's get out of here."

Maddie looked up at him in concern and he felt his gut twist. What had he just done?

"What's wrong?" she asked.

"Reporter hounding me in the bathroom. We need to get out of here."

Marcus took some hundred-dollar bills from his wallet and tossed them on the table while motioning to the waiter that they were leaving.

"I'll get it next time," Jake commented as they walked out.

"Whatever, man," Marcus replied with a huff. "You can't even go to the men's room. This is getting ridiculous. Let's go to my place."

"Good idea."

CHAPTER TWENTY-NINE

It was Friday. The Friday of the trial. Christmas had come and gone in a short-lived bright spot within the stretch before the trial began. Max had been so cute this year, old enough to really tear into his gifts and shout with glee over a new truck or talking Muppet. His little face was the only thing helping her keep her sanity. Him and Jake's daily call.

Maddie drove to the courthouse and concentrated on thinking about Christmas. Christmas had always been a magical time in her childhood. Her dad had decorated the outside of the house with a plethora of lights—from Santa and his reindeer on the glittering, light-edged roof to yard decorations that had changed throughout the years with the comings and goings of fads. Blow-up Frosty, make-believe igloos with gleeful penguins, dancing ice-skaters on a fake pond, robotic deer that Simon had placed under their apple tree just like the occasional real deer they saw and Maddie's favorite, a life-sized nativity, all in lights, Mary with her blue gown, the shepherds and animals with their heads bowed, the elegant wise men bearing their gifts and Joseph. For some reason she had always loved Joseph best, his lighted face staring down at the Christ child in seeming awe. Had he been frightened of the call on his life? Had he wondered how in the world he had ended up the adoptive father of God's only son?

The courthouse was crowded. She wished Jake could have been there, but the team was keeping him very busy this week in an effort to keep them apart. It seemed every eye turned on her as she walked in. She was wearing an ivory suit with tiny black pin stripes, black pumps and a simple black clutch beneath her right arm. Her hair was long and loose, her head held high.

She had nothing to hide.

She found a seat behind the prosecutor. She really didn't care which side she was assigned to or which side thought she could help their case. She was there for one reason. To tell the truth. The truth as she knew it when she was married and the truth as she knew it today.

The trial dragged on. Maddie waited in the hall outside the courtroom for them to call her, trying not to think about how it would go, trying to keep her heart from pounding so hard. Her head snapped up when her attorney came out and motioned her toward him. It was time to take the witness stand.

Maddie placed her hand on the Bible. She looked into the man's eyes and pledged to tell the truth, the whole truth. Yes, it was time for the truth.

"Mrs. Goode," began the prosecuting attorney. "Have you ever seen that woman sitting there?" He pointed at Sabrina.

"Yes, she called me a few weeks ago and asked that I meet with her."

"And what did she want with you, Mrs. Goode?"

Maddie took a breath. "She told me that she had been having an affair with my husband. She also told me about the embezzlement and that the bank suspected Brandon had stolen over a half a million dollars."

"What was your reaction to this?"

"I was shocked. I didn't believe her at first. I thought she must be crazy, but I couldn't understand why she would tell me such a thing if it weren't true."

"Mrs. Goode, do you now believe her?"

Maddie nodded, looking at the jury. "Imagine learning your significant other had another life that you knew nothing about. At first I flatly denied it. Then, as the evidence came out, as I learned more details from other sources, I was forced to believe that

Brandon had, indeed, led this other life. I can't fathom it. I can't reconcile it to the man I knew as my husband. He seemed so normal, a good husband and partner with me working toward the goals that we had, a father that loved his child, that...pretended, I guess now, to miss me when he had to be away on business. But everyone is telling me that they have this evidence. That it's true. So," she shrugged sadly, "what am I left to think? What am I left to tell his son?"

"So your husband gave you no cause to believe he had another, secret life?"

"I had no idea," Maddie said simply. She looked at Sabrina and repeated. "I had no idea until she told me."

"That will be all."

She stepped down from the stand.

"Congratulations, Maddie. It's definitive. It's over."

"It is?" She looked up at her attorney standing in the hall outside the courtroom.

He nodded, pale blue eyes pleased. "The bank was still considering prosecuting you, depending on this trial, but you were believable and they have no evidence they can pin on you. Now that Miss Bridgestone has been found guilty and they have someone to blame this on, they are satisfied. It helped that you were so credible on the witness stand. Excellent job today."

Maddie took a deep breath. "I'm relieved to hear it. Will Sabrina go to prison?" She couldn't help but feel a little sorry for her. They had loved the same man, a man neither of them had really understood.

"They gave her a three-year prison sentence, but suspended it. She'll serve about 180 days in jail, be placed on probation and have to repay some of the bank's remaining losses."

"That sounds terrible, but she probably got off pretty light, didn't she?"

He nodded. "She could have been sentenced to ten years in prison. I would say she is relieved."

"I would like to talk to her. Is there any way I can see her?"

Her attorney looked at her for a moment and then nodded. "I'll see what I can do. Wait right here."

He was back within ten minutes. "She's in a holding cell. They've given you a couple of minutes before transporting her. Be careful what you say, they may be recording it."

Maddie nodded and followed her attorney down a long hall, up an elevator to a floor with cells. She shivered walking by them. It wasn't the same as in the movies. There were no scantily dressed, lounging prostitutes, no catcalls or whistles—there was little sound at all. Instead Maddie felt despair seeping into her with each click of her shoes across the shiny tiled floors.

Her gaze met a woman's and she found helpless fury there. Another sneered at Maddie, but as Maddie gave her a small smile filled with all the compassion that she felt for her the woman's face changed to hopelessness and she turned away. They finally came to Sabrina's cell.

She had changed and was wearing a white t-shirt tucked into the elastic waistband of plain gray cotton pants and black tennis shoes. Her hair had been pulled back into a ponytail, revealing the sharp lines of her face. Her head jerked up, her gaze haunted as she stared at Maddie.

"You've lost weight," Maddie said her thoughts aloud.

"Here to gloat?" Sabrina said in a dead voice.

"No," Maddie said softly. "I wouldn't wish this on anyone."

"Yes, well, you got lucky. I'm taking the heat for both of us."

"I guess you could look at it that way. But the truth is, I'm not guilty of anything." Maddie stopped, stared at the gorgeous woman in front of her. "What happened? I just don't understand. You're beautiful. You had a successful career. You could have probably had any number of men. Why would you settle for a married man?"

Sabrina shrugged. "He was a challenge…and I wanted him."

Maddie felt the anger rise within her, white and hot. "You just took what you wanted then, never thinking about the consequences, about me or Max."

"I'll have plenty of time to think about it now, won't I? What do you want, Maddie? I thought you would be off somewhere celebrating. Why are you here?"

Maddie looked down at the shiny squares of marble. "I want to forgive you. I'm trying to forgive you and I thought it would help if I could understand why you did it." She looked back up at Sabrina. "Are you at all sorry?"

Sabrina stood up and walked over to the bars. "What do you think? Of course I'm sorry." She clutched two bars with either hand.

"Only because of this? Because you're being punished?"

Sabrina laughed. "I know what you want to hear. You want me to say that I've changed, that I've learned my lesson and wish I had never looked twice at Brandon. You want me to be good…like you. Well that's not going to happen, sweetheart. I don't regret going after Brandon. I don't regret falling in love with him. I do regret letting him talk me into signing my name to some papers and turning away and ignoring the signs when I suspected he was up to something. I do regret being a typical weak woman who protected him when I should have blown the whistle on the no-good weasel. I wouldn't be behind bars. A woman doesn't get punished for stealing a husband."

Maddie's breath stopped at the speech. She backed away from the angry woman, her knees feeling suddenly weak and wobbly. "Yes, they do. There are many levels of pain in such a relationship. You settled. I'm sorry you can't see your mistake," she said with sadness, "and I'm sorry for the next wife it happens to once you get out." Maddie turned and walked away, hoping never to see Sabrina Bridgestone again.

More news reporters were outside the courthouse, but Maddie refused to notice them. Head held high, she blocked out their questions and made her way to her car. Getting inside, one question penetrated her stoic wall.

"Maddie, have you heard that there is talk of Jake Hart being traded and it's because of you? Do you realize the impact you've had on Jake's career?"

Maddie turned to stare at the woman while a camera blinked at her. Quickly coming back to reality, she shut the car door and jammed in the key as fast as she could. She started the engine and hit the accelerator with her elegant shoe as hard as she dared. Her tires screeched as she pulled out of the parking lot and speed down the street toward Bankers Life Fieldhouse.

Maddie burst through the doors of the practice court, immediately able to pick Jake from the other players. As the doors closed behind her, a couple of the players saw her and stopped, causing the coach to look her way. She saw something on the man's face that made her heart sink—a mixture of revulsion and pity. Didn't he know she was innocent? Why did these men hate her now?

Everyone stopped playing as she walked over to the coach. "I need to speak to Jake, please."

Jake jogged over to her, looking grim. "Jake is practicing. Can't it wait until after?"

A couple of the men snickered. Maddie stared at them and they quickly looked at anything but her. "Please. It will only take a few minutes."

"Come on, coach. I have to tell her."

"All right, hurry up."

Jake walked with Maddie out the double doors, down the hall to the media room and shut the door behind them.

Maddie walked into the center of the room. "Is it true? Are they trying to trade you because of me?" Tears gathered in her eyes.

Jake tilted his head to one side, hesitating. "I think so. They are talking about a trade."

"You love this team. They can't make you leave just because of a trial that doesn't have anything to do with you, can they?"

"I had hoped it would have blown over by now, but it's gotten even worse." He lifted his hand to his head and leaned on it for a minute.

"What? What's happened?"

Jake walked over to a table and picked up one of several of the newspapers lying there. He flipped the paper around and handed it to her. Maddie looked down and saw a photo of her and Jake in an embrace, her chest barely blurred out, and read the huge headline. "Marriage Over: Jake Hart Admits Gold Digger Duped Him."

She gasped, heat rising to fill her face. Her gaze scanned the article, which quoted some of their wedding and wedding night descriptions from her diary.

"Oh, Jake," she whispered as she read. "This is worse than anything I imagined they might do with it." She looked up at Jake, his face white and stark.

Placing the paper on the table next to her, Maddie looked at the floor. "I'm sorry," she rasped out. "I'm so sorry."

She ran from the room, stumbling down the hallway, blinded by tears. When she arrived outside, it began to sleet.

~~~~~~~

Jake stared at the paper on the table, everything inside him wanting to go after her, wanting to wrap his arms around her and tell her he loved her, and they would get through this. But he couldn't make his feet move. That reporter from the men's room had twisted his words but this was his fault, not hers.

It had been the worst day of his life. The entire team had come down on him about the embarrassing press. He'd had to feign indifference against the jokes, the sideways looks and snickers of his teammates, the embarrassed anger of his coaches. The feeling that they wanted to get rid of him grew and grew until he might as well have not been on the floor practicing with them.

Then his parents had called—outraged. If he had thought they were going to have a hard time with Maddie before, well, this made him realize that in all likelihood, they would despise her for what they perceived she had done to their iconic son. No amount of explaining had changed their ranting against her. Jake hung up feeling helpless and angry.

He walked down to the locker room and opened his locker, his head down, his stomach hollow. "How am I going to fix this?"

CHAPTER THIRTY

FOUR MONTHS LATER

Maddie walked into the club carrying her new Taylor electric guitar with its awesome acoustic sound that she'd fallen in love with at the music store. She edged through the chairs of the dark club, making her way to toward the back where her lead guitarist, Neko, was leaning against the wall, tuning, his long dark hair hanging in his eyes, his shirt tight against his muscled chest. Sam, a stocky black man who wore a knitted beanie cap to cover his bald head and the best bass player in the Midwest, came in right behind her, lugging in his bass amp, laughing with the drummer, Nate, who was similarly loaded down with band equipment.

It would take them about thirty minutes to set up. They'd gotten it down to a science in the last few months since Rick had helped Maddie put together a band. Rick had become something of a manager to them. Maddie didn't know how an NBA player had time to babysit her career and set up gigs for a band, but he seemed to love it and they were booked to play every weekend, and even had a gig at the state fair in August. It helped to have a famous band manager, she supposed, but every time Maddie tried to give Rick the credit for one of their accomplishments, he would look her in the eyes and ask if she'd listened to her own demo tape recently. And Maddie would smile and nod and admit, "It *is* pretty good." That and the talent scout who had immediately liked her and was finishing up a recording contract for them, well, the career part of her life had turned out really good.

The place started filling up, her name drawing the regulars and a plethora of fans.

"Maddie." A blond-bearded guy named Rex waved her over. "Come meet some friends."

Maddie smoothed down her rhinestone-studded t-shirt and walked over. It still felt strange to be so popular for something like music. People thought they knew her, and Maddie guessed that in a way they knew that deep and exposed side of her that she poured into her music even better than her parents knew the everyday Maddie. But in other ways, day-to-day living ways, they didn't know her at all.

"This is Bobby and RJ and Cody."

Maddie shook their hands and smiled, seeing one of them look pointedly at her bare left hand, causing the pain of nothing being there to strike her—a white hot, lancing pain in the region of her heart, but short-lived as she distracted herself from it. She had insisted on a divorce so that she wouldn't ruin Jake's life but he had steadfastly resisted it. She'd stopped taking his calls, sent him back his ring and had gone ahead with the paperwork, determined to do what was right for him. As far as she knew, he would get the divorce papers any day.

"Thanks for coming, guys. I hope you enjoy the show."

The first set was fast and happy people-pleasers. She'd learned how to get the crowd into the cheering, dancing party mood. It was still amazing to her, the way she had instinctively known how to work a crowd, and every crowd was a little different. There were the twins, Dora and Danika, who danced to every song until sweaty and laughing, the other women giving them envious glares and the men staring with admiration. They were always a fun addition to the crowd and Maddie learned to play it up, letting them come on stage and sing with her, letting them bring up the shy guys to dance and have a great time.

The biggest shock had been the men who, after hearing her sing with a voice that swept the crowd into wide-eyed silence, wanted ask her out afterward. She'd always resisted, knowing what they were really attracted to, knowing that it was a God-given gift, and that while it was real and good and beautiful, it wasn't all of who she was, it wasn't anything that would ever belong to those men who thought they wanted her.

The second set slowed down a bit. People were starting to find someone in the crowd they wanted to get to know, and a slow one or two gave them a nudge to take a chance. Her favorite song was coming up.

The band quieted down, the lights dimmed except for one spotlight as she pulled up her stool and sat on the edge, one foot propped on a rung, her guitar in her hands. She'd learned about twenty songs on the guitar, but this was one of her favorites— Anna Nalick's Wreck of the Day. It was the story of the last year of her life. She closed her eyes and began to sing it.

As she neared the end, she opened her eyes and looked out beyond the embracing dancers to the crowd and then up, past the bright spotlight to those standing toward the back. There, by the door, was someone tall, his suit jacket hanging in effortless ease from his shoulders. Familiarity slammed into her. She faltered, the strumming on her guitar missing a beat, then she hurriedly regrouped, singing the last the verse, not able to look away from his shadowed face.

The song faded away, the notes slow and soft coming to an end from the speakers, and she found she didn't know what to say.

Neko filled the space. "We'll be taking a short break now." He dialed up the filler music.

"What's up?" He walked up next to her.

Maddie shook her head, unable to look up and see if he was still there. "I don't know. Just someone I used to…I think he's here."

Neko looked into the crowd and then Maddie could see him look up and up as a tall figure materialized in front of them. "Ah," he said simply. "Take all the time you need."

Maddie sat frozen on her stool.

"Maddie?"

Her head lifted, her gaze locked with his. "Jake."

"I forgot. I forgot how beautiful you are."

She exhaled a breath, heart pounding. "How are you?"

"I'm...I'm terrible. I got the papers."

She let the guitar slide from her hands, hearing a twang as it knocked against the floor.

She shook her head, fighting tears. "I'm sorry. It's for the best...I won't let a rush to the altar ruin your life."

Jake reached for her hand. "Dance with me?"

"Jake...what are you doing? I can't. Someone will record it. It will be on the internet, magazines. You know they will make it into something terrible for you." Her insides quivered with the effort to hold it together.

"Dance with me." His voice was low, certain.

She looked at the outstretched hand of her husband. Those beautiful hands. Those long fingers, elegant in their execution. She let out another breath and closed her eyes, remembering how much she loved holding his hand.

An old classic started from the speakers. She nodded. She couldn't help the melting feeling as he pulled her into his arms, smelled the familiar smell that she'd cherished and remembered everything she loved about him in a flash of insight, smell, touch and sound. She looked at his lips, wanting to kiss him more than she could ever remember wanting anything.

They danced on the stage while the crowd watched on. She closed her eyes, feelings of love and heartbreak warring within her. The song wound down and they stood there in the colored lights, staring at one another. Finally, Maddie backed out of his arms and asked, "What do you want, Jake?"

"I want my wife back."

It was the answer she wanted and yet couldn't bear to hear.

"What about your parents? What about your career?"

Jake shrugged. "I'm retiring. And my parents will just have to come around."

"What do you mean you're retiring? You love that game." She couldn't tear her gaze from his eyes.

"I love you more. I miss you. You are my other half. Without you and Max…I'm lost." He pulled her close with one hand, saying into her ear. "Come back. Be my wife."

Maddie pulled back. She looked up at him, stopped and really looked at him. He might miss her now but what if his parents really came against him. How could she ask that he turn away from them? And she knew, deep inside, that she didn't want to be that girl. That woman who would be rejected and abhorred for making him something other than what they wanted him to be. "I can't." She turned and walked quickly away.

At the bar she motioned to the bartender for a glass of water. Taking the glass, she downed several gulps. He was behind her. He turned her by her elbow.

"I'm not giving up, Maddie. I don't want to live my life without you, okay? I've tried. I've tried to tell myself we were going too fast, that people can't fall in love like that. I've tried to convince myself that everyone was right about us. But they aren't right. We were right all along."

Maddie shook her head and looked down, trying not to cry in front of the listening people around them. "It won't work, Jake. You'll resent me sooner or later." She said it so softly she didn't think he heard her.

"For giving up basketball? No, I won't. If I ever again have to choose between you and anything, I will choose *you*," he stated with conviction.

"But don't you see? I don't want you to have to."

He took her by the arms then slid his hands down to grasp her hands. "I don't want anything in my life as much as I want you. It is a huge mistake, this separation." He made her hold his gaze. The intensity of his voice and face forced her to let the words sink in. He was waiting for her to accept or reject him, looking so bare…so full of pain-filled hope. "Give us another chance, Maddie."

"I just can't." Maddie tried to breathe and found she couldn't. Pulling her hands out of his, she turned and ran toward the back of the building. Opening the back door, she stumbled out onto the gravel alley. She pressed the sides of her head as she stood, smelling the dumpster next to her, trying to get a grasp on reality.

The door behind her opened.

It was Neko. "You okay?"

She nodded, leaning against the brick wall, hugging herself. "I just needed a few minutes."

"That was Jake, wasn't it?"

"Yes."

"He seemed pretty intense. You want me to do something?"

She laughed, a short, harsh sound. "He's nearly six foot seven and in top physical shape. You think you can take him?"

Neko grinned back at her and shrugged one shoulder. "I've got cunning on my side. A roll of duct tape? The other guys in the band helping me?"

Maddie went over and gave him a quick hug. "Thanks. But I can handle it. Is it time to go back on?"

"Past time."

"Okay, let's go. This is a job, remember?"

"Yeah. A good job."

She knew what he meant. Neko and the others had been in a lot of bands, but there had never been this sweet meshing that had magically occurred with this group. They loved playing together and getting a recording deal was a dream come true for all of them.

Maddie walked back on stage determined to do her job and do it well. Her gaze scanned the crowd as she began the next song. Jake was nowhere to be seen.

"You've got to be kidding me!" Sasha yelled into the phone at one in the morning after Maddie's final set. "You let him go after he said that to you?"

"I can't go through it again. Sasha, you know me, I can't do it."

"Yes, you can."

"Love hurts too much."

"That's life and you know it. Quit hiding from it. You found something so great...something a lot of people long for their whole lives and you are being a coward, telling yourself that you're taking the high road when really you're just afraid. Maddie, I know I'm being tough here but you can do this. You can trust him and have a wonderful life with him if you will just let your fears go and love him back with all your heart."

Maddie was sitting in her car in the dark parking lot. She paused, letting the words sink in. "What if he isn't who I think he is? What if he leaves me?" She wailed it, beating on the steering wheel.

"What if he doesn't?" came Sasha's soft reply. "Go to him."

"I don't know...I just don't know."

256

"Yes, you do. You've been miserable without him. Now put that car into drive and go. Right now. Don't talk about it anymore. Don't think about it anymore. Just drive."

Maddie let out a laughing sob, shaking her head back and forth against the headrest. "Okay. Okay, I'll do it."

She hung up, put the car into drive and began the trek downtown.

She'd forgotten about the gate and the security guard she would have to get through to enter Jake's condo. Did he still live here? Her heart was beating so hard her hands shook.

The guard must have remembered her. He grinned at her, walked over to her rolled down window and said, "How you doin', Miss Maddie?"

"I'm okay, Darrell. Is Jake home, do you know?"

"Well, he came though over an hour ago, looking dog sick, but he left again about twenty minutes ago. Would you like to go in and wait for him?"

Maddie's heart sank. The last thing she wanted was to sit in a dark parking lot with lots of time to think and grow more nervous. "Uh. No, I'll just talk to him tomorrow."

"You do that," he said, like he meant it. "He misses you."

"I miss him too," she said softly.

The drive home was long and Maddie was tired as she pulled onto her street. She would call Jake tomorrow when she was fresh and able to put her feelings into words.

As she approached her driveway she saw it—Jake's SUV. Her heart began to gallop in her chest, her palms sweating. She pulled into the driveway and saw him sitting on the front porch of her parent's home.

He stood up as she got out of her car, walked toward her and she walked toward him. They both stopped just a few feet away from each other.

"Jake," she whispered, brokenly.

She came into his arms. Felt them reach around her. Felt how right they were, like coming home.

"I'm not going away, Maddie," he whispered into her hair, the warm June breeze growing stronger, moving her hair around them. "I'm not ever letting you go again."

Maddie nodded into his chest. "You promise?"

He took a box out of his pocket and knelt down in the grass on one knee. "Will you be my wife again, Madeleine Hart?"

Tears sprang to her eyes. She nodded. "Yes."

He stood, opened the box and slid her glittering diamond engagement ring back onto her finger. He pulled her toward him and she reached up on tiptoes to meet him halfway for a kiss—a sensual, branding kiss that left her breathless and dizzy.

He pulled back and took a piece of paper out of his pocket. "I wrote this for you. My true vows." He cleared his throat and began to read:

"I, Jake Alexander Hart, take you, Madeline Faith Goode, to be my wife, from this day forward. I bestow on you all my earthly possessions, my body and my heart. There shall never be another to take your place for as long as we both live. I promise to protect you from anything that might seek to harm you. I promise to love and cherish you wholeheartedly and remember what my life was like without you. As God is our witness, from this time forward, I will be your lover and your friend. I will be your loving husband."

Maddie stared in awe, trying to hold back the tears that were clogging her throat. Taking his vow as a pattern, she began.

"I, Madeline Faith Goode, take you, Jake Alexander Hart, to be my husband from this day forward. I bestow on you all my earthly possessions, namely and most importantly to me, my son, Max, to be your son. I give you my body and my heart. There will never be another to take your place for as long as we both shall live. I will always remember…" Her throat clogged completely and she leaned back her head waiting for it to pass before continuing. "I will always remember what my life was like without you. I promise to love you wholeheartedly, be your helper and cherish our time together. As God is our witness, from this moment on, I will be your lover and friend, your wife."

Jake pulled her into his chest, kissed her, both of them laughing with the joy of it, then he wiped the tracks of her tears from her cheeks with his hands, an anointing of emotion that covered them both.

"I'll be a good father."

"Yes." She nodded. "I know that you will."

She decided, right then and there, to make the vows true. She would never let the poison of her past sully this marriage with Jake. She would not doubt him if he came home later than expected. She would not listen in suspicion to his phone calls, always wondering if there was another woman. She would not doubt him or his love for her. She would not fear the worst and think the worst and expect something bad to happen. No. She would blindly trust again, letting life carry them on God's wind. Because blind trust was the only way to love another person and begin a marriage.

He groaned. "I don't want to wait another day. How soon can you and Max come home with me?"

"Let's go get him now."

"You would do that?" Jake looked like *he* might cry.

Maddie nodded. "It's where we both belong."

259

Other Books by Jamie Carie

Snow Angel

Please . . . God . . .

She whispered before collapsing.

When Noah Wesley hears the faint sound outside the door of his remote Alaskan cabin during a violent nighttime blizzard, it is no less than the voice of God that urges him to take a closer look, to discover there his snow angel.

Unconscious and more than half frozen to death, her name is Elizabeth, a beautiful young woman, fragile yet fierce, intent on discovering gold like so many others rushing headlong toward the Yukon.

But why Elizabeth is so drawn to the gold, and why she would chase it even through a pounding storm that no man would dare face, is a secret to be shared with no one, not even at the invitation of Noah's deep-blue, trusting eyes.

Jamie Carie has penned a can't-up-down debut novel in Snow Angel, a masterfully romantic story wherein cold and lonely hearts risk everything to be forever warmed.

The Duchess and the Dragon

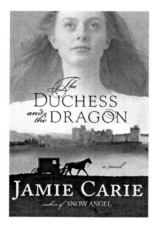

"To those who choose the path of passion, and the costs and rewards therein."

Two Worlds, One Destiny

Drake Weston, Duke of Northumberland, is heir to wealth, prestige, and power. But when his rage pushes him to a tragic mistake, he must leave everything behind. Not just his home, but England herself. Cloaked in a false identity, Drake slips aboard a ship bearing indentured servants to America.

Serena Winter lives out her Quaker beliefs tending the sick who arrive on ships in the Philadelphia harbor. But never before has she seen such squalor and misery as she finds on the latest ship from England. Nor has she ever met such a one as the half-conscious man with the penetrating eyes and arrogant demeanor. Though she saves his life, even taking him into her family home, there is little gratitude or humility in this man. And yet Serena is certain that beneath the brash exterior is a heart in search of peace.

Against the rich backdrop of Regency-era England and a young America, two passionate, seeking hearts find in each other the strength to face hard truths and confront an insidious web of deceit that may destroy all they hold dear.

Wind Dancer

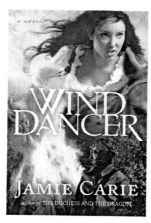

A love story beyond imagination …

Isabelle Renoir is different. A free spirit who dances alone in the moonlight as a praise offering to God, she\'s more at home in the woods with her long rifle and knife than cooking and cleaning like the other women in her wilderness town.

But as the shadow of the American Revolution stretches to the frontier, Isabelle finds herself on a journey that may overwhelm even her fearlessness and strength. And when the raven-haired beauty meets mysterious Samuel Holt, sparks fly. It takes an unthinkable attack and capture at the hands of Indians to push them together in a fight against deep spiritual forces …

Forces no physical weapon could ever conquer.

Love's First Light

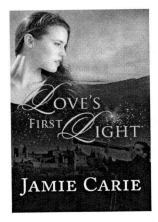

Christophe', the Count of St. Laurent, has lost his entire family to the blood-soaked French Revolution and must flee to an ancient castle along the southern border of France to survive. But the medieval city of Carcassonne proves more than a hiding place. Here Christophe' meets the beautiful widow Scarlett, a complex and lionhearted woman suddenly taken by the undercover aristocrat's passion for astronomy and its influence upon his faith. Although their acquaintance begins brightly enough, when the Count learns that Scarlett is related to the man who murdered his family, he turns from love and chooses revenge. Heaven only knows what it might take for Christophe' to love again, to love his enemy, and to love unconditionally

Angel's Den

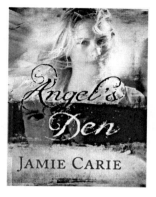

In 1808, when Emma meets and marries Eric Montclaire (the famed "most handsome man west of the Appalachians"), this young daughter of prominent St. Louis citizens believes a fairy tale has just begun. Instead, her husband's angelic looks quickly prove only to mask a monstrous soul all too capable of possessive emotions and physical abuse. Praying for mercy, she is devastated when Eric insists on her joining his yearlong group expedition to the Pacific Ocean, following the trail Lewis and Clark blazed just a few years earlier. By the time cartographer Luke Bowen realizes Emma's plight, it's too late to easily untangle what has become an epic web of lies, theft, murder, courtroom drama, and a deep longing for love. Only God can show them the way out.

The Snowflake

Ellen Pierce and her brother are determined to reach the Alaska gold rush. But when ice stalls their steamship, all seems lost, until Buck Lewis makes a decision: he'll lead all who dare to follow on foot toward Dawson City. Buck is determined to leave behind a heartbreaking past. No amount of ice or weather will stop him. But he never counted on a woman joining a dangerous wilderness trek—or on falling in love with her.

As their journey unfolds and Christmas approaches, Ellen and Buck discover that the greatest gift of all can't be wrapped in paper and tied with a bow. It comes from, and is received in, the heart. Come share in a soul-deep romance that gives a joyful reminder of a redeeming God who makes us each unique, yet loves us all the same

Pirate of My Heart

She gave up everything for a chance at true love . . .

When her doting father dies, Lady Kendra Townsend is given a choice: marry the horrid man of her uncle's choosing or leave England to risk a new life in America with unknown relatives.

Armed with the faith that God has a plan for her, Kendra boards a cargo ship and soon finds herself swept away by the rugged American sea captain Dorian Colburn. But this adventurous man has been wounded by love before and now guards his independent life.

He wasn't prepared to give up anything for anyone...

No swashbuckling man needs an English heiress with violet-hued eyes to make him feel again or challenge his faith with probing questions—or so he thinks. It is not until Dorian must save Kendra from the dark forces surrounding her that he decides she may be worth the risk.

The Guardian Duke

"Someday I will meet you and see your face."

Gabriel, the Duke of St. Easton, is ordered by the king to take guardianship over Lady Alexandria Featherstone whose parents are presumed dead after failing to return from a high profile treasure hunt. But the heart-driven Alexandria ignores this royal reassignment. Believing her parents are still alive, she travels to faraway lands to follow clues that may lead to their whereabouts. Gabriel, pressured by the king's ulterior motives, pursues Alexandria across windswept England and the rolling green hills of Ireland but is always one step behind.

When they do meet, the search for earthly treasure begins to pale in comparison to what God has planned for both of them.

The Forgiven Duke

Tethered by her impulsive promise to marry Lord John Lemon—*the path of least resistance*—Alexandria Featherstone sets off from Ireland to Iceland in search of her parents with a leaden heart. Her glimpse of her guardian, the Duke of St. Easton—*the path less traveled by*—on Dublin's shore still haunts her. Will he come after her? Will he drag her back to London, quelling her mission to rescue her treasure-seeking parents, or might he decide to throw caution to the wind and choose *Foy Pour Devoir*: "Faith for Duty," the St. Easton motto. The Featherstone motto *Valens et Volens*: *"Willing and Able"* beats in her heart and thrums through her veins. She will find her parents and find their love, no matter the cost.

The powerful and wing-clipped Duke of St. Easton has never known the challenge that has become his life since hearing his ward's name. Alexandria Featherstone will be the life of him or the death of him. Only time and God's plan will reveal just how much this man can endure for the prize of love.

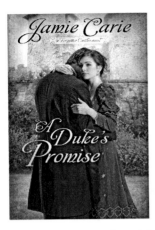

The Duke's Promise

Award-winning writer Jamie Caries concludes her most epic storyline with a wonderful twist in *A Duke's Promise*, the final Forgotten Castles novel.

From the Land of Fire and Ice back to England's shores, Alexandria Featherstone finds herself the new Duchess of St. Easton. Her husband has promised a wedding trip to take them to the place where her imperiled parents were last seen — Italy and the marble caves of Carrara — but a powerful Italian duke plots against Alex and her treasure-hunting parents.

Hoping to save them, Alex and Gabriel travel to Italy by balloon. Fraught with danger on all sides and pressured by Gabriel's affliction to the breaking point, they must learn to work and fight together. The mysterious key is within their grasp, but they have yet to recognize it. This journey will require steadfast faith in God and each other — a risk that will win them everything they want or lose them everything they have.

CPSIA information can be obtained at www.ICGtesting.com
Printed in the USA
BVOW012149260613

324453BV00007B/71/P